THE WIND ON THE MOON

THE WIND

ON

THE MOON

A Story for Children

by

ERIC LINKLATER

Nicolas Bentley drew the pictures

NEW YORK REVIEW BOOKS
New York

THIS IS A NEW YORK REVIEW BOOK
PUBLISHED BY THE NEW YORK REVIEW OF BOOKS
435 Hudson Street
New York, NY 10014
www.nyrb.com

The Library of Congress has cataloged the hardcover edition as follows:
Linklater, Eric, 1899–1974. The wind on the moon : a story for children / written by
Eric Linklater. Nicolas Bentley drew the pictures.
p. cm. — (New York Review children's collection)
Summary: In the English village of Midmeddlecum, sisters Dinah and Dorinda
struggle to keep their promise to try to be good when their father goes off to war, but
they soon get into a great deal of mischief.
ISBN 1-59017-100-4 (hardcover : alk. paper)
[1. Sisters — Fiction. 2. Fantasy.]   I. Bentley, Nicolas, 1907– , ill.
II. Title. III. Series. PZ7.L66286Wi 2004
[Fic]—dc22
2004004187

ISBN 978-1-68137-103-0
eBook ISBN 978-1-59017-433-3

Cover design: Leone Design, Tony Leone and Cara Ciardelli
Printed in the United States on acid-free paper.
1 3 5 7 9 10 8 6 4 2

FOR

SALLY, BOBBY, KRISTIN, SUSAN

AND

MAGNUS

Chapter One

A branch of the apple-tree, that was grey with old age, struck the window of the room in which Major Palfrey was packing his trunk. It made so brisk and startling a noise, like an angry postman on a cold morning, that the Major looked up with a sudden frown, while Dinah dropped the silver flask she was carrying, and Dorinda gave a shrill cry like a little owl.

The Major walked to the window and pulled back the curtain. 'Look at the moon,' he said.

Through the branches of the apple-tree the moon stared straight into the room. It was pale and wild, and round it clung a white collar of shining mist.

'There is wind on the moon,' he said. 'I don't like the look of it at all. When there is wind on the moon, you must be very careful how you behave. Because if it is an ill wind, and you behave badly, it will blow straight into your heart, and then you will behave badly for a long time to come.

So I hope you are going to be good to-night, because I shall be far away, in a foreign country, for at least a year, and I don't want you to be a nuisance to your mother, and worry her with mischief while she is all alone. Do you think you can be good, if you really try ? '

' It will be very difficult,' said Dinah.

' Very difficult indeed,' said Dorinda.

' I think,' said Dinah with a sigh, ' that we are quite likely to be bad, however hard we try not to be.'

' Very often,' said Dorinda, ' when we think we are behaving well, some grown-up person says we are really quite bad. It's difficult to tell which is which.'

' Would it help you,' asked their father, ' if I were to give you a thrashing before I go ? '

He often talked about thrashing them, because he himself, when he was a boy, had been beaten every week, and he thought it had done him good. But he was too tender-hearted to put his belief into practice.

' A truly severe thrashing,' he said, ' would almost certainly be good for you. It would help you to remember me.'

' It would make us cry,' said Dinah.

' We should cry as loud as we could,' said Dorinda.

' And that,' said Dinah, ' would upset Mother, who hates to hear us cry.'

' I shall be gone for a whole year,' said their father, ' and because the moon has a white collar round it, which means that an ill wind may be blowing, I am very worried about you.'

' I'm not worried,' said Dinah.

' Nor am I,' said Dorinda.

' My pigtails will be three inches longer when you come back,' said Dinah.

' And I shall have learnt to swim,' said Dorinda.

Their father looked unhappy, and went to find two pistols, which he wanted to put in his trunk, because the country where he was going was full of dangerous men, and he knew there would be plots and plans against him.

And when he had gone, Dinah said, ' Let's try to be good, just to please him, because Father likes to be pleased.'

' We could help him to pack,' said Dorinda.

' We could pack much better than he has been doing.'

' Look at all the things that have to go in yet.'

' There isn't much room for them,' said Dinah.

' We could make a lot more room if we rolled all his coats and trousers into long sausages, instead of hanging them up like that.'

So they took three ordinary suits and two suits of uniform off the hangers that held them neatly on one side of the trunk, and rolled them into long bundles like sausages. Then they pushed the sausages into the trunk, and stamped on them to make them smaller, and laid six white shirts in the middle, and put two pairs of boots on top of the shirts.

' I *think* that's better,' said Dinah.

But Dorinda was listening to the noise which the apple-tree made by beating its longest branches against the window. The wind was growing stronger, and the branch made an angry sound — *rat, rat, rat-a-tat* — and an ugly sound when the twigs came scraping on the glass.

' If apple-trees grew bells instead of apples,' said Dorinda, ' they would make a lovely noise whenever the wind blew.'

' Perhaps we could tie some bells on to it,' said Dinah.

' That's just what I was thinking,' said Dorinda.

' There's a big bell in the schoolroom, and seven silver bells in the drawing-room, and three bronze bells in the hall that Father brought home from China.'

' And I know where there's a ball of string,' said Dorinda.

' It will be very nice for Father,' said Dinah, ' to remember the apple-tree, ringing all its bells, on his last night at home.'

They went downstairs and got the silver bells, the bronze bells from China, and the big bell from the schoolroom, and went into the garden. The apple-tree, as if it were furiously angry, was waving its branches at the sky, and making a noise like a great crowd of people all muttering and whispering their most indignant thoughts. But it was not really angry, it was only playing its favourite game with the rising wind, and when Dinah and Dorinda came it stood quite still, and let them climb into its upper branches. They were adept at climbing trees, and they tied the silver bells to the topmost branches, the Chinese bells to the middle ones, and the big schoolroom bell to the lowest bough of all.

No sooner had they finished, and returned to the ground, than the tree gave its branches a little shake, and the bells began to ring.

In the room where their father had been packing his trunk, Dinah and Dorinda stood and listened to the concert.

Ding-dong, said the big schoolroom bell. *Ding-dong, come along. Twice two is bing-bang-bong.*

Millo, mello, catkin-yellow, sang the bronze bells from China. *Lillo lacquer, pull a cracker. Heigh-ho, heigh-ho! How far to old Hong Kong? Too long!*

And the silver bells, high in the tree, sang, *Twinkle-twankle stole some beef, catch his ankle, he's a thief. Lillo lily lady! Dapple apples in the moon, pick some cherries with a spoon, Saturday is pay-day!*

'What a lovely concert!' said Dinah.

'It's beautiful,' said Dorinda.

At that moment, however, their father and mother came into the room, and it was plain to be seen that both were alarmed and angry. Their mother was tall and handsome, but easily worried. She always wore a long string of beads. Sometimes they were white beads, sometimes green, and sometimes red, but always they swung to and fro when she walked, and often, if she turned in a hurry, they would swing out and knock something off the table.

'What is the matter?' she cried. 'What is making that awful noise?'

'It's a lovely noise,' said Dinah.

'I thought the house must be on fire,' said Mrs. Palfrey. 'Oh, what a fearful fright you gave me!'

Twice two is bing-bang-bong, shouted the schoolroom bell.

' The apple-tree is giving a concert,' said Dinah.

' Because it's Father's last night at home,' explained Dorinda.

How far to old Hong Kong ?   Too long ! sang the Chinese bells.

' You should have known how upset I would be,' said Mrs. Palfrey. ' It was very, very inconsiderate of you to do such a thing.'

' I have forbidden you to climb trees in the darkness,' said their father. ' It was a very dangerous thing to do. You are two naughty little girls.'

Twinkle-twankle stole some beef, chattered the silver bells on top of the tree. *Catch his ankle, he's a thief ! Lillo lily lady !*

' We were quite safe,' said Dinah. ' The tree stood perfectly still while we climbed it.'

' Oh dear ! ' exclaimed their mother. ' Look at this ! '

' Well, really ! ' said their father, and stared in amazement at the trunk, where his clothes lay neatly rolled into sausages, and his boots lay tidily upon his white shirts.

' This is too much,' said Mrs. Palfrey. ' This is more than I can stand.'

' Now, really,' said Major Palfrey. ' Really, really ! I don't know what to say. I think I must give you both a good thrashing.'

' We've been helping you to pack,' said Dinah.

' There wasn't much room in your trunk,' said Dorinda.

' But we found a place for everything,' said Dinah.

' My dress uniform ! ' exclaimed Major Palfrey, as he unrolled one of the sausages, and held up a scarlet tunic that was creased like a concertina.

' You wretched children ! ' cried Mrs. Palfrey.

Dinah looked sullen, Dorinda angry. Their parents, they thought, were most ungrateful. They had failed to appreciate some valuable help in packing a trunk, they had not enjoyed the splendid concert in the apple-tree. Their parents, thought Dinah and Dorinda, were behaving in a very stupid fashion.

' What's the use of trying to be good,' asked Dinah, ' if you never realise how good we are ? '

' We might just as well please ourselves and be bad,' said Dorinda.

' You are very bad indeed,' said their mother.

' Perhaps they can't help it,' said their father. ' There is wind on the moon, and if it is an ill wind, it may have blown into their hearts.'

' You had better go to bed before you do any more mischief,' said their mother. But it was a long time before Dinah and Dorinda fell asleep, for when they pulled up the blind, the moon looked through the window, and to both of them it seemed as if there was laughter on its face. So instead of being sorry for what they had done, they also began to laugh.

But in the morning just after breakfast they were very sad when their father kissed them good-bye, for they knew that he would be gone for a long time. All that day they sat quite still, doing nothing at all, either good or bad. And their mother thought they behaved very well indeed.

Chapter Two

The house where they lived was on the outskirts of a village called Midmeddlecum. At one end of the village was the Forest of Weal, and at the other a large estate, surrounded by a high wall, that belonged to the Squire, who had a private zoo. His name was Sir Lankester Lemon. There was a Square in the middle of the village, where the Doctor lived in a large house. His name was Dr. Fosfar, and he had a glass eye. He gave his patients bigger bottles of medicine than any other doctor they had ever heard of, and because of this he was very popular.

On the opposite side of the Square were a baker's shop, a grocer's shop, and a butcher's shop. The butcher was Mr. Leathercow, the grocer Mr. Fullalove, and the baker Mr. Crumb. Mr. Leathercow was a little fat man with a red face and no hair on his head. Mr. Fullalove was tall and thin, with a long neck and a sad expression. Mr. Crumb had a wooden leg. They all had wives who never stopped talking, and Mr. and Mrs. Leathercow had four sons, Mr. and Mrs. Crumb had three daughters, but Mr. and Mrs. Fullalove had no children at all.

A small river ran to the north of the village, and facing a bend of the stream were the Vicarage and a big house that belonged to Mr. Justice Rumple, who was one of His Majesty's Judges, and so fond of judging that he used to wear his wig even at the breakfast-table.

Mr. Steeple, the Vicar, who lived in the Vicarage, was a friendly man who loved to hear people singing, and gave all his money to the poor. His wife was more careful, and did not give him enough to eat. Her father had also been a vicar, and she had seven sisters, one of whom was governess to Dinah and Dorinda Palfrey. Her name was Miss Serendip.

Miss Serendip believed that knowledge was the most important thing on earth, and every hour of the day she did her best to make Dinah and Dorinda learn all manner of things, whether they were useful or not. Even at the breakfast-table, or the dinner-table, she would talk in this manner:

' Will you pass me the pepper, Dorinda ? Pepper, as I daresay you know, is a spice. There is black pepper, white pepper, and red pepper. Pepper used to be a monopoly of the King of Portugal. Much of it is now grown in Penang. Penang means the Island of Areca Nuts. At one time it was a penal settlement, or prison. The word prison is derived from the word *prehensio*. Our prisons used to be very badly conducted, but gradually reform was introduced. Newgate was a famous old prison, Sing Sing is a well-known modern prison. Thank you, dear. Put the pepper back in its proper place.'

One day, when she had been talking like this, Dinah said, ' I know something that's far more important than knowledge.'

' What is that ? ' asked Miss Serendip.

' Food,' said Dinah. ' Can I have some more pudding, please ? '

' I'm hungry too,' said Dorinda.

' I think I must ask Dr. Fosfar to come and see

Miss Serendip

you,' said their mother. 'You're eating far more than you used to, and you're both getting so fat.'

'We're fond of eating,' said Dinah.

'Very fond,' said Dorinda.

'Because food is the most important thing in the world,' said Dinah. 'I love food.'

At the very moment of saying this, Dinah realised that she was about to be very naughty indeed. She and Dorinda had talked a good deal about the wind on the moon, that might have blown into their hearts, and both of them felt that the time was coming when they were going to be naughtier than ever before. They were very excited about it, because they expected to enjoy themselves thoroughly. And now Dinah suddenly perceived that one of the best ways of being naughty was to be utterly and shamelessly greedy. At the same time she felt marvellously hungry, so that to be greedy seemed the most natural thing in the world.

'I *love* food,' she repeated.

'So does Mrs. Grimble,' said Dorinda, and Dinah laughed when she heard that, because Mrs. Grimble was a person about whom they were forbidden to speak. So Dinah knew that Dorinda now meant to be as naughty as herself.

'Children!' exclaimed their mother, 'I have told you never to mention that name. I do not believe there is such a person as Mrs. Grimble.'

'Yes, there is,' said Dinah.

'You must never contradict your mother,' said Miss Serendip. 'Every mother loves her children, and knows what is best for them. In ancient Greece there was a mother called Niobe who had no fewer

than twelve children, six boys and six girls. None
of them, I am sure, ever contradicted her.'

' Mrs. Grimble lives in the Forest of Weal, and I
went to see her yesterday,' said Dinah stubbornly.
' Can I have some more pudding, please ? '

Very few people had ever seen Mrs. Grimble,
though many had heard of her. Dinah said she was
an old woman with a hairy wart on her chin, and
one eye bigger than the other. She lived all alone,
said Dinah, in a little house, painted green with
yellow blinds and a red door, in the darkest part of
the Forest of Weal.

' The first time I met her,' Dinah continued,
' Mrs. Grimble was having a beautiful dinner. First
of all she had an omelette made out of twelve
partridge eggs that she had found. Then she ate
the partridge itself, roasted, with bread sauce and
cauliflower and fried potatoes. Then she had junket
and cream, and a piece of birthday cake with
almond icing on it.'

' If there is such a person as Mrs. Grimble,' said
Miss Serendip, ' why have we never seen her ? '

' Because she knows a lot of magic,' said Dinah,
' and she can make herself invisible to people whom
she doesn't like.'

' Now you are talking nonsense,' said her mother.
' You are talking wicked nonsense, and if your
father were here I would ask him to give you a
thrashing.'

' But he wouldn't do it,' said Dorinda. ' He
never did.'

' Oh, how naughty you are ! ' said her mother.
' You make me feel quite upset.'

Miss Serendip, still trying to be clever, said to Dinah, 'I should very much like to meet Mrs. Grimble. Won't you take me with you the next time you go to see her?'

'It wouldn't be any use,' said Dinah, 'because you are one of the people whom she doesn't like.'

'Then I am one of the people who must refuse to believe in her,' said Miss Serendip crossly. 'Because neither you nor she, it appears, can give me any proof of her existence.'

'Yes, we can,' said Dinah.

'How?' asked her mother.

'Give me some more pudding and I'll prove it.'

'Me too,' cried Dorinda.

'You've had far too much already,' said their mother, 'but I suppose I must give in to you.' And she gave each of them a large helping of pudding.

'And now for the proof of Mrs. Grimble's existence,' said Miss Serendip.

'Wait till to-morrow,' said Dinah. 'I'll prove it then.'

The following morning she and Dorinda went upstairs to Miss Serendip's room and knocked at the door. It was a pleasant room with a window facing south, a satinwood bed, a satinwood dressing-table, and a satinwood writing-desk at which Miss Serendip used to sit and write letters to her seven sisters. The walls had been newly papered with a paper of Miss Serendip's own choosing. The pattern was of small pink roses and large blue pigeons. The roses hung in wide loops, and in the middle of each loop sat a pigeon with a pink ribbon round its neck.

' Come in,' cried Miss Serendip, who was sitting at her satinwood desk writing a letter to one of her sisters. ' I suppose you have come to keep your promise,' she said, ' and prove to me that Mrs. Grimble really exists.'

' Yes,' said Dinah.

' That will be very interesting,' said Miss Serendip coldly.

Dinah showed her a little box full of yellow seed.

' This is pigeon-seed,' she said, ' and Mrs. Grimble gave it to me. When I throw it on the floor, all the pigeons in your wallpaper will come to life and fly away. You had better open your window.'

' I never heard such nonsense,' exclaimed Miss Serendip. ' You are certainly not going to make a mess of my room by throwing bird-seed all over it.'

But Dinah, with a sudden movement, scattered the seed on the carpet, and immediately all the pigeons in the wallpaper began to move their heads about, and lift their wings, and fill the room with their soft voices. *Coo-coooo-roo, coo-roo*, they said.

Miss Serendip was very much surprised, and she went quite white when first one pigeon, and then another, undid the little pink bows on their necks and threw them to the floor. *Coo-coooo-roo*, they said, while they were untying the bows, and from the tone of their voices it was quite clear that they had disliked those foolish ornaments.

Then they flew down to the floor and ate the pigeon-seed. The floor was covered with them, and when they rose again, the beating of their wings made a great wind in the room. Miss Serendip's

'Come in,' cried Miss Serendip

hair blew into her eyes, and Dinah's skirt flew up, and Dorinda was almost blown down.

But Dinah opened the window, and all the pigeons flew out and away to the Forest of Weal.

' Now do you believe in Mrs. Grimble ? ' asked Dinah triumphantly.

But Miss Serendip was quite overcome by her experience and did not know what to reply. Without even waiting to tidy her hair, she hurried downstairs and told Mrs. Palfrey exactly what had happened. Mrs. Palfrey did not believe her till she had seen for herself the wallpaper in Miss Serendip's room. The festoons of roses were still there, but all the pigeons had vanished, and on the floor lay the little pink bows they had torn from their necks. When she saw that, Mrs. Palfrey was very much upset, and had to lie down and rest for an hour.

For dinner that day the cook gave them tomato soup, cold tongue and salad, and gooseberry tart. Dinah had two plates of soup, three helpings of tongue, and three helpings of gooseberry tart. Dorinda had three plates of soup, one helping of tongue, and four helpings of tart. Their mother knew that this was far too much for them, but she had been so frightened by the flight of the pigeons that she dared not refuse to give them all they asked. Miss Serendip was still rather pale, and though she watched with dismay the enormous meal which the children ate, she hardly spoke. She did, however, say a few words about salads.

' The word *salad*,' she said, ' is derived from the Latin *salare*, which means to sprinkle with salt. For myself, I do not much care for salt, but Plato calls it a substance dear to the gods. In parts of Central Africa it is also much esteemed, and the use of it is confined to the rich. Few people realise the enormous size of the African continent. It covers nearly twelve million square miles, and from the north to Cape Agulhas in the south is a distance of five thousand miles. Among the most famous names associated with Africa are those of Cleopatra and Dr. Livingstone. . . .'

But nobody paid much attention to her, and after a little while she was silent.

As time went on, Dinah and Dorinda ate more and more. For breakfast they ate porridge and cream, fish and bacon and eggs and sausages and tomatoes, toast and marmalade, and rolls and honey. For dinner they ate roast beef and cold lamb, boiled mutton with caper sauce, Scotch broth and clear soup, hare soup and lentil soup, roast chicken with thyme and parsley stuffing, boiled fowl with oatmeal and onion stuffing, roast duck with apple sauce, apple-tart and cherry pie, Yorkshire pudding and plum pudding, trifle and jelly, potatoes and Brussels sprouts and cauliflower and French beans and green peas, and all sorts of cheese. For tea they had scones and pancakes, crumpets and pikelets, muffins and cream buns, plum cake and seed cake and cream cake and chocolate cake, and often some bread and butter as well. And for supper they had stewed fruit and fresh fruit, oranges and bananas and baked apples, and half a gallon of milk at the very least.

They got fatter and fatter. They got so fat, and quickly got fatter still, that every three or four days they burst their frocks and split their vests, and were quite unable to pull their stockings over their fat round legs. So every few days their mother had to buy new clothes for them. But if she bought them new dresses on a Tuesday, they were sure to burst the seams by Friday, or Saturday at the latest.

And still they went on eating. They knew it was wicked to be so greedy, but having started to be greedy, it was almost impossible to stop.

'Food,' they said, 'is the most important thing in the world. We love eating, and we mean to eat more and more.'

Their mother was very worried, and said she would have to call in Dr. Fosfar. A few of his largest bottles of medicine, she thought, might cure their dreadful appetite. But Dinah said wickedly, 'Dr. Fosfar has a glass eye, and if you send for him, I shall go to Mrs. Grimble and borrow her magpie.'

'She always has a magpie in her house,' said Dorinda.

'And magpies love to steal glass eyes from people,' said Dinah.

Their mother was so frightened by this threat that for a long time she never mentioned Dr. Fosfar's name.

So then, between breakfast and dinner, Dinah and Dorinda ate biscuits and strawberry jam, and Devonshire cream with raspberry jam, and sponge cake with damson jam. Between dinner and tea-time they usually ate a pound of chocolates and some candied fruit and a few caramels. And about midnight they often woke and went downstairs to the kitchen, where they ate whatever they could find, such as cold chicken and hard-boiled eggs and custard and plum tart and a slice or two of cake.

By and by they grew so fat they were almost completely round, like balloons. And one day they found they could hardly walk, so they rolled downstairs and bounced into the dining-room, just as if they were balloons.

Then their mother became so upset that she cared nothing for their threats, and so angry that she was no longer frightened of Mrs. Grimble.

' I am going to take you at once to see Dr. Fosfar,' she said. ' Your appearance is truly disgusting, and I am ashamed to be the mother of two little girls who look more like balloons than human beings. Not very long ago I used to think you were the prettiest children I had ever seen. You, Dinah, with your blue eyes and yellow pigtails, were a lovely child, and Dorinda, with her dark eyes and dark curly hair, was just as attractive. But now I can hardly bear to look at you, you are both so ugly. If you don't believe me, come into the hall and see for yourselves.'

So they rolled off their chairs and bounced into the hall, where a big round mirror hung over the fireplace. It was made of glass that looked almost black, but it reflected everything in clear bright colours, and when Dinah and Dorinda stood in front of it, and looked up, they too were shocked. For they saw that their mother had been speaking the truth, and they were indeed more like balloons than human children. They even felt a little frightened by what had happened to them.

' Quickly, quickly ! ' cried their mother. ' Put

on your hats, and I shall take you to Dr. Fosfar immediately.   There is no time to waste.   Miss Serendip, you must come and help me.'

Dinah and Dorinda got their hats, but now their hats were of no use to them.   They were so completely fat and round that their hats would not stay on.

' Who ever heard,' asked Miss Serendip coldly, ' of putting a hat on a balloon ? '

Chapter Three

It was a cold and sunny morning, and the road to Midmeddlecum was lined by great beech-trees, leafless now, because it was winter, the branches of which threw a tangle of thin shadows from side to side. It was a pleasant walk, and no more than half a mile, but neither Dinah nor Dorinda enjoyed it very much. Since they had taken to eating such a lot, they had had no time for walking, and they had not been to Midmeddlecum for several weeks. And now, being so fat and round, they could hardly walk at all, so their mother and Miss Serendip had to push them along. Sometimes they rolled and sometimes they bounced, and before they had gone very far they were covered with dust and extremely hot.

' I don't know what people will think, or what they will say,' said Mrs. Palfrey, ' when they see us pushing Dinah and Dorinda in this absurd and ridiculous manner. Perhaps we should not have come to the village. It might have been better to ask Dr. Fosfar to see the children at home.'

And she gave Dinah another push that sent her rolling along the pavement of the main street of Midmeddlecum.

' Let us hope that everybody is indoors, and will stay there,' said Miss Serendip, and gave Dinah a push that made her bounce three times on the pavement.

There was, indeed, nobody to be seen on the street, but that was not because the people were all

at home. It was too fine a day for that, and the
whole population of the village was in the Square
where Dr. Fosfar lived.

It so happened that the Vicar had come to buy

a bottle of hair-dye from Mr. Wax the chemist.
His hair, he thought, was turning red, which was a
most unsuitable colour for a Vicar, and he was on
his way to purchase a bottle of strong black dye
when, in the Square, he met the four sons of Mr.

Leathercow the butcher ; the three daughters of Mr. Crumb the baker ; Robin and Robina, the twin children of Mr. Wax the chemist ; and Mrs. Fulla-love the grocer's wife, who was giving them all sugar-plums because Christmas was coming.

It suddenly occurred to the Vicar that for at least two days he had not heard anybody singing, and because he was extremely fond of fine songs and choruses, he called to the children and Mrs. Fulla-love and said, ' I think it would be a good thing if we all sang *The Barley Mow.*'

Mrs. Fullalove, who had a pretty voice herself, at once agreed, and so did the children.

' Now all together ! ' exclaimed the Vicar. ' " Here's a health to the Barley Mow, my boys, A health to the Barley Mow ! " '

By the time they had finished that, there were forty-eight people and seven dogs in the Square. So then they started *Drink to me only with thine eyes*, and the lovely tune, sung very loudly, brought sixty-three other people and eighteen more dogs.

Climbing on to the statue of Queen Victoria, which stood in the middle of the Square, the Vicar, who by this time was very excited, shouted, ' And now a magnificent song that everybody knows ! *John Peel !* Open your lips, let the welkin ring ! Open your hearts, it's a song for a king ! " D'ye ken John Peel with his coat so grey. . . . " '

So great was the noise, and so beautiful, of *John Peel* being sung by a hundred and eleven people, all as loudly as they could, and of twenty-five dogs all beating the ground with their tails in perfect time, that everybody else in the village of Midmeddlecum came hurrying to join them. And when the whole population was in the Square, the Vicar made them sing *Funiculì Funiculà*.

This was about the time when Mrs. Palfrey and Miss Serendip and Dinah and Dorinda came into the village, and of course they met nobody in the streets because everybody was in the Square. They could hear the people singing *Funiculì Funiculà*, and Dinah and Dorinda went bouncing along the pavement — *bop-bump, bump-bop* — in time with the tune of it. Then the song came to an end, and for a while there was almost silence in the Square, because some people wanted to sing *Widdicombe Fair*, and others thought they should sing the *Volga Boat Song*, and the Vicar himself was in favour of *Fain would I change that note*. So they could not make up their minds which to choose.

Then Dinah and Dorinda came bounding into the Square, and a little way behind them appeared Mrs. Palfrey and Miss Serendip.

Tom Leathercow, the butcher's oldest son, was standing on the outskirts of the crowd, and beside him were Catherine Crumb, the baker's daughter, and Robin and Robina Wax. As soon as they saw Dinah and Dorinda, they all shouted at once, ' Balloons, balloons, balloons ! Look at the big balloons ! '

Every child in the Square at once hurried and thrust and scrambled and pushed a way through the crowd, and in less than a minute Dinah and Dorinda were entirely surrounded by fifty or sixty boys and girls, all shouting, ' Balloons, balloons, look at the big balloons ! '

Then the older people followed the children, and they also gathered round Dinah and Dorinda, and were very much surprised by their appearance.

The Vicar remained on the statue of Queen Victoria, but nobody paid any attention to him now except Mrs. Fullalove, who had climbed up in order to ask him if they could sing *Lily of Laguna*. And Mrs. Palfrey and Miss Serendip were on the other side of the crowd, and could not get near to Dinah and Dorinda.

Now it so happened that Catherine Crumb, the baker's daughter, had just bought a packet of pins from Mr. Taper the draper. She had very black hair, a white face, and long thin legs. She was quite pretty, but she had a wicked heart. Taking the packet of pins from her pocket, she gave some to Tom Leathercow, and some to Robin and Robina Wax, and told them to give pins to every other boy and girl in the crowd.

Then she said loudly, ' If they really are balloons, they ought to burst ! ' And she stuck a pin into Dorinda.

Tom Leathercow stuck a pin into Dinah, and all the other children cried ' Burst the balloons ! ' And those who were nearest Dorinda stuck pins into her, while others pricked Dinah.

Dinah and Dorinda began to cry. They cried so loudly that everyone was amazed, and all the dogs began to bark.

Mrs. Leathercow the butcher's wife caught hold of Tom and boxed his ears. Mrs. Taper the draper's wife, who was very short-sighted, seized Robin and

Robina Wax, thinking they were her own children, and knocked their heads together. So Mrs. Wax pulled Mrs. Taper's hair, and Mr. Taper was thrown to the ground by Mr. Crumb, who stood very firmly on his wooden leg and hit everyone within reach. Some of the children were still sticking pins into Dinah and Dorinda, who cried louder than ever, and seventeen dogs began to fight in eight different parts of the Square, while every other dog was barking with all his might to encourage them.

Mrs. Fullalove fell off the statue of Queen Victoria, but luckily fell on Mr. Horrabin the iron-monger, who was very fat and saved her from being hurt. The Vicar shouted, ' Peace, peace ! Silence is golden ! ' But no one could hear him, so no one paid any attention.

Then Constable Drum, the village policeman, blew his whistle. The first time he blew it, all the older people stopped quarrelling and looked around to see what was happening. The second time he blew it, the children stopped shouting and stuck no more pins into Dinah and Dorinda. The third time he blew it, the dogs stopped barking, and all was quiet.

' In the King's name ! ' shouted Constable Drum. ' If you do not behave yourselves, I shall put you all in prison. Let there be no more rioting, roister-ing, brawling or biting, barking or fighting. Be good people and go to your homes. Whoever is late for his luncheon shall feel the weight of my truncheon ! God save the King ! '

So all the people went home, feeling very much ashamed of themselves, and Mrs. Palfrey and Miss

Mrs. Taper knocked their heads together

Serendip did what they could to comfort Dinah and Dorinda. But nothing could make them stop crying, even though Mr. Whitloe the drayman took them home in his dray, which was much more comfortable than rolling home.

Chapter Four

Dinah and Dorinda would not stop crying. They cried for days and days. They lost their appetite, and wanted nothing to eat. But they drank lots of milk and water and lemonade and barley-water, and perhaps all this liquid turned into tears. Because as time went on they cried more and more. They cried all through the Christmas holidays, and every day they got thinner and thinner. They got as thin as a lamp-post, and then as thin as a walking-stick, and thinner than that. And their faces were always red with weeping.

One day when they were in the garden, crying under the apple-tree, their mother looked at them and said, ' They're as thin as match-sticks ! With their poor little red faces they look just like those big wooden matches that their father used to light his pipe ! '

' An early attempt to make sulphur matches,' said Miss Serendip, ' was directed by Robert Boyle, the natural philosopher, in the year 1680. Robert Boyle, whose father was the Earl of Cork, discovered Boyle's Law, which says that the volume of a gas varies inversely as the pressure. 1680, of course, was the year in which Parliament passed the Act of Exclusion, the object of which, as might be imagined, was to exclude the Duke of Monmouth.'

Mrs. Palfrey paid no attention to Miss Serendip, but sadly shook her head, and sighed, ' How you children do worry me ! I must take you to see Dr.

Fosfar — but will you promise me, Dinah, not to bring some horrid magpie who might steal his glass eye ? '

' I don't like Dr. Fosfar,' said Dinah.

' Nor do I,' said Dorinda.

' But you can't go about looking like match-sticks,' said their mother, and stood beside them, shaking her head very sadly. She was wearing one of her long necklaces, of yellow beads, and as she turned to look first at Dinah, then at Dorinda, it swung out and became entangled in a twig of the apple-tree.

' Oh, how annoying ! ' she exclaimed, and foolishly took a backward step. The string of the necklace broke, and all the beads fell into the grass.

' Beads,' said Miss Serendip, ' are probably the oldest form of ornament known to man. They have been found, not only in the ancient ruins of Babylon, but in primitive Stone Age dwellings in Northern Europe.'

' That doesn't make it easier to find them here,' said Mrs. Palfrey. Her voice was angry, and Miss Serendip hurriedly went down on her knees beside her. ' Let me help you,' she said.

' Dinah ! Dorinda ! ' called Mrs. Palfrey. ' Come and look for my beads ! '

'But Dinah and Dorinda had gone. They hurried through the garden, and past the kitchen-garden, to a rough lawn beyond it on which, every washing-day, the clothes were hung to dry. The lawn was surrounded by a holly hedge, a thick and sturdy hedge, a glittering green in the winter sun.

' Do we really look like matches ? ' asked Dinah.

'You do,' said Dorinda, screwing up her eyes. 'Well, not exactly, of course, but rather like.'

'So do you,' said Dinah. 'Go farther away. A little farther still. Yes, you look very like a matchstick.'

Dorinda began to cry again.

'Stop crying,' said Dinah. 'Crying makes us worse.'

'I thought we should enjoy being naughty,' sobbed Dorinda, 'but we haven't really enjoyed it so far.'

'We enjoyed eating too much,' said Dinah.

'But not having pins stuck into us,' said Dorinda, 'nor having to cry for days and days.'

'We did enjoy crying to begin with,' said Dinah. 'It was very nice and satisfying. Just to let yourself go, and howl and sob like anything, and make no effort to stop, is quite a luxury, I think.'

'But it lasted too long,' said Dorinda.

'Yes, we have cried too much. The trouble is — I have just thought of this — that we shall have to *learn* to be naughty. You know how hard it is to learn to be good. Well, it may be just as hard to learn to be naughty. To be naughty in a suitable way, I mean.'

At that moment they heard behind them a voice saying, 'There they are. Two match-sticks!'

'Matches on the washing-green,' said another voice. 'Well, I never!'

Quickly they looked round, and saw, leaning over the hedge, Catherine Crumb the baker's daughter, and Mrs. Taper the draper's wife. Mrs. Taper, who was very short-sighted, was determined to get as good a view as possible, so she thrust herself into the hedge, and the branches bent before her, and her face grew **red** with the effort she was making. Catherine Crumb was jumping up and down with her black hair flapping like a big black crow in a hurry to get home, but Dinah and Dorinda stood perfectly still. They were too frightened to move.

'Two match-sticks,' repeated Mrs. Taper. 'Well, did you ever ! '

'I told you so,' said Catherine Crumb.

She had indeed. She had been spying on Dinah and Dorinda for several days, and while they were crying under the apple-tree, she was hidden among the rhododendrons that grew beneath the garden wall. She had heard their mother liken them to match-sticks, and seeing at once a chance of mischief, she hurried away to make it. The garden gate led into a lane, and in the lane Catherine Crumb met Mrs. Taper the draper's wife.

'I've just seen something,' said Catherine Crumb.

'And what was that ? ' asked Mrs. Taper.

'Two big matches,' said Catherine Crumb.

'Well, that's nothing to boast about,' said Mrs. Taper.

'But these weren't ordinary matches,' said Catherine Crumb. 'They were two - legged matches.'

'I declare ! ' said Mrs. Taper.

'Would you like to see them ? ' asked Catherine Crumb.

'That I would,' said Mrs. Taper.

'They're on the washing-green,' said Catherine

Crumb, and they hurried down the lane till they came to the holly hedge. ' There they are,' she exclaimed.

' I never did ! ' said Mrs. Taper, when she had pushed her way into the very middle of the hedge. ' No, I never did expect to see a sight like that! Two-legged matches indeed ! It's a wonderful world we live in.'

' What do you think we should do with them ? ' asked Catherine Crumb.

Dinah and Dorinda, still too frightened to move, waited breathless for the answer.

Mrs. Taper thought very hard, and then with triumph in her voice declared, ' Why, strike them, to be sure ! If they're matches, we ought to strike them.'

' That's what I thought,' said Catherine Crumb.

' It's what matches are made for,' said Mrs. Taper. ' To be struck.' And she laughed again and again.

Now when Mrs. Taper laughed, she made a noise like someone rattling pebbles in a biscuit-tin, and Dinah and Dorinda, hearing that horrible noise, were more frightened than ever. But now their fright made them run, and they ran into the house as quickly as their shrivelled legs would carry them, and never stopped till they were safe in their own room with the door locked.

Then Catherine Crumb also ran away, leaving Mrs. Taper stuck fast in the holly hedge. Mrs. Taper, who was far too short-sighted to see where everyone had gone, was quite bewildered to find herself alone. She was still more worried when she found that she could not get out of the hedge. Branches stuck into her from all sides, and held her prisoner. Her face grew redder and redder as she struggled to get free. Her hat came off and fell into the garden, and she shouted for help.

' Help, help ! ' she cried, and presently heard heavy footsteps in the lane. ' Who's that ? ' she demanded.

' It's me, Mrs. Taper,' said a deep voice, which Mrs. Taper recognised as that of Constable Drum.

' Help me out,' she cried.

' Not so fast,' said the Constable. ' You must first tell me how you came to be in such a position. Were you by any chance contemplating a felony ? I perceive, hanging on the clothes-line, two pairs of silk stockings. Perhaps you were about to steal them, Mrs. Taper ? '

' Oh, how dare you ! ' she exclaimed. ' Why, the very idea of such a thing would never enter my head. I'm the very soul of honesty, which everybody knows.'

' That may be so,' said Constable Drum, ' but the Law pays no attention to what everybody knows. The Law is guided only by evidence, and the evidence, Mrs. Taper, is sadly against you. My duty is clearer than ink ; I shall have to put you in clink. In the name of the Law, Mrs. Taper, I hereby arrest you. God save the King ! '

Thereupon Constable Drum pulled Mrs. Taper out of the hedge, and handcuffed her right wrist to his left one. And in spite of all her protests, which were loud and many, he marched her away to prison.

Dinah and Dorinda, in the meantime, were having a very serious discussion.

' It seems to me,' said Dinah, ' that we have to make up our minds either to stop being naughty altogether, or to be naughty in a sensible way. Do you want to stop ? '

' No,' said Dorinda. ' Why, we've only just started. It would be cowardly to stop already.'

' Then we shall have to be sensible. There's no point in being naughty if it only makes us unhappy.'

' I want revenge,' said Dorinda.

' On Mrs. Taper and Catherine Crumb ? '

' And on all the village people who stuck pins in us as well.'

' Well, I think you're perfectly right. But how are we going to do it without getting more pins stuck in us, or being made to cry in some other way ? '

' I don't know. But you can think of something, Dinah. You always have good ideas.'

' I'm beginning to think of something already,' said Dinah. ' You remember how frightened all the village people were when a grizzly bear walked into Mr. Horrabin the ironmonger's ? '

' I remember,' said Dorinda. ' Though the bear didn't do anything except give Mr. Horrabin an envelope with Sir Lankester Lemon's name and address on it.'

' He just wanted to get into Sir Lankester's zoo,' said Dinah. ' But everybody was terribly frightened, and quite a lot of people climbed up trees to get away from him.'

' He was a very nice bear,' said Dorinda, ' and he's still in the zoo. I saw him there not very long ago.'

' Well, we're going to frighten people just as badly as he did.'

' Oh, how ? ' asked Dorinda. ' Do tell me how ! '

' I shall tell you to-morrow,' said Dinah, ' as soon as I have quite made up my mind.'

' It will be lovely to have our revenge,' said Dorinda.

Dinah went to a table on which stood a large blue-and-white jug of milk, and poured out two glasses. She gave one to Dorinda.

' You remember,' she asked, ' how Father was always drinking toasts ? To the King, and to Absent Friends, and to the Regiment, and the Memory of Nelson, and that sort of thing ? Well, we're going to drink a toast. To Revenge ! '

' To Revenge ! ' said Dorinda, and drank her milk so quickly that she nearly choked. When she was feeling better, she asked, ' What are you going to tell me to-morrow ? '

Dinah tiptoed to the door and quietly opened it

to make sure there was no one on the other side listening at the keyhole. Then she tiptoed back and whispered, ' As soon as we are better, and quite strong again, I'm going to Mrs. Grimble's, and she will help us to do something really dreadful ! '

Chapter Five

It was several weeks later. Lying between the roots of an oak-tree at the edge of the Forest of Weal, Dorinda waited patiently for her sister. She had wanted very much to go with Dinah to see Mrs. Grimble, but Dinah had said no. Mrs. Grimble, she explained, wasn't really fond of visitors, and it would be a pity to upset her by taking someone whom she didn't know. Because if that happened, she would simply make herself invisible, and they might waste the whole morning looking for her and finding nothing. And sometimes, to people who went to see her merely out of curiosity, she was extremely rude, and shouted at them in a very frightening way. Everybody was agreed that one of the most alarming things in the world was to be called rude names by an invisible Mrs. Grimble.

It would be wiser, then, said Dinah, for her to go alone ; and Dorinda, though naturally disappointed, agreed. Dorinda nearly always agreed with her sister, whom she admired very much because she was clever and had lovely yellow hair. And Dinah, for her part, admired Dorinda very much because she was brave and had beautiful dark hair.

So Dorinda waited patiently, and after a long time she saw Dinah walking along an aisle in the forest, and ran to meet her. Both of them were looking very well, and feeling perfectly strong, because they had long since stopped crying, and had eaten a good supper the night before and a still larger breakfast that morning.

'What did Mrs. Grimble say ? ' cried Dorinda.
'Is she going to help us ? What did she look like ?
When are we going to have our revenge ? What
shall we have to do ? Oh, do hurry up and tell me,
Dinah ! '

'You can carry this, if you like,' said Dinah, and
gave her sister a little box made of plaited grass.
'But take care of it, because it's very valuable.'

'Did Mrs. Grimble give it you ? Is it magic ? '
asked Dorinda.

'Yes,' said Dinah, and they both sat down
between the roots of the oak-tree.

'Now, listen,' said Dinah, 'and I'll tell you just
what happened. Well, to begin with, I found Mrs.
Grimble at home. She was having a cup of tea, and
talking to Willy her billy-goat and Moses her magpie. I don't quite know what they were talking
about, but it had something to do with one of the
animals in Sir Lankester Lemon's zoo. The golden
puma, I think.'

'I've seen it,' said Dorinda. 'It's the most
beautiful puma I've ever seen.'

'You haven't seen very many, of course,' said
Dinah.

'Neither have you,' said Dorinda.

'That's true,' said Dinah regretfully, 'but it
doesn't matter at the moment, because we're talking
about Mrs. Grimble, not pumas. Well, she made
Willy and Moses go outside, and she gave me a cup
of wild-strawberry juice, which was very nice, and
I told her about everything that had happened to us.
I told her that you wanted revenge on the village

people, and she said that showed you had a proper spirit, and that some day I could take you to see her.'

' How lovely ! ' said Dorinda in great excitement. ' When shall we go ? To-morrow ? '

' Not till you're a lot older,' said Dinah firmly. ' I never dreamt of going to see Mrs. Grimble when I was your age.'

' It's horribly unfair, the way people take advantage of being two years older than somebody else,' said Dorinda.

' No, it isn't,' said Dinah. ' It's quite natural.'

' It's unfair,' repeated Dorinda.

' You won't think so in two years' time, when you'll be as old as I am now,' said Dinah.

' Yes, I shall,' said Dorinda, ' because you'll still be two years older, and taking advantage of me in some other way.'

Dinah thought about that for nearly half a minute, and then she said : ' But think what will happen when we're quite old. When you're ninety, I shall be ninety-two, and at ninety-two it wouldn't be at all surprising if I were on my death-bed. But you, being only ninety, will still be going to parties, and taking a little walk in the morning, and having a good lunch, and telling your great-grandchildren about all the things you did when you were a girl. You'll be enjoying yourself when I'm on my death-bed, and that will be terribly unfair to me. So everything will be evened-up in time.'

' I suppose you're right,' said Dorinda, ' but I've got a good many years to wait. Well, tell me more about Mrs. Grimble.'

' She said that once when she was away from

home some of the village boys had thrown stones at her house, and broken a window. So she was very glad when she heard that we wanted to frighten them, and promised to help us in any way she could. Then I told her about the grizzly bear that went into Mr. Horrabin the ironmonger's, and how he frightened everyone so badly. And I asked her for a magic draught that would turn us into grizzly bears.'

' Not for always ? ' asked Dorinda.

' No, just for a few days, of course.'

' I wouldn't like to be a grizzly bear for the rest of my life,' said Dorinda.

' Well, you're not going to be one at all,' said Dinah, ' because Mrs. Grimble didn't think it a good idea. A grizzly bear has a very thick coat, and we would feel hot and uncomfortable, she said. We would probably come out in heat-spots under the skin, she thought. So she advised us to turn into crocodiles. A crocodile, she said, was always cool, and she couldn't think of anything that would give the villagers a worse fright than seeing a pair of enormous crocodiles coming up the street.'

' I don't think I want to be an enormous crocodile,' said Dorinda.

' Nor do I,' said Dinah, ' and I told her so at once. So then she said that a crocodile was her choice, and if we didn't like it, we should have to think of something for ourselves. She said she would give us a magic draught that would turn us into anything at all, but I would have to wait while she made it, because she hadn't any of that particular sort in stock. And that's why I was late, because it took her about an hour to make it. She put a pot on the fire, and while she was making it, she sang a song which was the recipe for the draught.'

' Does she sing well ? ' asked Dorinda.

' No, not very well,' said Dinah, ' but very clearly. You could hear every word.'

' Do you remember the song ? '

' I think so. Wait a minute, and I'll try to sing it.'

Dinah frowned and whispered to herself, rehearsing the lines, and then in a small clear voice she sang :

> ' A Cuckoo-clock and half a Leek,
> A Monkey's Paw and a Pigling's Cheek,
> Deadly Nightshade, a pinch of Salt,
> A Tiger's Whisker and some Malt,
> A Tadpole and a Stickleback,
> Something White and Something Black—
> Put in Pot and let 'em Simmer
> (Blow the Fire, it's getting dimmer),
> Put in Pot and let 'em Boil
> In the best Banana Oil.

> ' Feather of Bird that never Flew,
> A Rose and a Radish, a sprig of Rue,
> A Viper's Tongue, an Adder's Bile,
> A Worm from the Tooth of a Crocodile,
> Three Black Hairs from a Bull's Tail,
> A Sparrow, a Spider, and a Snail —
> Put in Pot and let 'em Simmer
> (Blow the Fire, it's getting dimmer),
> Put in Pot and let 'em Boil
> In the best Banana Oil.

> ' A Nightjar's Egg, the Blood of a Bat,
> The Naked Ear of an old Tom Cat,
> A Weasel's Brain and a Peacock's Eye,
> A Bunch of Nettles, a Warble Fly,

Puddle-water and Moonlight,
Something Black and Something White—
  Put in Pot and let 'em Simmer
  (Blow the Fire, it's getting dimmer),
  Put in Pot and let 'em Boil
  In the best Banana Oil ! '

' It's a nice song,' said Dorinda, ' but I don't think the medicine will have a very nice taste.'

' It will be quite horrible, I'm afraid,' said Dinah.

' But we can hold our noses and drink it very quickly,' said Dorinda, ' and then we shall become — well, what shall we become ? There are so many animals, it's very difficult to choose. I don't want to be a hippopotamus, or anything like that. I should love to be an antelope, but an antelope, of course, wouldn't frighten anyone. What shall we become, Dinah ? '

' I've been thinking about it very carefully,' said Dinah, ' and it occurred to me that there's one very big disadvantage in being an animal. Animals don't usually have pockets, and they can't carry a purse or a handbag. But if we are going to be away from home for a few days, we shall certainly want to take a tooth-brush and a clean pocket-handkerchief.'

' And some chocolate,' said Dorinda.

' And it would be a good idea to take a note-book.'

' And I shouldn't like to go away without my new watch,' said Dorinda.

' And we shall have to take the magic draught, of course, so that we can turn ourselves back into girls when we want to.'

' I suppose,' said Dorinda, ' that we could tie a little bag round our necks, to carry things in.'

49

' I've thought of something better than that,' said Dinah. ' There's one sort of animal that has got pockets.'

' I know ! ' said Dorinda. ' A kangaroo ! '

' Yes,' said Dinah. ' Of course the usual thing for a kangaroo to carry in its pouch is a baby, but I don't see why it shouldn't do equally well for a note-book and a pocket-handkerchief and a tooth-brush and some chocolate and anything else we may need.'

' We shall be far better off than the ordinary kind of animal,' said Dorinda, ' and the village people will get a terrible fright when they see us coming up the street, jumping twenty feet at a time.'

' We'll make them climb trees again,' said Dinah.

' It's going to be a lot of fun,' said Dorinda. ' But don't you feel a little bit strange to think that by this time to-morrow you'll be a kangaroo ? '

' Just a little,' said Dinah.

' When do we drink the magic draught ? Now ? '

' In the morning, after breakfast. And now let us go home and pack. Well, not exactly pack, because we haven't got anything to put stuff into yet.'

' I do feel excited,' exclaimed Dorinda, and just before they reached home she stopped and very solemnly said : ' I have often wondered what I shall be when I grow up, whether a teacher of dancing, or a circus rider, or a mother of ten, but never, never, never did I expect to be a kangaroo ! '

Chapter Six

In the Police Court at Midmeddlecum, Mr. Justice
Rumple was trying Mrs. Taper the draper's wife

for attempting to commit a felony, to wit, Larceny :
that is to say, in ordinary language, for trying to
steal two pairs of silk stockings. Mr. Justice Rumple
sat on a kind of throne with the Union Jack above

it, a picture of Britannia, another of the Duke of Wellington, and a Latin motto that said : *Fiat Justitia Ruat Coelum.* This terrible motto meant :

> Amid Thunder and Lightning and Earthquakes and Hail,
> I shall sit here just waiting to send you to gaol !

The Judge was wearing a red robe and a new wig covered with beautiful white curls, and he looked very magnificent.

Mrs. Taper, in the dock with a warder beside her, was weeping bitterly. Mr. Taper had just brought her a dozen new handkerchiefs, straight from the shop, and she had already used three of them.

The Counsel for the Prosecution was Mr. Hobson, and the Counsel for the Defence was Mr. Jobson. They were great friends, and they took it in turn to win cases. Mr. Hobson used to win on Mondays, Wednesdays, and Fridays, and Mr. Jobson on Tuesdays, Thursdays, and Saturdays. But this arrangement, of course, had to be kept a very strict secret, or nobody would ever have paid Mr. Jobson to defend him on a Monday, a Wednesday, or a Friday. This was a Thursday, and Mr. Hobson and Mr. Jobson were therefore both agreed that Mrs. Taper should be declared Not Guilty. But nothing went as they intended.

Mr. Hobson — Counsel for the Prosecution — said to Mrs. Taper : ' Did you intend to steal those stockings, Mrs. Taper ? '

' No ! ' said Mrs. Taper indignantly.

' Oh ! ' said Mr. Hobson, pretending to be very disappointed. ' I thought you did ! What a pity !

Well, that *is* a pity ! Because if you're not guilty, I'm afraid I can't think of anything else to say.'

And sitting down again, he took a large pinch of snuff.

But Mr. Justice Rumple, who was in a bad temper, shouted at Mr. Hobson, ' Then you're a poor fish ! A very poor fish indeed, sir ! ' And to Mrs. Taper he roared, ' What are you crying for, if you're not guilty ? '

This made Mrs. Taper cry louder than ever, which created a bad impression on the large audience.

Then Mr. Jobson — Counsel for the Defence — made a very good speech indeed. It was so good that every now and then Mr. Hobson clapped his hands and exclaimed, ' Well said, Jobson ! Oh, well expressed, sir ! ' It was such a magnificent speech that all the people who had come to listen to the trial, and were sitting in court eating sandwiches and hard-boiled eggs and drinking tea out of thermos flasks, stood up when it was finished, and applauded vigorously. Some of them even shouted ' Encore ! '

And Mr. Jobson, looking very pleased with himself, also stood up, and bowed several times, and handed round a lot of visiting-cards on which was printed :

MR. JOBSON, K.C.	
THE BEST LAWYER IN ENGLAND	
Reasonable Fees and Courtesy to All	Last Year's Record was 98 Wins, 14 Draws
Spécialité de la Maison : Defence of Murderers !	

But the Judge was now in a furious rage. For some time he had been shouting ' Clear the Court ! Clear the Court ! ' Nobody could hear him, however, because there was so much noise, and at last he came down from his throne, rolled up his sleeves, and borrowed a truncheon from Constable Drum. With this he started to bang and belabour everybody he could reach, including Mr. Hobson and Mr. Jobson, and drove them all out of court.

Then he returned to his throne, where he sat puffing and blowing, his wig askew, and his sleeves rolled well above the elbow. ' Now let's get on with the trial,' he said.

All this time the Jury had been sitting, very quiet and well-behaved, in the Jury-box. Some of them were playing Patience, some playing Noughts and Crosses, some were reading books, and some were knitting. They felt they were the most important people in court, and they were determined to pay no attention to anyone else. Long before the trial started, they had all decided how they were going to vote, and naturally they didn't want to hear anything that would make them change their minds. The Jury consisted of the following well-known, trustworthy, and highly respected citizens : Dr. Fosfar, Mr. and Mrs. Leathercow, Mr. and Mrs. Fullalove, Mr. and Mrs. Crumb, Mrs. Wax the chemist's wife, Mr. Whitloe the drayman, Mrs. Horrabin the ironmonger's wife, Mrs. Steeple the Vicar's wife, and Mr. Casimir Corvo, teacher of music and dancing. The Foreman of the Jury was Dr. Fosfar, who was, at this moment, polishing his glass eye with a silk handkerchief.

' Ladies and gentlemen of the Jury,' shouted the Judge. ' I shall give you five minutes to make up your minds and return a verdict. You have heard the evidence, you have heard Mr. Jobson talk a great deal of nonsense, and you have heard Mr. Hobson, that poor fish, say nothing at all. In my opinion Mrs. Taper ought to be sent to prison. But according to British Law, which is the best in the world——'

' Hurrah ! ' shouted Constable Drum.

' According to British Law,' continued the Judge, ' the verdict must be decided by you. Guilty or Not Guilty : one or the other. If you decide that Mrs. Taper is Guilty, then the wretched woman will go to prison, as she so richly deserves. If you decide she is Not Guilty, then I shall have to set her free, and she'll continue to go round the country stealing silk stockings wherever she can find them.'

' I never did and I never shall ! ' cried Mrs. Taper, but no one paid any attention to her.

' I shall say nothing, however,' proceeded the Judge, ' to influence you in any way. The responsibility is yours. You have five minutes, ladies and gentlemen, five minutes and not a second more ! '

The Judge took out his watch and laid it on the desk in front of him. Dr. Fosfar, who was sometimes absent-minded, put his glass eye in his waistcoat pocket and a piece of india-rubber where his eye should have been, and said to the Jury, ' Now I'm going to ask each one of you in turn whether you think poor Mrs. Taper is Guilty or Not Guilty, and I shall write down your answers on this piece of paper. Now you, Mr. Leathercow : what is your opinion ? '

' Not Guilty,' said Mr. Leathercow.

' Guilty,' said Mrs. Leathercow.

' Guilty,' said Mrs. Fullalove.

' Not Guilty,' said Mr. Fullalove.

' Not Guilty,' said Mr. Crumb.

' Guilty,' said Mrs. Crumb.

' Guilty,' said Mrs. Wax.

' Guilty,' said Mrs. Horrabin.

' Not Guilty,' said Mr. Whitloe.

' Guilty,' said Mrs. Steeple.

' Not Guilty,' said Mr. Casimir Corvo.

' And I,' said Dr. Fosfar, ' also say Not Guilty. Now if we add up the Guiltys and the Not Guiltys, we shall quickly discover which side has won.'

But a moment later he exclaimed, ' How very awkward ! Six of us think she is Guilty, and six of us believe she is Not Guilty ! Therefore neither side has won, and so we cannot deliver a verdict. I'm afraid the Judge is going to be rather angry about that.'

The Judge was.

' I insist on having a verdict ! ' he shouted. ' And you, sir ! ' — he meant Dr. Fosfar — ' take that piece of india-rubber out of your eye ! '

' Why ? ' asked Dr. Fosfar. ' It's much more comfortable than my glass eye.'

' Never mind why, do what I tell you. And I'll give your wretched Jury one more minute ! '

But the Jury, of course, had all made up their minds a long time ago, and nothing could now change them. All the men were quite sure that Mrs.

Taper was Not Guilty, because they were all sorry
for her. And all the women were equally sure that
she was Guilty, and ought to go to prison, because it
was disgraceful, they thought, that a draper's wife,
who could get stockings out of the shop without
paying anything, should go about the country trying
to steal them. So Dr. Fosfar had to give it up, and
tell the Judge they would not agree, and therefore
could not deliver a verdict.

' Then,' shouted the Judge in a mighty temper,
' I shall send you *all* to prison ! What for ? For
Contempt of Court, sir ! Six months in prison for
the lot of you ! That'll teach you to be sensible,
and give me a verdict when I ask for one. Put the
handcuffs on them, Constable Drum, and march
'em off. And as for Mrs. Taper, I remand her in
custody, so she'll have to go to prison too. Off with
the lot of them ! '

The Members of the Jury were completely dismayed by this dreadful sentence, but before they
could think of anything to say, Constable Drum had
handcuffed them together, two by two, and was
marching them away.

A large crowd of people were waiting outside.
There were those who had been expelled from the
court, and a lot of others who hadn't been able to
get in. They were very much surprised, and many
were indignant, when they saw the Jury all handcuffed together, and heard what was about to
happen to them. There was a great deal of shouting
and excitement, and Constable Drum looked rather
worried. Everybody was trying to get closer and
closer to the poor Jurymen and Jurywomen, to shake

hands and offer them sympathy, and the Constable feared that half his prisoners would get lost in the crowd.

Then the Rev. Mr. Steeple, the Vicar, did a noble thing. Though his own wife was in handcuffs and on her way to prison, he climbed on to a cart, and from this commanding position he declared in a loud voice : ' My dear people ! It is very sad for us to see so many of our friends being taken from us, but we must be patient ! We must not be cast down. We must remind ourselves of the many blessings that still remain to us. Let us be cheerful, let us face the future with brave hearts. And I think it would be a good idea to sing a song that we all know, which happens to suit the occasion very well indeed.'

So then, in a fine loud voice, the Vicar began to sing :

> ' Farewell and adieu to you, fair Spanish ladies,
> Farewell and adieu to you, ladies of Spain !
> For we've received orders to sail for old England,
> But we hope in a short time to see you again ! '

Before long the whole crowd was singing, and when that song was finished, they sang, with much feeling, *My Bonny Lies Over the Ocean*.

Then Constable Drum said that his prisoners would have to hurry, because in prison they always had dinner at twelve o'clock, and if they were late they wouldn't get any. So the Jurymen and Jury-women, and Mrs. Taper too, set off at a great pace, their handcuffs clinking and clanking, and all the other people, in two big columns, marched on either side of them.

But scarcely had they gone a hundred yards when they were brought to a halt by the most extraordinary sight. Coming up the street towards them, leaping high in the air and going twenty feet at a time, were two large grey kangaroos !

Chapter Seven

Dorinda had been the first to wake that morning.
She had dreamt that she was already a kangaroo,
and she was disappointed to find herself still in
human shape. She began to imagine, or try to
imagine, what it would feel like to be enclosed in a
furry hide, and to lean backwards, as if in a chair,
against the support of a long strong tail. And from
that position she would also be able to leap the
length of quite a long room. Kangaroos were very
lucky in some ways.

She slipped out of bed to practise a jumping
position, and at that moment Dinah got quietly out
of her bed with the same idea in her head. For she
too, as soon as she woke, had started to think about
the new experiences that were awaiting her. So she
and Dorinda both began to practise kangaroo jumps
on the bedroom floor, but found it difficult without
tails to help them. They had to wait, it seemed, a
very long time before breakfast was ready.

Then, as soon as they could get away, they left the
house and ran without stopping to the nearest part
of the Forest of Weal. That, they had decided, was
the best place in which to drink the magic draught,
because they did not want, of course, to turn into
kangaroos in the nursery, where they might frighten
their mother. And it might be difficult, added
Dinah, to get downstairs. She did not think that
kangaroos were very good on stairs.

So they hurried to the Forest, carrying the little

box of plaited grass with Mrs. Grimble's medicine in it, and two small bundles that held all the things they wanted to take with them. When they came to a suitable place, they stopped and looked all around to make sure there was no one within sight. Then they opened the grass box, and read the directions on the bottle. This is what Mrs. Grimble had written on the label :

DIRECTIONS FOR TURNING YOURSELF INTO
ANYTHING YOU WANT TO BE

1. Shake the Bottle.
2. Undress Yourself.
3. Fold your Clothes Neatly and Put in Safe Place.
4. Turn Three Times against the Sun and say : I Want to Be Whatever You do Want to Be.
5. Shake the Bottle again.
6. Drink one Dose.
7. Replace the Cork.
8. Go for a Little Walk.

(*Signed*) MRS. GRIMBLE

' This is a solemn moment,' said Dinah, as she began to take off her shoes.

' Very solemn,' said Dorinda. ' I'm glad it's a warm day.'

' There's a hole in that oak-tree,' said Dinah. ' We can put our clothes away there.'

They packed their clothes into the hole in the oak-tree, and shook the bottle for the second time. There were just four doses in it, and Dinah had remembered to bring a tablespoon. She gave Dorinda the first dose, and quickly took her own.

They packed their clothes into the oak-tree

' Oh ! ' cried Dorinda, turning quite pale.

' I have never in all my life tasted anything so horrible,' said Dinah. But she put the cork back in the bottle, and in a firm voice said to Dorinda, ' Now we must take a little walk. You go that way, and I'll go this.'

She wanted to be alone, because she thought she was going to be sick. But in a little while she felt much better, and curiously strong. She felt far stronger than she had ever been, or ever dreamt of being, and never, she thought, had all the leaves and the grass looked so nice. She put a few leaves in her mouth and chewed them, and to her surprise they tasted rather like bread-and-honey. Then, seeing a bush in front of her, she jumped over it, and thought : Well, I've never been able to jump as high as that before !

But then she got a terrible fright, because a few yards away she saw a wild animal. A tall grey kangaroo !

Her heart nearly stopped beating, for she had never expected to meet a real kangaroo, and she was just going to turn and run away as fast as she could when she remembered Dorinda. She must warn Dorinda.

So as loud as she could she shouted, ' Dorinda, Dorinda ! Take care, there's a kangaroo in the Forest ! '

Her voice sounded curiously unlike anything she had heard before, but that, she supposed, was due to the fright she had had.

The kangaroo, it seemed, had also been on the point of running away. But it stopped when it heard Dinah, and then Dinah heard Dorinda's voice. At least, she supposed it was Dorinda's voice, though it wasn't like her ordinary voice, because it said : 'Dinah, Dinah ! Take care, I can see a kangaroo !'

And the voice, which was Dorinda's, came from the kangaroo of which Dinah had been frightened. The kangaroo *was* Dorinda !

And Dinah, feeling rather hot and quite embarrassed, looked down at her own great legs, and over her shoulder at her long powerful tail, and realised that she too had become a kangaroo, and that she had made Dorinda equally frightened. The medicine had worked !

'Oh, Dorinda !' she exclaimed.

'Oh, Dinah !' said Dorinda.

'I got such a fright when I saw you,' said Dinah.

'So did I when I saw you,' said Dorinda.

'We certainly look exactly like real kangaroos,' said Dinah.

'Mrs. Grimble must be a very good sort of witch,' said Dorinda.

'I think it will be nice when we get used to it,' said Dinah. 'I've done one or two marvellous jumps already.'

'But it does feel strange to begin with,' said Dorinda.

In a few minutes, however, they felt perfectly at home in their new shape, and greatly pleased with themselves. They practised long jumping and standing on their tails, and found that their arms, though quite small in comparison with their great legs, were very useful. Almost as useful, indeed, as human arms and hands.

After practising running for about half an hour, they decided to go to the village. But first of all they returned to the place where they had drunk the magic draught, and carefully packed in their pouches the things they had brought from home.

Dinah had taken a note-book and a pencil and a rubber ; two pocket-handkerchiefs and a tooth-brush ; the key of the back door and a slab of chocolate. She put them all into her pouch, and also the bottle of medicine and the tablespoon.

Dorinda had taken some milk chocolate and her new watch ; a tooth-brush and a comb and a pencil-sharpener and a book called *Wild Life in Borneo*, which she thought might be useful, but it was too big to go into her pouch, and had to be left behind. She had forgotten to bring a handkerchief, but Dinah said she would lend her one if she needed it.

Then they set off for the village.

' Now for revenge ! ' said Dinah.

' Revenge ! ' said Dorinda, and jumped across a hedge and back again.

In the outer streets of the village they saw no one at all. The streets were deserted because everyone was waiting outside the Police Court to hear the result of the trial of Mrs. Taper. Not a soul was to be seen till they came into Elm Lane, and there, approaching them, was a great procession of people. All the people, indeed, who were escorting the Members of the Jury to Midmeddlecum Gaol. They were singing a very fine French song which the

Vicar had taught them only a few weeks before. It was called *Avec mes Sabots.*

Seeing so many people all at once, and hearing such a great noise of singing, Dinah and Dorinda became slightly nervous, and stopped for a moment. It needed, they felt, a lot of courage to charge the whole population of Midmeddlecum. They had not expected to see them all together like this.

But the people of Midmeddlecum, seeing two tall grey kangaroos coming towards them, were far more frightened than Dinah and Dorinda. They also stopped, and their fine song died away.

Then Dinah said, ' Father is a soldier. He would never flinch from the enemy. Charge, Dorinda, charge ! '

Bounding and waving their arms, they advanced at top speed. Never before had such a sight been seen in Elm Lane.

The villagers turned and ran in all directions, but the prisoners, who were handcuffed two by two, were rather at a disadvantage, and some of them were left in the lurch. Only one man tried to defend the village, and that was Constable Drum. He stood very bravely in the middle of the lane, and shouted to the kangaroos, ' Halt, in the King's name ! Halt, and be arrested ! '

But Dinah, with a kick as she passed, knocked him head over heels. She did this as gently as she could, because she was quite fond of Constable Drum who was a good man, but her great kangaroo legs were so strong that even a gentle kick made him turn two complete somersaults. Then she caught Tom Leathercow the butcher's son, and kicked him

into a ditch. And Dorinda caught Robin and
Robina Wax, who were trying to climb a tree, but
the tree was already full of people, so there was no
room for them, and Dorinda kicked them both into
a convenient garden.

All the trees in Elm Lane were crowded with
people who had climbed into their branches to get
away from the kangaroos. But a great many
villagers, including the prisoners who were handcuffed and therefore could not climb trees, were
running towards the Square, and Dinah and
Dorinda chased them across Elm Street, and up
Tulip Street, and round the statue of Queen Victoria.
As they passed the door of the Police Court, Mr.
Justice Rumple came out to see what all the noise
was about. His shirt-sleeves were still rolled up,
and he was smoking a cigar. When he saw the
kangaroos he retreated very quickly into the Police
Court, and slammed the door behind him, and
bolted it and locked it. Then he went to the telephone, and telephoned to Sir Lankester Lemon.

Dinah and Dorinda chased the people three times
round the statue of Queen Victoria. The Vicar,
who was good at climbing, was sitting on her lap
with Mrs. Fullalove, and the Vicar was saying, ' I
wish I had my camera ! Oh, I *wish* I had my
camera ! ' But everybody else had only one wish
in the world, and that was not to be kicked by the
kangaroos.

On their way round for the third time, Dinah
and Dorinda caught sight of Catherine Crumb, who
was riding a bicycle that belonged to Wilfrid
Leathercow, the butcher's second son.

' Look ! ' shouted Dinah. ' There's Catherine Crumb ! '

' Chase her,' shouted Dorinda.

So they chased her up Rose Street, and across Oak Street, and along Oak Lane. At the end of Oak Lane, Catherine Crumb turned left into Meddlecum Road, and Dinah and Dorinda were close behind her. But Wilfrid Leathercow's bicycle was a racing bicycle, and Catherine Crumb rode very fast, with her head right down over the handlebars, and her long thin legs going like pistons. Several times she was nearly caught, but she managed to keep ahead, and rode faster and faster. Dinah and Dorinda, because they had not had very much practice at being kangaroos, were by now somewhat tired.

Meddlecum Road led to Meddlecum Hall, where Sir Lankester Lemon lived. There were large iron gates at the entrance to his estate, and a little farther on the road went over a humpbacked bridge across the River Brill.

The iron gates were wide open, and Catherine Crumb rode straight on. She crossed the bridge, and Dinah and Dorinda were scarcely a yard behind her. But suddenly, from behind a tree that grew on the left-hand side of the road, a long coil of rope came leaping through the air, and a noose of it fell round Dinah's neck. At the same time, from behind a tree on the right-hand side of the road, another rope leapt into sight, and encircled Dorinda's neck. They were jerked from their feet, and rolled over and over in the grass. They came down with a bump, and they saw, as it seemed, the road and the bridge and the grass and the trees, and Catherine Crumb on her bicycle and the two men who had thrown the ropes, all going round and round. Then they stopped rolling, and sat up, and got a clearer view of the scene.

It was Sir Lankester Lemon and Mr. Plum, his keeper, who had lassooed and captured them. Warned by Mr. Justice Rumple that there were kangaroos in the neighbourhood, Sir Lankester had made the necessary preparations, and he and Mr. Plum were all ready when Dinah and Dorinda came chasing Catherine Crumb into his estate.

He was very pleased at having two fine kangaroos to put in his zoo, and he gave Catherine Crumb a shilling as a reward for her part in the capture. Catherine Crumb looked very hot and untidy, but she was glad to get a whole shilling for herself, and rode away with a great air of triumph.

But Dinah and Dorinda were by no means pleased. They were, quite naturally, a little frightened, and they were rather sore from their fall. And they felt extremely angry with Sir Lankester for giving money to Catherine Crumb. But they did not try to escape when Mr. Plum began to lead them towards the zoo, and they went meekly into the cage that had been prepared for them.

It was large and clean, with a little house behind it, and behind that a sort of small garden surrounded by a tall fence. It was a well-kept zoo, and everything in it was very tidy and comfortable. Mr. Plum took the ropes off their necks, and, locking the cage behind him, left them alone.

' And now what are we going to do ? ' asked Dorinda miserably.

' I don't see that we can do anything at all,' answered Dinah.

' Oh, look ! ' Dorinda exclaimed, and pointed to the next-door cage on the right.

From the house behind it, a much bigger house than theirs, came a tall Giraffe with bulging eyes, who stared at them in the most suspicious manner.

' And look there ! ' said Dorinda, pointing to the next-door cage on the other side. ' It's the Grizzly Bear that went into Mr. Horrabin the ironmonger's,' she whispered.

The Bear was looking at them in a rather surly way, as if he were a bear that did not like company. But he did not say anything.

' I don't like being stared at by a Giraffe and a Grizzly Bear,' said Dorinda.

' Neither do I,' said Dinah ; ' let's go into our house, where they can't see us.'

There was nothing in the house except a rack for food, but it gave them privacy, and they sat on the floor, leaning against their tails, and considered what to do.

At last, after thinking for a long time, Dorinda said, ' Well, we've had our revenge, and we've still got some of Mrs. Grimble's magic draught. If we take the other two doses, and change ourselves back into girls, Sir Lankester will have to let us go. He can't keep girls in a zoo.'

' It would be difficult to explain how we got here,' said Dinah.

' You could make up a story,' said Dorinda.

' It wouldn't be easy,' said Dinah, but all the same she felt in her pouch for the bottle of magic medicine. She took out the note-book and pencil, the tablespoon and a pocket-handkerchief. She felt again, and yet again. But there was nothing else in her pouch !

' Oh, Dorinda ! ' she exclaimed, ' I've lost it ! I've lost the key of the back door as well, and my chocolate and my tooth-brush, but that doesn't really matter. But what is going to become of us without Mrs. Grimble's medicine ? '

' Perhaps we shall have to be kangaroos all the rest of our lives ! ' said Dorinda. ' Oh, Dinah ! '

' Oh, Dorinda ! ' said Dinah.

Chapter Eight

Sir Lankester Lemon was a tall thin man with a small head and large pale-blue eyes that gave him a kindly but rather a goggling look. He was a great traveller, and in various far-away countries he had learnt to use such strange weapons as bow and arrow, blowpipe, bolas, lasso, throwing-spear, and boomerang. He used to practise with them, twice a week, in the park. He had a tall thin wife, who did not matter much, however. She did nothing but grumble because she didn't enjoy herself as much as she would like to, and Sir Lankester took no notice of her. All his attention was devoted to the animals in his zoo, and he did everything he could to make them happy. Most of them were quite contented with the life they led, but there was a Puma, a lovely animal of a fine golden colour, who could not forget the freedom of her native jungle, the hot sun by day and the hunting moon ; and she was not happy. And there was a Greenland Falcon, whose plumage was nearly as white as snow, who kept thinking of the crystal air of the Far North, and long bright views of the ice-edged mountains ; and he was not happy.

On the morning after the capture of Dinah and Dorinda, Sir Lankester came very early to see how they were getting on. Dinah and Dorinda were glad to see him. They knew him well by sight, and once, when he came to a tea-party at their house, they had actually spoken to him. It was comforting to remember that, and Dinah thought how surprised he would be if he discovered who his kangaroos really were.

Sir Lankester was wearing a tweed suit with a

yellow waistcoat and a green hat, he was smoking a pipe, and there was a copy of *The Times* sticking out of his coat pocket. In appearance, thought Dorinda, he was not very unlike her father. And wistfully she remembered how far away her father was, in a foreign country, and perhaps in danger.

Mr. Plum the keeper, who was with Sir Lankester,

was a short broad-shouldered man with a cheerful expression and red cheeks. He wore a canvas jacket, whipcord breeches, and a bowler hat. He and Sir Lankester, leaning against the next-door cage, where the Grizzly Bear was yawning in the early sun, gazed thoughtfully at the kangaroos, and Sir Lankester said to Mr. Plum : ' They are the finest kangaroos I have ever seen, but they don't look happy. Let us take them for a walk and show them the zoo. Perhaps that will cheer them up a little.'

So Mr. Plum unlocked their cage, and put collars like big dog-collars round their necks, and led them out. There were steel chains attached to the collars, and Sir Lankester led Dinah, and Mr. Plum led Dorinda.

' And now,' said Sir Lankester in a friendly voice, ' we are going to introduce you to our other members, and we hope you will become friendly with them. Most of them get on very well together, and those who do so come out every day to play in the park, and down by the river. You have already seen Bendigo the Grizzly Bear, of course, and Mr. Parker the Giraffe. They are among the most highly respected members of my zoo. And here is Marie Louise, a Peruvian Llama. She is rather proud, and from her expression you may think she is sneering at you. But she has, in truth, a heart of gold. Haven't you, Marie Louise ? '

The Llama, indeed, wore a very cold and disdainful look, but when Sir Lankester reached through the bars of her cage and scratched her neck, she smiled in her own way, and half-closed her eyes, and murmured, ' Hasn't he the most charming manners ? Don't you think Sir Lankester is quite the handsomest man you have ever seen ? '

Neither Sir Lankester nor Mr. Plum, of course, could understand what Marie Louise was saying, but Dinah and Dorinda, to their surprise, understood her perfectly. Being kangaroos, they now knew the language of animals, as well as English, and they had learnt it without any trouble to themselves. This was very gratifying when they remembered the weary hours they had spent with Miss Serendip trying to learn French.

And after all, thought Dinah, what is the point of learning French ? Because French people talk about the same things as we do, and why we should want to talk about the same things in two different languages I can't think. But a conversation with a camel or a leopard, for example, should be really interesting.

She and Dorinda grew more cheerful, and Sir Lankester introduced them to an Antelope, a Ring-tailed Lemur, an Ant-eater, and a Zebra. A very large Python, however, of whom he was particularly proud, was fast asleep and they did not disturb him.

' He sleeps a great deal,' said Sir Lankester, ' but if you ever manage to meet him when he's awake, you'll find him very interesting. He is certainly one of our most distinguished members.'

Then they walked across the park, in a corner of which was a small enclosure where a pair of Ostriches lived. They were called Sir Bobadil and Lady Lil.

' They recently had a great sorrow,' Sir Lankester explained. ' A few days ago Lady Lil laid her first egg. It was a most beautiful egg, and they were naturally very proud of it. So indeed were we all. But then the most dreadful thing happened. The egg disappeared ! We searched for it everywhere, but no trace of it could be found. It was a complete mystery. And Sir Bobadil and Lady Lil, poor things, were almost heart-broken. But yesterday she laid a second egg, and they were so delighted that both of them, I hope, have by now forgotten their sad loss. Because, after all, one egg is very like another. And there, beside the lime-trees, is where they live.'

' Something's up,' said Mr. Plum.

' What do you mean ? ' asked Sir Lankester.

' With the Ostriches,' said Mr. Plum. ' What are they making all that noise for ? '

As they came near the enclosure they could see the Ostriches striding up and down in a very agitated way. They were screaming at each other with anger in their voices, and Dinah and Dorinda were soon able to learn the reason for their quarrel.

' It's all your fault ! ' Lady Lil was repeating. ' Your fault entirely. *All* your fault. Oh, how I hate you ! '

' It wasn't my fault at all,' shouted Sir Bobadil. ' I just went out for a walk — not a long walk, just a little walk — and I wasn't away for more than half an hour.'

' After I had sat on it all night ! ' screamed Lady Lil. ' All I asked you to do was to look after it for an hour or two, while I went for my breakfast, and when I came back you were nowhere to be seen, and *it* was nowhere to be seen, and now my heart is broken. Oh, whatever shall I do ? First one, and then another ! My lovely eggs, my dear, dear eggs ! Oh, why did you go away ? Why didn't you stay and look after it ? '

' I just went down to the river to have a word with the Black Swan,' said Sir Bobadil. ' What harm was there in that ? '

' What harm ? ' exclaimed Lady Lil. ' How dare you say a thing like that ! My beautiful white egg has been stolen, because you wouldn't stay to look after it, and then you ask what harm you have done ! Oh, you wicked, wicked Ostrich ! '

' No, not wicked,' cried Sir Bobadil. ' Don't say I'm wicked. Please don't say that ! '

' Yes, you are,' said Lady Lil. ' You have made me so unhappy, I think I shall die.'

' It was my egg as well as yours,' said Sir Bobadil. ' You needn't think that you are the only one to suffer. I've got a very, very tender heart, and at this very moment I'm suffering acutely. Perhaps I did make a mistake, but if so I'm paying for it now. I'm just as unhappy as you are, I'm sure I am. Perhaps I shall die too. So don't let us make things worse by quarrelling. Please don't quarrel with me, Lil.'

' No, we shouldn't quarrel,' sobbed Lady Lil.

' Then say you forgive me ! ' begged Sir Bobadil.

' Are you truly sorry ? '

' Truly, truly sorry ! '

' Then I forgive you,' whispered his wife. ' But all the same it was terribly wrong of you to go and leave it. Oh, wickedly wrong, foolishly wrong. So wrong that I can't think how you did it. And what can have happened to our lovely egg ? To both our lovely eggs ? What black-hearted thief has robbed us of our dear ones ? Oh, where have they gone ? '

' If I had the miscreant here,' exclaimed Sir Bobadil, ' I would make him sorry for his vile behaviour. Oh, comfort yourself, dear Lil, pray comfort yourself. Perhaps we shall find them yet.'

' Never, never,' sighed Lady Lil, and hung her head, the picture of misery.

' Oh dear, oh dear,' muttered Sir Bobadil. ' Why was I so foolish ? ' And he too hung his head, and looked quite as unhappy as Lady Lil.

Though Dinah and Dorinda could understand the whole of this conversation, it meant nothing to Sir Lankester and Mr. Plum, and it was not until they had thoroughly searched the enclosure that they really knew what had happened.

' The nest is empty,' said Sir Lankester.

' Robbers,' said Mr. Plum.

' But how could they do it ? ' asked Sir Lankester. ' It's impossible for anybody to get into the park. The railings are charged with electricity : anybody who touched them would be electrocuted.'

' Aeroplane,' said Mr. Plum. ' Came down by parachute.'

' Nonsense,' said Sir Lankester. ' We should have heard an aeroplane, and if a parachutist did come down in the zoo, he couldn't get out again. No, no. The thief is in our midst ! '

' Don't ask me,' said Mr. Plum. ' I'm a keeper, not a detective.'

'A crime has been committed,' declared Sir Lankester. 'There can be no doubt of that.'

'Two crimes,' said Mr. Plum. 'Two eggs, two crimes.'

'Take the kangaroos back to their cage,' said Sir Lankester, 'and I shall make another search.'

So Mr. Plum took charge of Dinah and Dorinda, and Sir Lankester looked here and there for the missing egg, and Sir Bobadil went searching in one direction, and Lady Lil in another. And the Barbary Sheep and the Fallow Deer who lived in the park came to help, and the other animals soon learnt what had happened, because news travels quickly in a zoo, and all grew very worried to think that one of them must be a thief. When they were let into the park, to play and take their exercise, they all gathered round the Ostriches' enclosure, and Sir Bobadil and Lady Lil had to tell their sad story over and over again. And every animal looked at every other animal and wondered who was the horrid miscreant.

Dinah and Dorinda were not allowed into the park, because it was only their first day in the zoo, and Sir Lankester thought that new arrivals ought to stay in their cages to begin with, and settle down. So for a week they had a very dull time, and though they were sorry for the Ostriches, they were also very sorry for themselves.

'Lady Lil may have lost her egg,' said Dinah, 'but I don't think that's any worse than losing our magic draught. Because Lady Lil, I daresay, can lay another egg, but we can't get more medicine without going to see Mrs. Grimble. And if we don't

' Don't ask me,' said Mr. Plum

get any more, we shall have to be kangaroos for the rest of our lives.'

' Perhaps we can escape,' said Dorinda.

' Sir Lankester said that no thief could get into the zoo, or out of it either. All the railings are electrified. And if a thief can't get out, how shall we ? '

' We may find some way that **Sir** Lankester doesn't know about,' said Dorinda.

' We shall have a good look round, of course,' said Dinah, ' as soon as they let us out into the park. Sir Lankester *may* be wrong. People often are.'

' Very often,' said Dorinda.

Every day they ate a good dinner which Mr. Plum brought them. It usually consisted of some hay and some turnips, a few pounds of carrots, a couple of cabbages, and a bucket of beans. And carrots and hay, to their surprise, now tasted rather like roast chicken and chocolate pudding, so they enjoyed their dinner and often went to sleep for a little while afterwards. But when they woke up they generally felt very sad and lonely, and it was all they could do to keep from crying. They used to go to bed quite early.

One night when they had been sleeping for two or three hours, perhaps, Dinah woke and saw a light shining faintly through a chink in the left-hand wall of their little house. On the other side of the wall lived Bendigo the Grizzly Bear, and Dinah wondered why there should be a light in his house. Perhaps he was ill ?

She got up and peeped through the chink in the wall, and what she saw was most surprising.

A candle, about three inches long, stood in its own wax on the edge of the feeding-trough in Bendigo's house, and Bendigo himself, sitting comfortably in the corner beside it, was reading *The Times* !

She recognised the newspaper at once, because her father always read it when he was at home, and she had, indeed, seen a copy of it only that morning — a copy of it sticking out of Sir Lankester's pocket as he leaned against Bendigo's cage on his daily round. She remembered the look of it quite clearly. And then she remembered something else : there was no newspaper in Sir Lankester's pocket when he walked away again ! Where had it gone ?

There could be only one answer : Bendigo had stolen it. Bendigo was a thief ! And since he was a thief, perhaps it was he who had stolen the egg from Lady Lil ?

She was so excited by this possibility that she quite forgot how strange it was to see a Grizzly Bear reading a newspaper. She woke Dorinda and told her to keep very quiet and look through the chink in the wall.

Dorinda had a good look, and then she whispered, ' Did you know that bears could read ? '

' No,' whispered Dinah.

' It just shows,' murmured Dorinda, ' how much we *don't* know.'

' He must have stolen it from Sir Lankester,' said Dinah. ' *The Times*, I mean.'

' Perhaps he's only pretending to read it,' said Dorinda. ' Look again, and see if he's holding it the right way up.'

At that moment, however, the light in Bendigo's house went out.

' Do you think he heard us talking ? ' asked Dinah, and held Dorinda's hand.

For two or three minutes all was quiet, and then Dorinda whispered, ' I can hear somebody else talking ! '

They both listened, and from the cage on the other side, that belonged to Mr. Parker the Giraffe, they heard the low mutter of another voice.

Moving as quietly as they could, they looked out from the door of their house and saw against the starry sky the tall shape and the long dark neck of their other neighbour. He was pacing slowly to and fro, as if deep in thought, and talking very quietly to himself.

' A very baffling mystery,' he was saying. ' Very baffling indeed. The Case of the Stolen Ostrich Eggs. As baffling a case as I can remember. There were, to begin with, no footprints : that makes it baffling. There is, so far as I can see, no motive for the theft : that makes it more baffling. And as we don't know who the thief is, we can't ask him if he's got an alibi : and that makes it utterly baffling.'

Mr. Parker walked up and down for a minute or two without saying anything at all. But his head, nodding so wisely among the stars, showed that he was thinking very hard indeed.

' A note-book ! ' he suddenly exclaimed. ' If I had a note-book, I could write down the various clues, the names of everybody I have cause to suspect, and so on and so forth. But without a note-book, what can I do ? What could any detective do ? Nothing at all ! '

' If you please,' exclaimed Dinah, ' I've got a note-book, and if you really want it, I'll be glad to lend it to you.'

Mr. Parker was almost frightened out of his skin. He had not known that anyone was listening to him, and to hear a strange kangaroo making so curious an offer was quite unnerving. In a single bound he leapt into his house, and though the door was ten feet high, he knocked his head on the lintel, and at once began to shout, ' Oh, oh, somebody hit me ! I'm sure somebody hit me ! '

Half a minute later, very cautiously, he poked out his long neck and asked, ' Was it you who hit me ? '

' Of course we didn't,' said Dinah.

' Then who did ? '

' You hit yourself,' said Dorinda.

' My mother often told me that I didn't know my own strength,' said Mr. Parker sadly, and bending his head very low, he rubbed the sore place with his right hind hoof. Then abruptly he demanded : ' Who are you ? '

' My name is Dinah Palfrey, and this is my sister Dorinda.'

' Then you are in disguise,' said Mr. Parker.

' I suppose we are,' said Dinah.

' Why ? ' asked Mr. Parker.

' It's rather hard to explain,' said Dinah.

' A very suspicious circumstance,' said Mr. Parker. ' Very suspicious indeed. Are you fond of eggs ? '

' Not ostrich eggs.'

' I wonder,' said Mr. Parker. ' I wonder very much indeed. I wonder, I wonder, I wonder ! '

And suddenly withdrawing his head, he shut his door with a bang.

Chapter Nine

The morning was quiet. Dinah and Dorinda sat in their cage and nobody spoke to them till Sir Lankester came and said good-morning. 'We are going to let you out in the park this afternoon,' he said, ' and I hope you will enjoy yourselves.'

Mr. Parker walked up and down, and often looked at them with a very suspicious eye, but he said nothing, and they didn't like to speak to him unless he spoke first. Bendigo slept in the sun.

But in the afternoon, just before the animals were let out to play and take their exercise, Mr. Parker put his head over the bars of his cage and whispered to Dinah, ' Bring your note-book ! '

Then Mr. Plum came round, opening doors, and said to Dinah and Dorinda, ' Now see and behave yourselves, and if so you'll have a good time like the others.'

So they went out in a very quiet and modest way, though they were both excited by the thought of a little freedom and the prospect of meeting so many strange animals.

Mr. Parker was waiting for them. ' Follow me,' he muttered, and led the way to some willow-trees that grew beside the river. No other animals were near them there.

Mr. Parker looked at them very sternly and said, ' Tell me why you are disguised as kangaroos.'

So Dinah told him about Mrs. Grimble and the magic draught, but Mr. Parker interrupted her and said, ' I don't believe in magic.'

' Then how did we become kangaroos ? ' asked Dorinda.

' A baffling question,' said Mr. Parker. ' Very baffling indeed. I have often wondered how I became a giraffe.'

' Weren't you a giraffe when you were born ? ' asked Dinah.

' Indeed I wasn't,' said Mr. Parker indignantly. ' I was one of the most beautiful babies in England. I took first prize at a Baby Show ! Then I grew up and became a detective. I was one of the best detectives in the world. I used to capture murderers by the dozen, forgers by the score, and hundreds of burglars. But one day when I was trying to look over a very high wall — craning up and up, stretching my legs and stretching my neck — a strange thing happened. Suddenly I found that I could see over it quite easily. I had become enormously tall ! And there, on the other side of the wall, there was a burglar burying a lot of silver plate in a flower-bed. ' I arrest you ! ' I shouted, but my voice sounded strange, and when the burglar looked up he uttered an exclamation of intense surprise.'

' You had become a giraffe,' said Dinah.

' I had,' said Mr. Parker sadly.

' What happened then ? ' asked Dorinda.

' The burglar, who was a bold and quick-witted man, came out and stroked me,' said Mr. Parker. ' I was quite astonished, because, as probably you know, it is most unusual for a detective to be stroked by a burglar. I moved slightly away from him, and happened, at the same moment, to catch

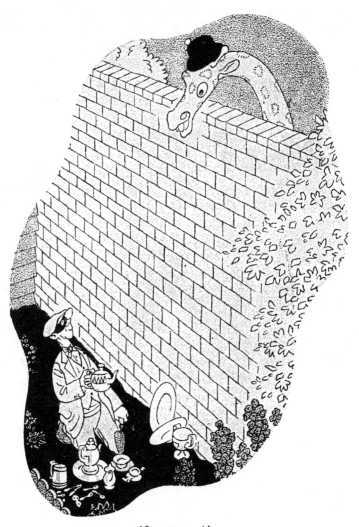

'I arrest you!'

sight of my legs. I looked round and saw my back. I was bewildered by the change in my appearance, and the burglar, taking advantage of my perplexity, led me away and finally sold me to Sir Lankester Lemon for fifty pounds.'

' It must have been magic that turned you into a giraffe,' said Dinah.

' I don't believe in magic,' said Mr. Parker stubbornly.

' Then how did it happen ? ' asked Dorinda.

' I don't know,' said Mr. Parker, ' but people often get what they want, if they want it long enough. Think of all the people who say, ' All I want is peace and quiet.' And sooner or later they die, and what could be quieter than that ? And I, you see, had always wanted to look over walls.'

' Do you think that many of the animals here were people to begin with ? ' asked Dorinda.

' Well ! ' said Mr. Parker, his big eyes bulging with astonishment. ' Well, that *is* a disturbing thought ! It never occurred to me that any of the others might not be the genuine article. I thought I was quite, quite different from everyone else.'

' Don't forget us,' said Dinah.

' I hope you didn't forget to bring your note-book,' said Mr. Parker severely.

' What are you going to do with it ? '

' Write down all my notes on The Case of the Missing Ostrich Eggs,' said Mr. Parker. ' It is one of the most baffling mysteries that I have ever known. And when I have solved it, I shall at once begin to investigate the private life of every animal here. Half of them, I now believe, may be human beings in disguise ! Even our nearest neighbour, Bendigo the Grizzly Bear, may really be a man ! '

' I expect he is,' said Dorinda. ' Last night we saw——'

' Never mind that,' said Dinah sharply. ' That's not a bit important. What we have to do, without wasting any more time, is to help Mr. Parker find the missing eggs.'

' How right you are ! ' said Mr. Parker. ' One thing at a time, and first things first. That's how to go about it. Now if you'll write down what I dictate — have you got a pencil ? Good. If I dictate my notes, and you write them down, we'll get a much clearer view of this difficult case than we have at present.'

So Dinah took out her note-book and pencil, and this is what she wrote :

THE CASE OF THE MISSING OSTRICH EGGS

A. People I suspect : Everybody.
B. Clues : None.
C. Object of crime : Don't know.
    N.B. (1) It may be kidnapping. Wait and see if anyone demands a ransom from Sir Bobadil.
    (2) The eggs were *fresh.*
D. Alibis : Everybody will have to prove one.
E. Nature of Case : Baffling.

' There,' said Mr. Parker. ' That makes it a lot clearer, doesn't it ? '

' What is an alibi ? ' asked Dorinda.

' Well,' said Mr. Parker, ' if I were to say to you,

" Were you in Birmingham on the night of the crime ? " you would have to answer, " No, but I was in Blackpool." And that's an alibi.'

' It's like playing Happy Families,' said Dorinda.

' In a way it is,' said Mr. Parker doubtfully, ' but in another way it isn't, if you see what I mean. — Hush ! What's that ? '

They all stood up. They were not very far from Sir Lankester's house, and from the lawn in front of it they could hear angry voices. There was a woman's voice, and a curious noise that was half a scream and half a choke. Then they saw Sir Bobadil running towards them, and Lady Lemon chasing him with a croquet mallet. But she was a long way behind, and soon, being short of breath, she gave up the pursuit.

' Come,' said Mr. Parker. ' Come quickly. This may be important. It may be a Clue ! '

So they hurried to meet Sir Bobadil, who appeared to be somewhat ashamed of himself.

' What have you been doing ? ' asked Mr. Parker sternly.

' Oh, nothing much,' said Sir Bobadil, and turned aside to cough.

' There's something in your throat,' said Mr. Parker, and bent his head to examine more closely a large round lump in the very middle of Sir Bobadil's neck.

' Merely a crumb,' said Sir Bobadil, and choked as he said it.

' It looks more like a cake than a crumb,' said Dinah.

' It's a ball,' said Dorinda.

' A croquet ball ! ' exclaimed Dinah. ' It's just about the right size, and it was a croquet mallet that Lady Lemon was chasing him with.'

' They do play croquet sometimes,' said Mr. Parker thoughtfully. Then, with a sudden appearance of anger, he bent and whispered to her, ' I say, that wasn't fair ! I'm the detective, not you. You should have let me guess first.'

' I'm sorry,' said Dinah. ' I was only trying to help.'

' Well, you shouldn't help so quickly,' said Mr. Parker.

Sir Bobadil, in the meantime, had been gulping and swallowing, and the lump was gradually moving down his neck. It disappeared completely just as Mr. Parker turned again to question him.

' Why was Lady Lemon chasing you ? ' asked Mr. Parker.

' It's her idea of fun,' said Sir Bobadil.

' You stole her croquet ball,' said Mr. Parker.

' Nonsense,' said Sir Bobadil. ' Where's your evidence ? ' And proudly he stretched his long neck to show how smooth and thin it was.

' Aha ! ' said Mr. Parker. ' You've swallowed it.'

' Swallowed what ? ' asked Sir Bobadil.

' The evidence,' said Mr. Parker.

' How do you know it wasn't a potato ? ' asked Sir Bobadil, and with a loud hoarse laugh he walked slowly away.

' Quickly,' whispered Mr. Parker to Dinah. ' Take this down in your note-book. Quickly, quickly. Ready ? — Clue Number One : Sir Bobadil has eaten a croquet ball. — Have you written that ? Then leave me. I must work alone now. I am going to shadow him ! '

Walking softly and slowly, on the tip of his hooves, Mr. Parker began to follow Sir Bobadil, who was by now some eighty yards away, and Dinah and Dorinda were left alone.

' Do you think it was Sir Bobadil who stole the eggs ? ' asked Dorinda.

' If he can swallow a croquet ball, I suppose he can swallow an ostrich egg,' said Dinah.

' He must be terribly wicked if he ate an egg that his own wife had laid,' said Dorinda.

' He looks quite wicked on one side of his face,' said Dinah.

' It's a most exciting case,' said Dorinda.

' And it's very interesting to meet a real detective,' said Dinah, ' even though he is a giraffe.'

They had been walking towards another part of the zoo, and now, in one of two cages set apart from the others, they saw a lovely animal, gleaming like gold, moving swiftly out of shadow into sunlight, out of sunlight into shadow. It was the Golden Puma.

In a very high cage, a few yards away, there was a pinnacle of rock between two trees, and on top of the rock sat a marvellous bird as white as snow. It was the Greenland Falcon, but in the zoo it was generally called the Silver Falcon.

They were both so beautiful that Dinah and Dorinda stood between their cages and could not decide which to look at first.

' Good afternoon,' said the Puma.

' Hail ! ' cried the Falcon.

' How do you do ? ' said Dinah and Dorinda.

Chapter Ten

' I think I ought to tell you,' said Dinah, ' that we aren't genuine kangaroos. We are really human children who have been turned into kangaroos by a magic draught.'

' How interesting ! ' said the Golden Puma.

' It's very honest of you,' said the Silver Falcon, ' to admit such a lowly origin.'

' A *lowly* origin ? ' said Dinah. ' I never thought of it like that. Do you despise human beings ? '

' Well,' said the Falcon, ' you can hardly expect me to admire them. In Greenland, of course, where I used to live, there weren't very many human people, but I saw enough to form a pretty accurate opinion, I think. There were some Eskimos, and trappers, and traders, and fishermen, and people of that sort, and I don't deny that they were very enterprising creatures. They tried to do a lot of things, but they couldn't do anything properly. They could see a little, hear a little, run a little, swim a little, but they couldn't do anything really well.'

' I like human beings,' said the Puma. ' I like the sound of their voices, and the way they can laugh or look sad. I often wanted to make a friend of one.'

' And that didn't do you any good,' said the Falcon. ' That's what put you in a zoo.'

' I know,' said the Puma in a melancholy voice. ' I was very foolish. I didn't realise that human beings could be treacherous.'

' Don't you like being in a zoo ? ' asked Dorinda.

The Puma's cage looked very comfortable, and behind it there was an outrun with bushes and a bare stony rise and a little brook.

The Puma was silent for a while, and then she said, ' I used to live in a forest in Brazil, and in every part of the forest there was something new to look at. Every tree had a different shape, and some were smooth as a young leaf, and some were rough and deeply crinkled. Their branches made pictures against the sky, and at night they became a fishing-net and caught the stars like a shoal of little fishes. Flowers like trumpets grew upon the trees, sweet-smelling, and among the huts of an Indian village were small brown children playing in the sun. There were long winding paths in the forest, I could run for fifty miles. There was a river, sometimes brown and swirly, sometimes clear and smooth. I used to lie on a branch above the water and look at my reflection in a greenish pool. And when I was hungry I went hunting, and that's the loveliest thing in life, to go hunting in the moonlight, and feel your blood like quicksilver in your veins. Not a bird wakes but you hear it. Not a leaf closes but you see the edge turn in. Nothing moves but you smell the wind of its movement. And you go like a shadow through the trees, and even your skin and your claws are laughing and alive.'

' I suppose a Brazilian forest is good in its own way,' said the Falcon, ' but I wish you could see Greenland. There's nothing in the world so beautiful as that enormous tableland, covered with snow, peaked and shining in the sun, cut by great ravines, and patched with blue shadow. I used to ride upon a breeze, a mile above it, in air like crystal, and on either side I could see a hundred miles of snow and sea, and icebergs shipwrecked on the beach, and the pack-ice moving, and the Eskimos in their kayaks, fishing. Then I would close my wings and dive like a bullet through the diamond sky, down to the little bushes and the glinting rocks, the heather and dwarf-willow getting bigger and bigger, yellow poppies rising like bursts of fire to meet me, and the quartz in the granite boulders like pinpricks of light. Headlong down, the thin air screaming, then *crash* — wings out, head up, and halt two feet from the heather — when I struck stiffly, straight-legged, at a fine fat ptarmigan, too slow to escape, and dashed him to the ground. Ha ! the delight, the swiftness, and the freedom ! '

' Freedom ! ' sighed the Puma. ' Life without freedom is a poor, poor thing.'

' Do they never let you out of your cages ? ' asked Dinah.

' Never,' said the Puma. ' They don't trust us.'

The Falcon stood tiptoe on his rocky pinnacle and slowly stretched his lovely wings, as if to remind himself of his power. Then, folding them again, he looked at Dinah and Dorinda and said, ' I suppose you are quite happy to be here ? You cannot regret the loss of your freedom, because, having only been human children, you never knew what freedom was.'

' Oh, I'm sure we did,' said Dinah. ' We had to do lessons, of course, and be punctual for dinner, and go to bed at half-past seven, but in between times we had quite a lot of freedom. Hadn't we, Dorinda ? '

'Not nearly enough,' said Dorinda. 'You remember how often Mother used to make us wash our hands, and how Miss Serendip made us wear shoes when we wanted to go barefoot. I think we had very little freedom.'

'But we weren't locked up,' said Dinah.

'No, we weren't locked up.'

'So even you aren't contented with life in a zoo?' said the Puma.

'It's interesting,' said Dinah, 'but we don't mean to stay here.'

'How are you going to get out?' asked the Puma.

'We shall escape,' said Dorinda.

'How?' demanded the Puma and the Falcon, both speaking together.

'We haven't decided yet,' said Dinah, 'but somehow or other we shall find a way. You said yourself that human beings were very enterprising, and Dorinda and I get more and more enterprising every day.'

'Will you help us to escape?' asked the Falcon.

'Of course we shall,' said Dorinda.

'O great and glorious Kangaroos!' cried the Falcon, stretching his wings again as if tasting already the joy of flight. 'You promise that? Ah, Greenland, Greenland! I shall see the snow again, and the pack-ice melting in the green, and the Arctic Sea. Do you hear that, Puma? We shall be free!'

'Yes, I hear,' said the Puma. 'But it is more difficult for me. You can fly to Greenland, but I cannot run to Brazil.'

'There's a very large and beautiful forest not far

from here,' said Dinah. 'It's called the Forest of
Weal. Couldn't you live there?'

'Of course she could,' said the Falcon.

'Is it a real forest?' asked the Puma.

'Indeed it is,' said Dinah.

'Miles and miles and miles of it,' said Dorinda.
'You could easily get lost in it.'

'And if I did,' asked the Puma, 'would you come
and look for me?'

'We should love to!' cried Dinah and Dorinda.

Chapter Eleven

Just then they heard Mr. Plum ringing a large bell, which was the signal for the animals to go back to their cages, so Dinah and Dorinda said good-bye, and presently, when they were alone together, Dinah said thoughtfully, 'We seem to be in the very thick of exciting events. I never thought that life in a zoo would be so thrilling.'

'We've certainly got plenty to do,' said Dorinda, 'what with helping Mr. Parker to find the missing ostrich eggs, and arranging the escape of the Golden Puma and the Silver Falcon.'

'We've got to arrange our own escape first,' said Dinah, 'and I don't see how we are going to do that unless we can find the bottle I lost and drink what's left of the magic draught.'

'Do you think Mr. Parker could find it? He is a detective.'

'I wasn't thinking about Mr. Parker. I was thinking about the Silver Falcon. Do you remember his saying that in Greenland he could see a hundred miles on either side, and from a mile in the air he could aim at a ptarmigan almost on the ground? He must have marvellous eyes.'

'You mean that if we could let him out of his cage, he might fly round and round, looking for the bottle, everywhere between here and Midmeddle-cum?'

'Well, I must have dropped it somewhere,' said Dinah.

For a little while they sat without speaking, thinking of the tasks that awaited them, and of the difficult situation they were in. They had had a pleasant day, talking to the Falcon and the Puma, and helping Mr. Parker, and to both of them it seemed that being a kangaroo was quite a good sort of life so long as there was plenty to do. But merely to be a kangaroo in a cage, without books or a paint-box or a jigsaw puzzle, with nothing in the way of amusement but sitting and thinking, would be a very dreary existence indeed. They looked at each other, and each saw the same doubt and worry in the other's eyes.

Presently they heard, from the house next door where Mr. Parker lived, a noise like someone tearing linen sheets — *rrip, rrip, rrip* — and at the end of every three *rrips* there was a piercing whistle. Mr. Parker had fallen asleep in an uncomfortable position and was snoring loudly.

' Shadowing Sir Bobadil must have made him very tired,' said Dinah.

' We shall never get to sleep if he goes on like that,' said Dorinda.

The noise grew louder and louder, and then, with a tremendous whistle like a train going into a tunnel, Mr. Parker woke himself up. They could hear him tumbling and turning and rising clumsily to his feet. Then came a little cough, twice repeated.

' He wants us to go and talk to him,' said Dinah.

' Perhaps he's got a clue,' said Dorinda.

They went out, and there in the darkness was Mr. Parker's head leaning over the railing of his outer cage, and the small light of a star was reflected in his large and melancholy eyes.

' Got your note-book ? ' he whispered.

' Here it is,' answered Dinah.

' Then take down a few items, will you ? I'll dictate them quite slowly, and be careful, because every word is important.'

It was rather difficult to write in the dark, but Dinah did her best, and this is what Mr. Parker dictated :

At 2.30 P.M. on 13th inst. began to shadow Sir Bobadil the Ostrich, whom I suspect of being the criminal. Shadowing successful. Didn't lose sight of him once. —

Query : Did he know I was following him ? *Answer :*
Don't think so, because I was walking very quietly. — He
proceeded to river, where there is sandy ground, and
stopped. He stood as if thinking about something. Then
quite suddenly he buried his head in the sand. I watched
him intently, but he made no other movement. I sat
down and waited. I waited for a long time. Nothing
happened. Then I got hungry so I came home. When
last seen Sir Bobadil was still there with his head in the
sand. Had something to eat and thought about case. —
Query : Was I baffled ? *Answer :* Yes. — Thought harder
and fell asleep. But when I woke up, everything was
clear ! ! ! Sir Bobadil is the criminal, as I suspected. He
stole his wife's eggs and buried them. This afternoon
(13th inst.) he meant to dig them up again. But he dug
in the wrong place, hit his head on a rock, and stunned
himself ! That is why he stood so still. *N.B.*—This is
only a theory, and will have to be proved before it becomes
evidence.

' I should think so, indeed,' said Dinah. ' Don't
you know that ostriches always bury their heads in
the sand when they want to hide themselves ? '

' And how does that help ? ' asked Mr. Parker.

' It doesn't,' said Dinah, ' but they think it does.'

' How do you know what they think ? '

' Because Miss Serendip told us so.'

' And who is Miss Serendip ? '

' She's our governess,' said Dorinda gloomily,
' and she knows everything.'

' Does she know the whereabouts of the Missing
Eggs ? ' asked Mr. Parker.

' Of course she doesn't,' said Dinah. ' How
could she ? '

' Then she doesn't know everything,' said Mr.
Parker sharply. ' And if she doesn't know every-

thing, we can't be sure that she knows anything. And if she doesn't know anything, she doesn't know what ostriches think. And you know less, because you only know what she tells you. That's called Logic, and it proves that what you said isn't evidence. And if a thing is not evidence, I'm not interested. Not INTERESTED, do you hear?'

And Mr. Parker, whose voice had become louder and louder, went stamping into his house in such a temper that he forgot how tall he was, and once again hit his head on the lintel.

'Who did that?' he cried.

'You did!' said Dinah and Dorinda, and Mr. Parker, though extremely suspicious, couldn't prove they were wrong, and went to bed in a very bad mood.

Presently Dinah said, 'I don't think he's a very good detective.'

'He can't have had much practice since he became a giraffe, of course.'

Leaning close to Dorinda, Dinah whispered, 'If I were a detective, I would watch Bendigo. He stole *The Times* from Sir Lankester, and therefore he's a thief. And if he's a thief, it's quite likely that he stole the eggs.'

'Is that what Mr. Parker would call Logic?' asked Dorinda.

'I think so,' said Dinah. 'Anyway, if there's a light in Bendigo's house to-night, we ought to take turns to watch, and learn as much as we can about him.'

Dorinda agreed, and though they found it difficult not to fall asleep, they waited hopefully for a long time. After about an hour, Dorinda began to nod and doze, and to dream she was at home again, and Miss Serendip was talking over the breakfast-table about ostriches and ostrich feathers and ostrich farms. Then Dinah gave her a gentle pinch, and she woke up.

' Look ! ' whispered Dinah.

It was so dark that the shape of their room was quite invisible, but in the darkness on one side there was a little patch of light like a glow-worm ; Bendigo had lit his candle, and very faintly it was shining through the chink in their wall.

' I'll watch first and you sleep,' whispered Dinah. ' Then, when I'm sleepy, I'll wake you and it will be your turn.'

' All right,' Dorinda answered, and in two minutes she was dreaming again about Miss Serendip. But Dinah, making no noise when she moved, was peeping through the hole in the wall.

Bendigo's candle was burning on the edge of his feeding-trough, and Bendigo was feeling and fumbling under the heap of straw that was his bed. The copy of *The Times* which he pulled out was by now rather dirty and crumpled, but with a grunt of satisfaction he made himself comfortable in a corner and began to read.

He was really behaving in quite a human way, thought Dinah. He didn't look like a bear pretending to be a man, but like a man who had become a bear without forgetting all the things that men like to do. ' And that, I suppose,' said Dinah to herself, ' is the real truth of the matter. Well, I never knew that human beings could be turned into animals so easily. But it makes life much more interesting, of course.'

Bendigo went on reading *The Times*. Then he turned to another page, looked up and down the columns, and began to grumble. He looked at the front page, and the back page, and all the inside pages, and grew more and more impatient. He was muttering to himself, and by listening very hard Dinah could hear most of what he said.

' I've read that before,' Bendigo grumbled. ' I've read that, and that, and that. And that and that. And the whole thing's a day old, anyway. What's the use of a paper that's a day old ? Confound that man Lemon ! Why didn't he have a *Times* in his pocket when he came round this morning ? It's a nuisance not getting your paper every day. If I get one a week I'm lucky nowadays. Oh, I'm tired of being a bear ! '

Bendigo folded *The Times*, which had become very untidy, and sat puffing and grunting. Then he began to mutter again : ' Well, I'd better go out and get rid of it. Can't leave it lying about. Got to get rid of it in the usual way. Thank goodness it's a fine night.'

He suddenly turned his head and blew out the candle. Then Dinah could see nothing, but she heard him moving around. She heard him leaving his house and going into the cage in front of it. She followed his example, moving very quietly, and in the darkness she could see his great shadowy bulk at the door of the cage. He was stooping down. She heard a click. The door opened, and Bendigo walked out !

' He has a key ! ' murmured Dinah, who, if she
had not been a kangaroo, would certainly have felt
extremely frightened to see a grizzly bear going out
for a walk. ' But where can he have got it, and
how ? Did he steal it from Mr. Plum ? He must be
a *professional* thief ! '

Chapter Twelve

Bendigo had left the door of his cage open, so Dinah concluded that he did not mean to be out for long. It would be a good idea, she thought, to stay up till he returned and give him a fright. But then it occurred to her that she might be the one to get a fright, for Bendigo would be fearfully angry when he knew that his secret had been discovered, and because he had a key which would open his or her or Mr. Parker's cage — Mr. Plum always used the same key for all three of them — he might even come in and hug her. Bears did hug people when they were annoyed with them. She knew that, because Miss Serendip had told her so.

It was a frightening thought, and Dinah was on the point of going back to bed when she saw something which made her change her mind immediately. Bendigo had not only left his door open, but he had left the key in the lock.

If she could only reach it !

She put her arm through the railings between her cage and Bendigo's, and stretched her fingers as far as she could. She could just touch the edge of the door. She managed to give it a little pull, and made it move inwards till it was nearly shut. The lock was a few inches nearer now. She reached again, pressing her shoulder against the bars till they hurt her, and she felt the end of the key.

She wriggled it in the lock, and it came out. But her fingers were stretched so straight that she couldn't hold it. It fell with a tinkle to the floor, it gave a little jump, and lay farther away than ever.

Dinah nearly began to cry. Their hope of escape had been so near, and now it had vanished again.

But she made up her mind to be brave, and no sooner had she done that than she remembered that she had a tail. And her tail was much longer than her arm.

She turned round, with her back to the railing, and put her tail between the bars. Then, looking over her shoulder, she began to fish for the key. She got the tip of her tail round it and pulled it towards her. Nearer and nearer it came. Then she could reach it with her hand, and a moment later she had unlocked the door of her own cage.

She wondered for a moment whether to go in and wake Dorinda, but she knew that she must not waste time, so without more than a moment's hesitation she set off in the direction that Bendigo had taken. She went quickly, using her tail to leap far ahead into the darkness. How well she could see in the dark, now that she was a kangaroo ! She wondered if her eyes were shining, as the eyes of other animals gleam at night, and if so what colour they were.

She felt that she was being very brave, and at the same time she could not deny that she was rather frightened. For no one could say that pursuing a grizzly bear was not a dangerous thing to be doing, even though he was a highly educated bear who read *The Times*. But somehow she was convinced that it was most important to find out where he had gone, so she did her best to stop feeling frightened, and to think instead how excellent a thing it was to be brave.

Suddenly, in the middle of a long jump, she heard a kind of hoarse whistle, and twisting herself round in mid-air she landed softly on the grass, and then went forward very, very cautiously.

A few yards farther on she peeped carefully round a holly-tree, and saw Bendigo. He was sitting up, and in the darkness he looked enormous. Low in the sky there were a few stars, and the brightest of them seemed to be resting on top of his head. Then Bendigo put one paw into his mouth and whistled through his claws. It must be a signal, thought Dinah.

She waited patiently, and presently against the starlit sky she saw a tall creature with long legs and a long nodding neck and a big pale body. It was Sir Bobadil the Ostrich. He and Bendigo had a whispered conversation, and then Bendigo gave him *The Times*. Sir Bobadil immediately began to eat it, and appeared to enjoy his meal very much indeed.

' So Miss Serendip was right,' murmured Dinah.

Miss Serendip had often told her that an ostrich will eat anything, but neither she nor Dorinda had quite believed such a story. Here, however, was the proof of it, and this was how Bendigo got rid of his stolen newspapers. Bendigo and Sir Bobadil were in partnership, and it was, in a way, a partnership of crime. Mr. Parker, thought Dinah, will be interested to hear about this.

Then to her horror she saw that Sir Bobadil had nearly finished *The Times*, and she knew she must hurry, for Bendigo would be going home at any minute now. So quietly and carefully she crept away, and when she felt safe took a great leap, and another, and another, and speedily got back to her cage, which now seemed very safe and comfortable. She went in, and closed the door, and locked it carefully, and put the key in her pouch. She lay down beside Dorinda, and waited.

In a few minutes' time she heard Bendigo closing his door with a gentle click. Then came a deep growl of astonishment and dismay. He had discovered that the key was missing! She could hear him shuffling about, and breathing hoarsely. Then she heard the gate click again.

The key hung on a loop of tarry string, and Bendigo had probably worn it round his neck, where it would be hidden by his thick hair. 'He probably thinks that he dropped it in the park,' said Dinah to herself, 'and now he has gone back to look for it. Poor Bendigo!' And suddenly she felt sorry for him, because it struck her that he must now be almost as worried as she and Dorinda had been when they discovered the loss of Mrs. Grimble's bottle.

'Poor Bendigo!' she repeated. But she was very tired, as well as sympathetic, and before she knew how it happened she was fast asleep.

Bendigo had indeed gone back to look for the key. He searched everywhere for it, but naturally could not find it. He was about to call Sir Bobadil to come and help him, when the suspicion occurred to him that he might have dropped the key at the same time as he gave Sir Bobadil *The Times*, and Sir Bobadil had swallowed both of them. The Ostrich, he knew, had a perfectly insatiable appetite, and he was probably just as fond of old iron as he was of paper.

The more he thought of it, the more strongly was Bendigo convinced that this had actually happened, and he became so furiously angry that all the hair on his neck stood out as stiffly as the bristles of a new hair-brush. He put his paw to his mouth and whistled through his claws. He whistled three times, and then Sir Bobadil, thinking that here was another meal, came running to him.

' You swallowed my key,' growled Bendigo.

' No, I didn't,' said Sir Bobadil.

' Then where is it ? '

' How should I know ? '

' It's in your stomach.'

' Nothing of the sort ! I never eat keys.'

' You're a liar. You eat everything you can get.'

' No, I don't. I've got a very delicate digestion, and you're a rude old bear ! '

Then they began to quarrel in earnest, and Bendigo chased Sir Bobadil all round the park, but couldn't catch him, and while they were still arguing the sun came up and it was broad daylight.

Bendigo suddenly remembered that he had no business to be out of his cage, and without another word he turned and went lumbering home as quickly as he could. But he was too late.

Mr. Plum had got up early, and was taking a walk round the zoo. Just as Bendigo was approaching his cage from one side, Mr. Plum approached it from the other. Mr. Plum was extremely astonished to see Bendigo, and Bendigo was totally dismayed to see Mr. Plum. So they stood and looked at each other for half a minute without speaking or moving.

Then Mr. Plum said in a very angry voice, 'What are you doing out at this time of the morning?'

And Bendigo hung his head, and Mr. Plum put a rope round his neck and led him off to a dark uncomfortable cage that stood all by itself in the loneliest corner of the zoo.

Chapter Thirteen

As soon as they woke, Dinah told Dorinda everything that had happened the night before, and Dorinda looked at Bendigo's key and said, ' Now we can escape.'

' Not immediately,' said Dinah. ' There's not much use in escaping before we have found Mrs. Grimble's bottle. And don't you think it's our duty to stay till Mr. Parker has solved the mystery of the missing eggs ? '

' He may take a long time to do that,' said Dorinda.

' He'll take much longer if we're not here to help him,' said Dinah. ' I think the first thing we ought to do—— '

' I know ! ' said Dorinda. ' Let out the Silver Falcon ! '

' Yes,' said Dinah. ' Give the Falcon his freedom, and he'll look for Mrs. Grimble's bottle while we're looking for the missing eggs.'

' He may fly away altogether,' said Dorinda.

' I don't think so. I feel sure that he's an honourable falcon, and he wouldn't go away and leave his friend the Puma in captivity.'

' Suppose we do find Mrs. Grimble's bottle, and turn ourselves into girls again : how are we going to get the Puma out of the zoo ? '

' I haven't thought of that yet,' said Dinah, ' but we'll find a way. And now I think I must have a talk with Mr. Parker.'

Before she could call Mr. Parker, however, Sir Lankester and Mr. Plum came to pay their usual morning visit to the animals, and they stood before Bendigo's cage talking gravely about his wicked behaviour.

'You were perfectly right to put him in solitary confinement,' said Sir Lankester. 'I should have done the same myself.'

'I got the shock of my life when I saw him standing there,' said Mr. Plum. 'But luckily I had a bit of rope with me, so I put a noose round his neck and led him off to the solitary cage right away. He came quietly, I'm glad to say.'

Dinah and Dorinda listened to this conversation with great surprise, for they had been sound asleep when Bendigo was discovered by Mr. Plum, and it had never occurred to them that he was anywhere but in his own house. As he was often late in getting up, there was nothing unusual in not seeing him out in his cage. Now again Dinah felt sorry for Bendigo in his misfortune, even though he was a newspaper thief, and possibly worse.

'I wonder how he got out,' said Sir Lankester for the seventh time.

'If we knew that,' said Mr. Plum, 'we'd know a lot.'

'Are you *sure* that his door was locked?'

'I've been locking doors for eighteen years,' said Mr. Plum, 'and I've never made a mistake yet.'

'It's a complete mystery,' said Sir Lankester.

Slowly they walked on to the next group of cages, and as soon as they were out of earshot Mr.

Parker demanded excitedly, ' What is it all about ? What is the mystery now ? '

Dinah told him the whole story, and Mr. Parker's great dark eyes grew so large with amazement that Dinah and Dorinda could see their whole reflection in them.

' Quickly, quickly ! ' he exclaimed. ' Get out your note-book. Write it all down. Write down CONSPIRACY to begin with. Do you know how to spell it ? C–O–N–S–P . . . S–P . . . Well, call it a Plot. P–L–O–T, Plot.'

' I can spell Conspiracy, thank you,' said Dinah, and wrote it down.

' It's very bad manners to use a difficult word when a simple word will do just as well,' said Mr. Parker. ' And what is worse, you've interrupted my train of thought.'

' Oh, all right,' said Dinah. ' I'll call it a Plot.'

' Good,' said Mr. Parker. ' Now write this : There is a Plot between Bendigo and Sir Bobadil. Therefore Bendigo is Sir Bobadil's accomplice. A–C–C–M . . . No, that's not right. A–C–U–M . . . Oh, call him a Partner. Therefore Bendigo is Sir Bobadil's partner. Have you written that ? '

' Yes,' said Dinah, and this time she didn't argue, because she herself wasn't quite sure how to spell *accomplice*.

' Alternatively,' said Mr. Parker, ' Sir Bobadil is Bendigo's accomplice — or partner, as we have agreed to call it.'

' I've written that,' said Dinah.

' Good,' repeated Mr. Parker. ' And what can we deduce from that ? '

' I don't know,' said Dinah.

' Neither do I,' said Dorinda.

' Nor do I,' added Mr. Parker after a minute or so of hard thinking. ' It's baffling, isn't it ? Very baffling indeed. But we have two suspects now instead of one,' he went on more cheerfully, ' and it's always a good thing to have several suspects. Because if you're disappointed in the first, you may still be lucky with the second.'

Mr. Parker scratched his right ear with his right hind foot, and a new thought seemed to strike him. ' Have you ever,' he asked, ' seen egg stains on Bendigo's chest ? '

' I don't think so,' said Dinah.

' A pity,' said Mr. Parker, ' because an egg stain would be a very good clue. Well, I must go in and think about this new development. Hard thinking will be necessary before we solve this most baffling of all my cases. There's no rest for a detective, just hard work and hard thinking.'

Taking a good look at the lintel of the door, Mr. Parker carefully lowered his head and disappeared from view. A few minutes later Dinah and Dorinda heard a familiar noise : *rrip, rrip, rrip*, and then a long shrill whistle.

' That's what he calls thinking,' said Dinah.

' Father used to call it meditating,' said Dorinda.

' Father didn't *snore*,' said Dinah.

' Well, not loudly,' said Dorinda. ' Poor Father, I wonder where he is now ? '

' I hope he isn't in danger,' said Dinah.

In the afternoon, when the animals went into the park, there was a great deal of excited conversation, for the news had already gone round that Bendigo had been out all night and was now in solitary confinement.

Nearly everybody took it for granted that the Grizzly Bear was the criminal, and the Ant-eater, a Toucan, and a Sacred Baboon were all saying loudly, and repeating it to anyone who would listen, that from the very beginning they had been sure he was the thief.

' *Quite* sure,' said the Toucan.

' And if anyone had ever cared to ask my opinion, I would have had no hesitation in saying so,' added the Ant-eater.

' In consequence of which,' exclaimed the Sacred Baboon, ' we should all have been saved a great deal of trouble and anxiety.'

A rather gloomy-looking Reindeer was telling two Kinkajous that a person's life depended entirely on a good upbringing, and nowadays, he thought, parents weren't nearly strict enough with their children. ' If Bendigo's father and mother,' he said, ' had been as strict and careful as my parents were, I'm sure he wouldn't be in prison to-day. Let this be a lesson to you young people ! ' And the Kinkajous were so impressed they began to cry.

A Black Bear from the Himalaya, with two Pandas and a Malayan Honey-bear, were very angry because a member of their family had brought such disgrace upon their honourable name. *Bear*, they said, was one of the noblest names in the world, and in all their long experience, they affirmed, they had never even heard of a Bear committing theft before. It just showed what the world was coming to.

Lady Lil, however, was delighted by the news. She was walking up and down with a Dancing Cassowary who was a friend of hers, and telling her what a relief it was to feel safe. ' So long as I knew there was a thief at liberty in the zoo,' she said, ' I should never have had the heart to lay another egg. Never ! What was the use of laying eggs simply to have them stolen ? All that trouble, and no reward but sorrow ! Never again : that's what I said to Bobadil, and I meant it too. But *now* I'm going to lay another just as soon as ever I can.'

' How brave you are ! ' said the Dancing Cassowary. ' I do admire you ! '

One of the very few animals who refused to believe in Bendigo's guilt was Marie Louise the Llama. She was talking to a group that consisted of an Antelope, a Fallow Deer, a young Dromedary, a Zebra, and a Gnu. Dinah and Dorinda were there as well. Marie Louise said she had known Bendigo for a long time, and throughout their acquaintance he had always behaved towards her with perfect courtesy and consideration.

' Bendigo is a gentleman,' she said, ' and a gentleman *cannot* be a thief. No, indeed. I have my own theory as to the criminal, but I don't suppose that my poor opinion would interest anybody.'

' Pooh, pooh ! ' said the Gnu. ' Tell us, do ! '

' Well,' said Marie Louise, ' I lived for a long time in France, as I daresay you know. I was in a very select private zoo near Lyons, and I soon learnt to understand the language of the country.

—Such charming people, the French ! They have lovely manners, rather like Sir Lankester's, I always think. — Well, whenever there is a crime in France, the policemen always say " Cherchez la femme." And that means——'

' I know,' said Dinah. 'It means : Find the lady.'

' Why do they want to do that ? ' asked the Antelope.

' I never bothered to enquire,' said Marie Louise in a haughty voice. She was annoyed because Dinah also knew French.

' Perhaps,' said Dorinda, ' it's because there are more ladies in the world than men, and so they are easier to find.'

' That's a good reason,' said the Zebra.

' But who,' asked the young Dromedary, ' is the lady whom you suspect ? '

' Ah, who ? ' said the Gnu.

' Lady Lemon, Sir Lankester's wife,' said Marie Louise in her most impressive manner. ' And my reason is this : one day, rather more than a week ago, she and Sir Lankester stopped outside my cage and had a short but far from agreeable conversation. She was grumbling. She grumbles a great deal, though why a woman who is married to so charming, sensitive, handsome, exquisite a man as Sir Lankester should have *any* cause for complaint, I simply cannot think. But there you are ! Some people never know when they're well off. And that morning Lady Lemon was complaining bitterly about eggs. About the boiled eggs they often have for breakfast. They were too small, she said, and they seemed to be getting smaller and smaller.

What she wanted, she said, in a very brutal way, was an egg with something in it.'

' Coo ! ' said the Gnu.

' You all see the significance of that ? ' asked Marie Louise.

' I don't,' said the Fallow Deer.

' It means,' said Marie Louise, ' that she wanted bigger eggs. Much bigger eggs. And what is the biggest of all eggs ? An ostrich's egg ! Therefore *that* is what she wanted ! And if she wanted it enough, being the sort of woman she is, she would take it. And so, in all probability, she is the thief.'

' An interesting view,' said the Gnu. ' It may be true.'

The other animals were also impressed by Marie Louise's theory.

Mr. Parker, who had joined the group, enquired, ' Have you ever seen egg stains on her chest ? '

' A lady's chest,' said Marie Louise, ' is *never* egg-stained.'

' What a pity ! ' said Mr. Parker. ' Because an egg stain would be a very useful clue.' And lowering his head he carefully examined the chests of all the animals there.

While he was doing this, Dinah whispered to Dorinda, ' Let us go and talk to the Golden Puma and the Silver Falcon.'

They said good-bye to Marie Louise, the Antelope, the Fallow Deer, the young Dromedary, the Zebra, the Gnu—' Adieu,' said the Gnu — and to Mr. Parker. Then, leaping twenty feet at a time, they crossed the park and quickly came to the cages where the Golden Puma and the Silver Falcon lived.

' Hail ! ' cried the Falcon.

' Welcome,' said the Golden Puma. ' Tell us your news.'

' We've got the key of the cages,' said Dinah and Dorinda in one voice.

Then the Falcon flew down from his perch and thrust his head between the bars, and the Puma pressed her soft muzzle hard against the railings of her cage, and both stared longingly at the key which Dinah so proudly showed them.

' Freedom ! To be free in the windy, silvery sky ! ' cried the Falcon. ' Ah, let me out, now, before another minute goes to waste ! '

' Freedom ! ' purred the Golden Puma. ' To go freely on green turf, among the shadows of great trees ! Ah, let me out ! I am thirsty for freedom.'

' But if we let you out of your cage,' said Dinah to the Puma, ' you will still be in the zoo. You can't get out of the zoo unless we find some way of getting you out. And we can't help you to get out until we become human children again, when we shall be able to ask the gate-keeper to open the gates.'

' And we can't become human children again,' said Dorinda, ' unless we find Mrs. Grimble's bottle that Dinah lost somewhere between here and Midmeddlecum, and drink some more of the magic draught.'

' Let me out,' cried the Silver Falcon, ' and I shall find your bottle. I have eyes that can see a heron standing stilly in the shadow of a rock five miles away. I can see the eyes of a field-mouse shining in the ling when I am so high above that you could see me only as a mote in the sky. I can see fish moving on the bottom of the sea, and the vole running in tunnels of the heather. Give me freedom to mount the sky, and from a great height I shall search for ten miles around and find your bottle in less than two days from now.'

'He is right,' said the Puma. 'Give him his freedom first, and he will help us all. I must be patient.'

'You won't fly away altogether?' asked Dorinda anxiously.

The Falcon, his eyes gleaming, whispered fiercely, 'Do you doubt my word?'

'No!' cried Dorinda. 'I'm sorry!'

'In all the history of our race, a Greenland Falcon has never yet broken faith.'

'Of course we trust you,' said Dinah, and looking round to make sure that no one was watching them, she unlocked the Falcon's cage.

He flew out, straight to her shoulder, and spreading his wings about her head he murmured, 'I am your friend and your brother from now until the day of my death.' Then, very softly for so great a bird, he kissed her.

'Me too!' exclaimed Dorinda, and the Falcon, with a leap into the air, came gently down upon her shoulder and kissed her also.

Then, turning to the Puma, he said, 'You have no fear that I may desert you?'

'None,' said the Puma. 'Go your way into the sky, and I shall wait for your return. But remember that every hour I wait is an hour of bitter hunger for my liberty.'

'I shall remember,' said the Falcon, and with a

great scream of triumph he rose into the air and climbed the breezy sky so swiftly that in less than a minute he was out of sight.

' Go now,' said the Puma to Dinah and Dorinda.

' It is near the time when you must be back in your cages, and you should not be found here when his cage is discovered empty. Take care of the key.'

' You will be lonely now,' said Dinah.

' I shall not be very happy,' said the Puma, ' but you and the Falcon will return before long. Go quickly now — and take care of the key ! '

Chapter Fourteen

The following day, which was a Wednesday, they saw nothing of the Falcon, but all the animals were very much excited when it was learnt that he had escaped, and Sir Lankester and Mr. Plum had a long and heated argument about the proper way to lock a cage.

Mr. Plum said again that he had been locking cages for eighteen years, and if he didn't know how to do it, then nobody did. Sir Lankester said that he wanted a better explanation than that, and Mr. Plum said that he would have to find it for himself. Sir Lankester then said that Mr. Plum was being impertinent, and Mr. Plum replied that he was so worried he didn't know whether he was on his head or his heels. Sir Lankester admitted that he felt exactly the same, and for the rest of the day they walked about looking quite bewildered, and muttering.

In the afternoon, when most of the animals were at liberty, Sir Lankester was amazed to find Mr. Parker lying flat on the ground in front of the Python's cage. The Python, as usual, was fast asleep, but Mr. Parker, his long neck stretched towards the cage, was squirming and wriggling in the most extraordinary way.

'Whatever are you doing?' exclaimed Sir Lankester. 'Are you ill?'

Mr. Parker looked round, and was deeply embarrassed. As a detective, of course, he had often been compelled to do the most unusual things, but he had always hated being seen at work, and now he would certainly have blushed if giraffes were able to behave in such a way. He felt hot all over, and couldn't think what to do. Then he had a brilliant idea. He raised his body about three feet from the ground, and slowly lowered it. Then raised it again, and lowered it again. Up and down, as if he were doing a physical exercise to strengthen his legs and his chest. Then rising quickly to his feet, he galloped away, leaving Sir Lankester looking more bewildered than ever.

Later, when they all returned to their cages, Mr. Parker told Dinah and Dorinda what had happened, and boasted about his cleverness in concealing from Sir Lankester what he had really been doing.

' But what were you doing ? ' asked Dinah.

' I was trying to look at the Python's chest,' said Mr. Parker.

' Why ? '

' To see if it was egg-stained, of course. I have now examined the chest of every animal in the zoo except the Python and the Alligator. But to look at their chests is very, very difficult indeed, especially if they don't want to help you.'

' And have you found any egg stains ? ' asked Dorinda.

' None,' said Mr. Parker with a sigh. ' Not a single stain. The mystery remains as baffling as ever.'

' I wonder,' said Dinah to Dorinda when they were going to bed that night, ' if the Falcon will come to wake us, very early in the morning, and say that he has found Mrs. Grimble's bottle ? '

' I wonder,' said Dorinda. ' Oh, I hope he does ! '

But the Falcon did not come, and the Puma, when they spoke to her in the afternoon, said that she had not seen him either.

' But he *will* return,' she continued. ' Have no fear about that. Last night in my dreams I was hunting again, and I woke in the certain faith that my dream would come true. Have patience. The Falcon will return.'

But Friday dawned, and still he did not come, and all that morning Dinah and Dorinda felt very gloomy. They were quite sure that the Falcon would keep his word if he could, but they began to think that he might have had an accident. Perhaps he had been shot, or attacked by some larger bird such as an eagle.

' I never heard of there being eagles in the Forest of Weal,' said Dinah, ' but there might be.'

' There are eagles in Scotland,' said Dorinda, ' and one of them may have come to the Forest for a holiday.'

' Or the Falcon may have lost his way,' said Dinah.

' Perhaps he couldn't find anything to eat, and has fainted from hunger,' said Dorinda.

By the time they had thought of half a dozen other calamities, they were in the very depths of despair, and their neighbour, Mr. Parker, did nothing to make them more cheerful. Mr. Parker was also depressed. He had failed to find any evidence that would convict Bendigo of the theft of the missing ostrich eggs, and equally he had failed to prove him innocent. In spite of all his work he had been unable to find a single piece of evidence against anyone at all. And walking up and down his cage he repeated again and again, ' I am baffled. I am utterly baffled. I am totally and horribly bewildered. I am absolutely and abominably baffled. *Baffled !* '

In the afternoon, however, they all went to congratulate Lady Lil. For she had laid another egg.

Quite naturally, she was very proud of herself, and she sat upon her nest like a queen on her throne, while the other members of the zoo stood round her like courtiers and made polite remarks.

' How clever of vou ! ' exclaimed the Dancing Cassowary.

' Bless you, my dear,' sighed Marie Louise the Llama.

' What a *lovely* egg ! ' cried the Kinkajous.

' Let me see it too,' begged the young Dromedary.

' As handsome an egg as I have ever met,' said the Toucan.

' It looks good enough to eat,' said the Sacred Baboon.

But everyone was shocked by this last remark, and most of the animals exclaimed, ' What a dreadful thing to say ! ' Lady Lil went pale with emotion.

' I think she is going to faint,' said the Reindeer.

' But I didn't *mean* anything,' shouted the Baboon, at whom Mr. Parker was now glaring in the most suspicious manner.

' It was a very ill-bred and inconsiderate remark,' said Marie Louise, and the Dancing Cassowary screamed, ' Give her air, give her air ! '

Then the Dancing Cassowary fanned Lady Lil, who recovered fairly quickly, and the animals began to congratulate her all over again. And presently Lady Lil, sitting on her nest exactly as if it were a throne, made a little speech to them.

' Thank you very much,' she said, ' for all your kindness and good wishes. I appreciate them very deeply, and I am very glad to think that when my little Ostrich is safely hatched, he will have so many kind neighbours to live among.'

' Hurrah ! ' cried the animals.

' I need not remind you,' continued Lady Lil, ' how bitterly disappointed I have been in the past, but I ought to tell you, I think, that I had almost made up my mind that I would never, never, never lay an egg again. Then, happily, the whole situation changed. Bendigo was caught and put in prison. And if Bendigo was the thief, then the danger to my eggs had been removed. I could lay another without fear, and hope to hatch it in safety. I felt positive, a few days ago, that Bendigo *was* the thief. But after what I have heard to-day, I am not so sure.'

Lady Lil paused in her speech, and looked very hard at the Sacred Baboon, who again protested that he hadn't meant anything objectionable by what he said. But the other animals showed themselves so unfriendly towards him that he suddenly grew frightened and ran away. And Mr. Parker, pretending that he was only going for a little walk, proceeded to shadow him. Then Lady Lil went on with her speech.

' It seems to me,' she said, ' that my poor little

The Sacred Baboon ran away

egg is still in danger. It will have to be guarded with the greatest care, and I propose to guard it entirely by myself. I shall not leave my nest until my egg is hatched.'

Lady Lil paused again, and went on more slowly. 'I do not want to say anything against Sir Bobadil. He is my husband, and I love him. But he is *not* as considerate as I could wish him to be. He is *not* a good father. He thinks entirely of his own pleasure. He is not wicked — at least I hope he is not — but he is idle and weak-willed. He is easily led astray. Why, this very afternoon, when it is clearly his duty to be standing here beside me to receive your kind congratulations, he has gone and left me all alone. He is down by the river, I suppose, talking to the Black Swan. That is the sort of husband I have! Though I would never deny that he has a good kind heart, and though everybody admires him for his handsome figure and charming manners, he is NOT to be trusted! I shall never ask him to keep our egg warm, even for half an hour. I mean to hatch it entirely by myself!'

As a result of this speech, most of the animals grew very angry with Sir Bobadil, and some of them again began to wonder if it was he who had stolen the other eggs. A few of them thought that the Sacred Baboon had worn a guilty look when he ran away, and many of them were now convinced that Bendigo was innocent, and had suffered a great injustice in being imprisoned. All were full of sympathy for Lady Lil, and everyone devoutly hoped that this time her egg would be preserved from danger.

Chapter Fifteen

Another morning came, and still there was no sign of the Silver Falcon. Dinah and Dorinda tried their hardest to keep cheerful, but they could not help feeling woefully disappointed, nor looking rather sadder than kangaroos usually look. That day seemed to be the longest they had ever known.

But in the late evening, just as they were going to bed, they suddenly heard the sound of great wings beating the air, there was a scuffling noise in their cage, and then the voice of the Falcon calling hoarsely to them.

They hurried to the door, and Dinah cried, ' Oh, how glad we are to see you again ! '

' You've no idea how glad ! ' exclaimed Dorinda.

' We've been longing for your return.'

' We've been *aching* for you to come back.'

' And the first thing you want me to tell you, I suppose,' said the Falcon, ' is whether I have found Mrs. Grimble's bottle.'

' Have you ? ' asked Dinah.

' Don't say you haven't,' pleaded Dorinda.

' I know where it is,' said the Falcon.

' Come in and tell us all about everything you have been doing,' said Dinah. ' We'd better go inside in case we wake Mr. Parker, though I don't think he'll wake very easily to-night, because he was trying to shadow both Sir Bobadil and the Sacred Baboon all afternoon, and he's quite exhausted in consequence. But we'll be safer inside.'

So they went into their house, and the Silver Falcon was like a patch of light in the darkness, so bright was his plumage. And this is the story he told.

' For four days,' he said, ' I have been searching for the bottle. Twice or three times I have flown so high that I was caught in the tide of the upper winds, and carried far to north or south or east or west ; but that was merely for the joy of flight after having been so long a time in prison. And three or four times I have gone a-hawking over the Forest of Weal, and struck down three or four fine pigeons, strong on the wing ; but that was only for the joy of hunting, after having been so long in a cage where they fed me like a tame cat. For the rest of the time I have done no hawking, save the getting of my dinner, and no farther flying than from here to Midmeddlecum. Every day I have been searching for your bottle, in field and ditch, under bush and tree, in copse and garden, by road and river. I have searched every inch of the ground, and day after day was a blank and useless day. Night after night I flew to roost in the Forest, tired and disappointed. Dawn after dawn I was on the wing again, but all my searching brought no profit. Till an hour ago my quest was vain. I could not find it. And then, barely an hour since, I was quartering the field by the gate-keeper's lodge for the tenth or the twelfth or the fourteenth time, though the light was going fast, when I saw, not the bottle, but a plump young rabbit, and I thought to myself, There is my supper. So I stooped upon the rabbit, but the light being bad I nearly missed, and I barely gripped him by the hinder parts as he was vanishing down a hole. I pulled him out, he was squealing like a baby, and as I pulled I could see, beyond him in the hole, the bottle that you lost. It was too deep for me to reach, but the hole is near the edge of the field, on the far side of the road, eighty yards from the gate-keeper's cottage, and so that you will find it easily I have stuck in the soil beside it the rabbit's white tail.'

' What a clever thing to think of ! ' said Dorinda.

' Poor rabbit,' said Dinah.

' A fat and tender rabbit,' said the Falcon. ' I enjoyed my supper very much.'

' To-morrow afternoon,' said Dinah, ' we shall go and get the magic draught, and then, just as soon as we like, we can become girls again. Think of it, Dorinda ! '

' I've been thinking about it for a long time,' said Dorinda.

' I can't tell you how grateful we are,' said Dinah to the Falcon.

' Don't try to,' said the Falcon, ' for I have not finished my own story yet. I have learnt, by chance, who is the thief who has put all the zoo in turmoil by stealing the eggs of those silly Ostriches, Sir Bobadil and Lady Lil.'

' She has just laid another,' said Dorinda.

' She has ? Then you had better warn her to take good care of it or she will lose it like the others.'

' But who is the thief? ' asked Dinah.

' Let me tell the story in my own way,' said the Falcon. ' It began when I killed, early one morning, a cock Pheasant in a gaudy suit of feathers, of the

sort called the Amherst pheasants, I think, and that
was behind the farm which lies beyond Sir Lankester's mansion-house. No sooner had I killed than
a little Bantam Hen came running from the farmyard crying, " Well done, Falcon ! That was a very
proud and dangerous bird, who should have been
killed long ago, for he has done much mischief about
the farm with his boasting and fine feathers. We
are grateful to you, Falcon, and we shall be still
more grateful if you will kill another of our
enemies." '

' Who is that ? ' I asked.

' Then she spoke the name of one who lives in the
zoo, who is a notorious robber, and goes by night
to steal eggs, a whole clutch at one swallow, from
the Bantams who dwell in the farmyard. " Is it
only the eggs of a Bantam that he relishes ? " I
asked. " No indeed," she answered, " for lately we
have been spared, because he has been finding much
greater eggs, the eggs of an Ostrich, so I have heard,
but when that supply is finished he will return to
us, for eggs of one sort or another he must and will
have. And therefore, Falcon, I ask you, who are a
brave and noble killer, to kill him as you have killed
this naughty Pheasant, and save us Bantams from
further loss and sadness."

' Then I told her that he whom she had named
was too large an adversary for me to conquer, strong
and well-armed though I am. But I would see to
it, I said, that his thieving was made known, and
brought to a finish. And that, I think, is what you
can do.'

' But who,' asked Dinah, ' who *is* the thief ? '

The Falcon whispered his name.

' But,' said Dinah, ' I thought . . .'

' I never dreamt of it being him ! ' exclaimed Dorinda.

' How does he get out ? ' asked Dinah.

' I do not know,' said the Falcon, ' but he is the criminal, and you must contrive the means by which he may be caught. And now I am going. My dear friend the Golden Puma will have been waiting for my return even more eagerly than you, and she will rejoice to learn that I have found the magic draught. What other news shall I tell her ? Have you made a plan for her escape ? '

'If we find the bottle to-morrow afternoon,' said Dinah, ' we can take a dose at once, and we shall turn into girls again in about five minutes' time, I think. Now to-morrow is Sunday, and that is Visitors' Day, and there will be lots of other children there, so we shan't be noticed. We shall go to the Puma's cage . . . Oh, but we can't ! '

' Dinah ! ' cried Dorinda. ' I've just thought of it too ! '

' Thought of what ? ' asked the Falcon.

' Our clothes ! ' said Dinah. ' We haven't got any clothes ! '

' And if we turn ourselves into girls again, we shall be naked,' said Dorinda.

' You poor humans,' said the Falcon. ' How helpless you are ! '

Dorinda began to cry. ' It isn't our fault,' she sobbed.

' It's no good blaming *us* for being human,' said Dinah.

' Are you sure,' asked the Falcon, ' that you wouldn't prefer to remain kangaroos ? '

' Quite sure,' said Dinah.

' It seems to me,' said the Falcon, ' that a kangaroo has many advantages over a human child. As kangaroos you haven't the daily nuisance of getting dressed and then undressed. You aren't required to learn a lot of dull lessons, you can run faster and leap farther than any mere girl can hope to do. Why not stay as you are ? '

' No, no, no ! ' cried Dorinda.

' You are determined to change ? '

' Yes,' said Dinah. ' Absolutely determined.'

' Then it is indeed a pity,' said the Falcon, ' that you will have no clothes to wear.'

Overcome by this new disaster, Dinah and Dorinda sat in a miserable silence till, from the darkness of the house, there came a curious sound. It was harsh and low, like two river pebbles being rubbed together, then softly clapped together, but in a certain way it resembled laughter. Could it really be ? Was the Falcon mocking them ?

' Are you laughing at us ? ' asked Dinah indignantly.

The strange noise stopped. ' Forgive me,' said the Falcon. ' I do not often laugh, but the fact is that I have been making a little joke with you.'

' I don't think it's a very good joke,' said Dorinda glumly.

' Wait till you have seen the point of it.'

' Well, what is the point ? '

' You know where the Black Swan lives ? A hundred yards from his home there is a row of willow-trees. The third tree from the left has a hollow crown. Go there to-morrow afternoon and look for what you will find.'

' Not our clothes ? ' cried Dorinda.

' They are somebody's clothes,' said the Falcon, ' and whoever owns them had hidden them in a hollow oak in the Forest of Weal.'

' But however did you find them ? '

' I can discern a field-mouse in a cock of hay,' said the Falcon complacently. ' Do you think I would fail to see two bright dresses in a rotten tree ? '

' But how kind of you to bring them here ! ' said Dinah. ' How kind and thoughtful ! '

' It's the most thoughtful act I ever heard of,' said Dorinda.

' Thank you again and again,' said Dinah. ' We shall *always* be grateful to you.'

' Remember the Puma,' said the Falcon. ' We cannot leave without her, and it is your part to make a proper plan for her release.'

' You can trust us,' said Dinah solemnly.

' Then good-night,' said the Falcon. The silver gleam of his plumage went out of the darkness, and then they heard the first strong wing-beats of his flight.

' Dinah ! ' said Dorinda, ' what are we going to do first ? '

' We are going to have the busiest night of our lives,' said Dinah. ' And first of all, go and call Mr. Parker. Then I shall tell you my plan.'

Chapter Sixteen

Dinah took charge. She let Mr. Parker have no time to argue, but gave him his instructions as calmly and clearly as if she had been her father issuing orders to his battalion. Mr. Parker was full of admiration for her plan, but even more impressed when she admitted that she had a key which would open all the animals' cages, and he was positively awe-stricken when she divulged the name of the criminal who had been stealing Lady Lil's eggs.

'What put you on his trail?' he whispered. 'What was the final clue which enabled you to solve this baffling mystery?'

'There weren't any clues,' said Dinah. 'Someone told me who he was.'

'Ah, yes,' said Mr. Parker wisely, 'that is often the way. A clue is a very good thing to have, and a lot of clues are still better, but an informer is best of all. The police are very fond of informers, because if they know the name of the criminal, and where he lives, they can solve the most difficult cases quite quickly and with perfect efficiency.'

'Look at that cloud,' said Dorinda. 'As soon as it blows a little more to the east, the moon will shine.'

'It is full to-night,' said Mr. Parker.

'Then we have no time to lose,' said Dinah, 'for everybody should be in position before the moon comes out.'

Without another word she unlocked the door of

their cage, let the Giraffe out of his, and went swiftly
to the next block of cages, where Marie Louise the
Llama, the Zebra, the Ant-eater, and the Kinkajous
lived. She woke them all, opened all their doors,
and leaving Mr. Parker and Dorinda to explain
what they had to do, she proceeded to call many
other animals in their turn. Finally, she went to
the prison cage where Bendigo the Grizzly Bear was
confined. She had a long conversation with him.
He was very ill-tempered about being wakened,
but Dinah pacified him at last, and when he heard
what was about to happen, and what she wanted
him to do, he became very cheerful, and laughed
in his throat with the sound of a little thunderstorm
in a ravine.

By now the great dark cloud, the only one in the
sky, which had covered the moon, had blown away
to the east, obscuring a few thousand stars on its
way but leaving the full moon shining bright and
clear like a vast silver tray which had been polished
by ten thousand housemaids for ten thousand years.
The sky itself was a dark smooth blue, like the skin
of a grape, and the park, towards which Dinah was
now hurrying with long swift leap-after-leap, was
flooded with milky light ; but trees and shrubs cast
inky shadows. Here and there in the shadow she
could see the bright eyes of animals on guard.

Her plan had been to release all the animals who
could be trusted — but not the Puma, because many
of the others were afraid of her — and post them
like sentries round Lady Lil's nest. She had told
Mr. Parker that they must not go too near the nest,
for Lady Lil should not be unnecessarily disturbed,

The animals were on guard

but they had to be close enough to each other to prevent the thief from slipping through the ring unseen. He was strong and cunning : they must keep a good look-out.

She found the animals in position in a great circle surrounding the nest. They were all wide awake and eager to be the first to catch sight of the criminal. But a good many of them were rather frightened. They were all well concealed in the shadow of trees and bushes, and they stood perfectly still, as animals can.

Within the circle, and only about twenty yards from the nest where Lady Lil was calmly sleeping, there stood a group of lime-trees, and Mr. Parker was standing between them with his long neck among the branches and his head looking over the topmost leaves. He stood so still that he was almost invisible, but Dinah could see that he had a good view of the nest, and he at least, she thought, was bound to see the thief if he came. 'If he doesn't fall asleep, that is,' she added, 'for he is leaning against a tree in a very comfortable-looking way, and he is shamefully fond of going to sleep.'

She hoped for the best, however, and after she had visited all the sentries, and encouraged them to be alert and brave, she went to look for Dorinda.

She had told Dorinda to wait for her on the far side of the sentry-ring. On the side farthest from the cages, that is, and nearest to the gate-keeper's cottage and the field where Mrs. Grimble's bottle lay in a rabbit-hole. She had said nothing about the bottle to Mr. Parker, of course, but she had told Dorinda, 'If the animals behave intelligently, and seem as though they can be trusted, then you and I will go and look for the rabbit-hole which the Falcon marked with the rabbit's tail. It should be easy to find in the moonlight, and we may be away for only a few minutes. Then we'll return and keep watch till morning if need be.'

So she and Dorinda waited for perhaps a quarter of an hour a little beyond the sentry-ring, and everything was quiet. The moonlight lay so thickly that Dorinda thought she could see it dripping off the leaves, and the moon, she said, was bulging out of the sky like the old mirror in the hall at home.

'After all,' said Dinah thoughtfully, 'he may not come to-night. The thief, I mean. Let's go and look for the bottle. But be careful! We must move as quietly as possible, for on a night like this the smallest sound will be heard——'

She was interrupted by a loud and fearful shriek that would have been heard in the midst of a winter gale.

'What's that?' cried Dorinda.

'Lady Lil!' said Dinah. 'Hurry, hurry!'

The nest, when they reached it, was already surrounded by some twenty or thirty feverishly excited animals, and Lady Lil, in a hoarse high voice, was weeping and bemoaning her loss. She was waving her head to and fro in agitated movement, and her eyes were sprinkling bright tears in the moonlight as though they had been watering-cans.

'It's gone, gone, gone!' she cried. 'My latest, loveliest, littlest egg is for ever gone.'

'It was quite a big egg when I saw it,' said Mr. Parker suspiciously.

'What does that matter now,' screamed the Ostrich, 'when it's gone, gone, gone?'

'But how did it go?' asked the Cassowary. 'You have been sitting on it all night, and we have been watching you.'

'There was a pair of eyes,' said Lady Lil. 'I woke in a fright, and two great yellow eyes were staring at me. They were as yellow as, as . . .'

'As butter?' asked one of the Kinkajous.

'No, no!' said Lady Lil. 'They were hard and yellow, like, like . . .'

'Like cheese?' asked the young Baboon.

'*No!*' shouted Lady Lil. 'They were bright and hard and yellow . . .'

'Like a topaz,' said Marie Louise.

'Yes, like a topaz, and they glittered in the moonlight only a yard from mine. And then, I think, I fainted. I rose a little way from my nest, and fell again. And when I came to my senses, my egg was gone. My latest, loveliest egg, for ever gone. Ah me, I am the most miserable Ostrich that ever lived! Why, if this was to be my fate, did my poor mother sit so long and patiently to hatch me? In such a world as this, an Ostrich has no hope of happiness.'

'Mr. Parker,' said Dinah in her most efficient voice, 'did you see this happen?'

'I saw nothing,' said Mr. Parker. 'Absolutely nothing! I am completely baffled by this wholly unexpected development.'

'You were asleep,' said Dinah.

'I resent that,' said Mr. Parker. 'I strongly resent it. I bitterly and deeply resent it. I resent it from the depths of my being. I am not unduly sensitive, but——'

' You were unduly sleepy,' asid Dorinda unkindly.

' Anyway,' said Dinah, ' we are only wasting time standing here and talking. We should be looking for the thief. We all know who he is, and he has been too cunning for us. I believe that most of you were keeping a good look-out, but he has beaten you. He got through between two sentries and stole the egg. But he may not have eaten it yet, and perhaps he isn't far away. He may have gone towards home, but he won't get home very easily, for I've seen to that, and he is just as likely to be hiding somewhere quite near. So scatter and look for him. Some of you should go towards his cage, but all the others must hunt in every direction.'

' Admirable advice,' said Marie Louise. ' Scatter, my friends, pray scatter ! Two or three of you, however, may come with me.'

She spoke rather coldly, for she strongly disapproved of a young kangaroo like Dinah, who had so newly come to the zoo, setting herself up as a leader ; but though Marie Louise was inclined to be jealous, she was also fair, and she knew that Dinah's plan was the proper one. So she offered a good example to the other animals, who quickly began to search for the criminal in all directions. But they were, by now, far too excited to keep quiet, as they had been while they stood sentry round the nest, so presently the moonlit air was trembling with the wild noises of the hunt, with baying and barking and crying and grunting and chattering and twittering and hissing and hollering and hip-hip-hurrahing and view-hulloing. But Lady Lil, entirely forgotten, sat alone upon her nest and wept.

Then Mr. Parker, regarding the scene from his superior height, uttered a sudden tremendous shout and attracted nearly everyone's attention. ' Tally-ho, tally-ho ! ' shouted Mr. Parker, with his fore-legs stiffly braced and wide apart, his long neck stretching like the jib of a crane, and his great dark eyes ashine. The other animals looked in the direction to which he was pointing, and all were completely astonished. For there in the moonlight stood Sir Bobadil, and Sir Bobadil was obviously embarrassed. Sir Bobadil wore a guilty look, and midway between his beak and his breast, in the very middle of his neck, there was a sinister, suspicious bulge !

But Sir Bobadil was *not* the thief they had expected. It was not Sir Bobadil against whom they had been on guard and for whom they were now searching.

That, however, did not worry Mr. Parker. Mr. Parker forgot everything that Dinah had told him, and looking only at the bulge in Sir Bobadil's neck, exclaimed joyfully, ' A clue, a clue at last ! '

' After him ! ' he shouted. ' Don't let him get away. Surround him, cut him off, capture him, there he goes ! '

Mr. Parker led the pursuit at a gallop, and Sir Bobadil might have been taken almost immediately if Mr. Parker had looked where he was going. But in his excitement he tripped over the Ant-eater and fell heavily, which disorganised the chase. So Sir Bobadil got a good start and fled towards the wide lawn in front of Sir Lankester Lemon's mansion.

Now Sir Lankester had been wakened by the noise of the hunt, and was standing on the broad steps in front of the main door, wondering what it was all about. He was wearing a suit of yellow silk pyjamas with red braid on the jacket, a girdle with red tassels, and red Turkish slippers ; and he carried a bolas and a boomerang.

Sir Bobadil the Ostrich ran frenziedly on to the lawn. Sir Lankester stepped forward, swung the bolas three times round his head, and let fly. His aim was sure. The iron-weighted rope wrapped itself round and round the base of Sir Bobadil's neck, who staggered, swayed, and fell.

At this very moment, however, the rest of the animals, a wild hunting pack led by Mr. Parker, came charging across the lawn.

' Rebellion ! ' cried Sir Lankester. ' They have broken loose, we are attacked ! Down, rebels, down ! Virtus semper Viridis — Ma Foi et mon Droit — Du bleibst doch immer was Du bist ! '

These foreign phrases were the mottoes of the Lemon family, and Sir Lankester used often to encourage himself by repeating them. They always made him feel even braver than before, so now he did not flinch from the charging animals, but instantly threw his boomerang at Mr. Parker.

But this time his aim was not so good. The boomerang missed, by three yards at least, Mr. Parker's head, and began its return flight. It was not easy to see it in the moonlight, and Sir Lankester did not observe its approach. He was amazed when something struck him on the forehead. Or rather, he would have been amazed if he had had time to think about it. But he had no time, for immediately he fell to the soft turf, stunned.

Well in the van of the pursuing animals was Marie Louise the Llama, and when she saw her beloved master fall, she uttered a piercing scream and raced towards him. He made, indeed, a very handsome and pathetic sight as he lay in the moonlight in his yellow silk pyjamas, with their red braid and red tassels, and the red Turkish slippers, and a trickle of blood on his noble brow.

Marie Louise, kneeling beside him, laid her head on his chest and was convulsed with sobs. The young Baboon began to chafe his feet, the Kinkajous to rub his hands, while the Gnu blew gently on his face to give him air. He was surrounded by his animals, who all revealed, in various ways, the intensity of their grief and their utter devotion. Sir Bobadil was entirely forgotten.

There on the moonlit turf before his stately house lay Sir Lankester among the weeping animals, while a hundred yards away, on the open lawn, the poor silly Ostrich, choked by the bolas and gasping for air, felt sure he was about to die. Twice he struggled to his feet, and fell again. He tried a third time to get up, but rolled on to his back, kicking feebly with his long legs.

At this moment a kangaroo appeared on the edge of the lawn. It was Dorinda.

When Mr. Parker set the animals off in pursuit of Sir Bobadil, Dinah and Dorinda with a Howler Monkey called Siren, who had a very loud voice, were already on their way to the main part of the

Sir Lankester looked very handsome

zoo. There, they had thought, was the most important place to watch. But then, for a moment, they were undecided. Perhaps it would be as well for one of them to join Mr. Parker's hunt, while the other kept to the original plan ? So Dorinda said that she would go with the Giraffe, and as swiftly as she could she hurried after the disappearing animals.

She arrived on the lawn too late to see the collapse of Sir Lankester. The first thing she saw was Bobadil waving his legs in the air.

' Who did this ? ' she asked, as she began to unwrap the bolas from his neck.

' Urgk, urgk ! ' croaked Sir Bobadil, who could say no more.

' And what's this ? ' she demanded, as she felt the lump in his neck, which was about eighteen inches higher up.

' Urgk ! ' said Sir Bobadil.

Dorinda felt it more carefully.

' I do believe,' she said, ' that it's something belonging to me ! And if it is, then you *are* a thief, as everyone thought, because eating other people's property is only another form of stealing, and it's greedy too. It serves you right that it stuck in your throat, and though you couldn't swallow it, you're going to *unswallow* it, and unswallow it this minute, or I shan't take this rope off your throat.'

' Urrurgk. Urrugagrurgk,' said Sir Bobadil.

' You mean you can't unswallow it unless I take the rope off first ? '

' Brurrugh.'

' But you promise you will ? '

' Grurg.'

' All right then, I'll trust you.   But if you don't
— well, something much worse than a bolas is going
to hit you ! '

Then Dorinda unwrapped the rope that was
wound so tightly round Sir Bobadil's throat, and
after some wriggling, writhing, and coughing for a
little while, the Ostrich laid on the turf the bottle
containing Mrs. Grimble's magic draught.

' Excuse me,' he said.

Chapter Seventeen

Bendigo the Bear lay in the shadow of a rock beside a group of cages, waiting. Here was where the thief lived, and Dinah, when she let Bendigo out of prison, had said : ' If the animals guarding the nest fail to capture him, he's almost certain to make for home. Then you will have to stop him. He'll be in a desperate mood, but you're very strong. Do you think you can do it ? '

' Let me get my arms round him,' Bendigo had growled, ' and I'll crush him to death ! '

During his imprisonment he had been, naturally enough, in a very bad temper, for he had no *Times* to read, and he was being punished for a crime which he had not committed. But now he had a chance to get rid of his anger upon the real thief. A glorious, honey-sweet revenge ! With all his wrathful heart he hoped and prayed that the other animals would fail to find or hold the criminal, so that he, Bendigo, might have the exquisite pleasure of halting him, wrestling with him, and, if possible, breaking his abominable back.

That is what Bendigo promised himself as he waited in the shadow. ' I'll break his abominable back,' he growled, and grew impatient because the thief did not come at once.

In front of the cages, and in front of the rock beside which Bendigo lay, there was a narrow strip of grass, and before that a road about ten feet broad. Beyond the road there was more grass, with shrubs and bushes, and behind them could be seen a few trees, their leaves in the moonlight as still as the leaves on a Chinese scroll.

Suddenly Bendigo stiffened, and the coarse hair on his neck rose harsh and bristling. In the bushes beyond the road, only a few inches above the ground, he saw, like tiny yellow lamps, two palely glittering eyes. He lay perfectly still, and slowly, very slowly, the eyes came nearer. They left the darkness of the bushes, and drew close to the farther edge of the road. But only the eyes were visible. There seemed to be nothing else.

Then, with unbelievable speed, they were over the road, and behind them, with a fast-flowing movement, came a thick round body. Bendigo, with a roar, hurled himself upon it. It was the Python. The Python was the thief.

Now there began a fearful battle.

The Python was about twelve feet long, and first of all Bendigo seized it by the middle and tried to lift it off the ground. The middle came up in a great loop, but quickly the Python coiled its head-end round one of his legs, its tail-end round the other, and threw Bendigo off his feet. They rolled over and over on the road, the Bear tied up in the snake. Then the Python broke loose, and tried to escape into its house by a secret hole under the wall which it used, unknown to Mr. Plum the keeper, for going in and out whenever it wanted. But Bendigo caught it by the tail, and there was a tug-of-war with Bendigo hauling and pulling in one direction, and the Python straining with all its length of mighty muscle to get away in the other.

Bendigo was unable to drag it away from the hole, but the Python couldn't get away from the Bear, so after three or four minutes of desperate pulling it suddenly turned, and its head, like a battering-ram, leapt straight at Bendigo's throat.

Just in time, Bendigo struck. His rough right paw hit the Python a dreadful blow on the side of the head, and the front end of the snake — some four or five feet of it — fell limply to the ground. But Bendigo, of course, had been obliged to let go the tail in order to hit the head, and before he could avoid it, the tail-end — some five or six feet of it — coiled itself round his waist and tried to squeeze him to death, while the head-end, recovering its breath, again struck at him like a battering-ram.

But again and again, now with his right paw and now with his left, Bendigo clouted the darting head, beating it to one side, then to the other, and at last the Python fell senseless to the ground, and its tail uncoiled from Bendigo's waist. Then Bendigo, picking up the loose body and holding it about three or four feet from the head-end, struck its skull against the wall of the nearest cage and killed it.

' Oh, well done, well done ! ' cried Dinah. ' Brave Bendigo ! '

She had arrived, with Siren the Howler Monkey close beside her, in time to see most of the fight, and though she had been afraid, she had watched every blow and throw, every trick and turn of the struggle.

' Oh, brave Bendigo ! ' she repeated. ' How magnificently you fought ! But I was terribly afraid for you. Every time that dreadful head struck at

Bendigo struck its skull against the wall

you, I felt sure you were going to be killed. My heart almost stopped beating.'

'Nonsense,' said Bendigo, puffing and panting. 'It was just the sort of fight I like, and I feel all the better for it. Did you see that first punch I gave him?'

'It was wonderful,' said Dinah.

'You've got to know how to time your punches,' said Bendigo. 'Balance and timing — that's the secret of a good punch. I used to do a lot of boxing when I was a boy.'

'When were *you* a boy?' asked Dinah.

But Bendigo, in spite of the brave way in which he had been talking, was very tired. His last words had been no louder than a whisper, and now he was sitting on the grass with hanging head and shoulders relaxed, looking like the oldest and most weary bear in the world. He paid no attention to Dinah's question.

Siren the Howler had been examining the dead Python, and now he called softly to Dinah.

'Look!' he said, pointing to a round swelling in the snake's body. 'There's the egg, Lady Lil's egg. He swallowed it, but it doesn't seem to be broken.'

'But how can we get it out?'

'I don't know,' said Siren.

'If we had a knife,' said Dinah, 'we could do an operation and cut it out. Bendigo! Do you know where we can get a knife?'

'I've got a little one,' said Bendigo in a weary voice. 'I use it for cutting cigars. People some-times give me a cigar on a Sunday afternoon.'

'I didn't know that bears could smoke cigars,' said Dinah.

'Didn't you?' asked Bendigo, and slowly, with a groan at every movement, he got up and shambled towards them.

He had a little knife on a chain round his neck. He opened it and made a long neat cut in the Python's hide. The egg was unharmed.

'You'd better take it back to Lady Lil while it's warm,' said Bendigo. 'I'm going to my bed. I'm just a trifle tired, I think. Don't forget to come and lock me in. And you'd better hurry up and get the others back to their cages, for it's nearly morning, and there'll be trouble if old Plum finds them out and about when he gets up.'

'But what are we going to do with *this*?' asked Dinah, pointing to the body of the Python.

'Let it lie,' said Bendigo. 'It isn't any good to anyone.' And limping and groaning, he went off to his cage.

'It seems very untidy to leave it lying there,' said Dinah, 'but what else can we do? Let's take the egg back to Lady Lil.'

The moon by now was low in the east, and its light was duller, as though it were dimly reflected from a silver tray that no one had cleaned for a long time. But already there was a little dawn-grey in the sky, and that made them hurry.

They found Lady Lil beside her nest. She was all alone, and with drooping head she looked at the empty place where the egg had lain. She was sobbing bitterly, and her long neck quivered, and now and then she touched with her beak the dry grass in the bed of the nest. Dinah herself could hardly keep from crying when she saw her, and quite forgot the little speech she had intended to make. She had meant to return the egg with a gracious gesture and a few polite words of congratulation, like Lady Lemon presenting Mrs. Fullalove with the First Prize for Dahlias at the Midmeddlecum Flower Show, but all she could do was to hurry forward and exclaim, 'Stop crying! We've found your egg; here it is, stop crying *please*!'

For a moment Lady Lil stared at the egg as if she could not believe her eyes, but then she began to dance up and down with excitement, and asked twenty questions, and told Dinah what to do, and what not to do, and laughed for pure joy, and cried for no reason at all.

'Where did you find it?' she demanded. 'Who was the thief? Where has he gone? Put it down there. Oh, be careful with it! No, not there, *there*. Is it all right? It's quite warm. Why is it still warm? Oh, my egg, my darling egg, where have you been? Oh, I'm so happy! You're the cleverest kangaroo that ever lived! Darling Kangaroo, where did you find it? No, don't tell me now, I mustn't get excited. I must keep quiet and calm for *its* sake. My dear, dear egg. . . .'

So they left her, and then Dinah said to Siren the Monkey, 'Howl as loudly as you can, for it's time we all got back to our cages.'

Then Siren opened his mouth and howled, and the noise was heard far and wide, and all the animals obeyed and went back to their cages.

Marie Louise and the others, who had gathered round Sir Lankester when the boomerang hit him, were rather reluctant to go, because Sir Lankester had by now recovered consciousness, and was talking to them in the most friendly way. He couldn't quite remember what had happened, but the first thing he had seen when he opened his eyes was the loving face of Marie Louise, and then the other animals, all of whom, in one way or another, were showing their affection for him. So he sat up and told them what a happy man he was to have so many good kind friends.

' There is only one recipe for happiness,' he said in his most solemn voice, ' and that is to make others happy. I have done my best, and I have every intention of doing more and more to give you pleasure and promote your welfare.'

But what it was that he intended to do they could not wait to hear, because at that moment they heard Siren the Howler Monkey. And a few seconds later Sir Lankester, in his yellow pyjamas, was left alone upon the lawn. The rapid disappearance of the animals bewildered him, and when he tried to think of all that had happened, and find a meaning for it, he grew still more bewildered. His head was aching, he was feeling cold, and there was no one to talk to. So he decided to go to bed.

Dinah was already hurrying from cage to cage and locking the doors. Bendigo was fast asleep, but she spoke a few words to all the other animals, praising them for what they had done, and telling the news that Lady Lil's egg had been safely restored and the Python was dead. She talked for several minutes to the Golden Puma, who had been anxiously awake all night, and she had to spend twice as long with Mr. Parker before he could be made to understand what had happened.

Then she went to her own house, and there was Dorinda with Mrs. Grimble's magic draught.

They were both far too happy to feel sleepy, so they lay talking till it was broad daylight. And then, without meaning to, they did go to sleep.

Chapter Eighteen

About ten o'clock in the morning Sir Lankester and Mr. Plum were standing outside Dinah and Dorinda's cage, arguing about the events of the previous night. Sir Lankester, who wore a large piece of sticking-plaster on his forehead, had by then remembered the alarming sight of the animals charging on to the lawn. He remembered throwing his boomerang, and he remembered waking up to see Marie Louise bending over him. But Mr. Plum refused to believe a word of this fantastic story, and said that in his opinion Sir Lankester had had a nightmare.

' Then how did I get this cut on the forehead ? ' demanded Sir Lankester.

' You must have fallen out of bed,' said Mr. Plum.

' I never fall out of bed ! ' said Sir Lankester. ' And even if I had fallen downstairs, how would that account for the Python's death ? How was he killed ? '

' Ah ! ' said Mr. Plum, ' that's a different story altogether. Now if you ask me what happened to the Python——'

' I do ask you,' said Sir Lankester.

' Then my answer is that I don't know, and I don't believe we ever shall know.'

' That isn't very helpful.'

' Wait a minute,' said Mr. Plum. ' We have had a criminal in the zoo : we do know that. An egg-thief. And the Python's dead : there's no disputing that. So if you ask me why he was killed — not how, but why — I should say because he was the thief, and whoever discovered the truth about him, took the law into his own hands and punished him.'

' In that case,' said Sir Lankester, ' Bendigo is innocent.'

' Of course he is,' said **Mr.** Plum.

' Then he must be released immediately and returned to his own cage.'

' A very good idea,' said Mr. Plum.

So Bendigo was removed from the dark and narrow prison cage to his own comfortable house, and ten minutes later he was reading, with great contentment, the copy of the *Observer* — for it was Sunday — that he had cleverly taken from Sir Lankester's coat pocket. And Sir Lankester went to church, and when the Vicar began his sermon, he was very angry to find that he had nothing to read.

Dinah and Dorinda waited with the utmost impatience till afternoon. Visitors were admitted to the zoo on Sundays at half-past two, and the main gate would be open for them. The gate-keeper, of course, would be there all the time to see that none of the animals went out, but Dinah had a plan for smuggling the Golden Puma past him. She and Dorinda, having drunk Mrs. Grimble's magic draught and resumed their ordinary shape, could, if they liked, walk out with the other visitors and no one would suspect them.

' Oh ! ' she suddenly exclaimed.

' What's the matter ? ' asked Dorinda.

' The medicine,' said Dinah. ' I hope it hasn't

gone stale and lost its strength.'

Dorinda took out the cork, smelt, and shuddered. ' It's all right.'

' We'll soon know if it is,' said Dinah. ' Oh, I wish it was time to be let out ! '

Mr. Plum came at last, and unlocked the cages of all those animals who were allowed into the park. Dinah and Dorinda first said good-bye to their particular friends, and then hurried to the cluster of willow-trees where their clothes were hidden. They found the Silver Falcon waiting for them.

' Well done ! ' he cried. ' That was finely managed, that campaign of yours last night, and Bendigo fought a brave fight. But his bravery would have served no purpose had you not made the plot. I saw it all, and I say you did well. Very well indeed, my children.'

' We were lucky,' said Dinah, ' but it was really clever of Dorinda to find Mrs. Grimble's bottle before we expected to.'

' Good luck often comes to those who deserve it,' said the Falcon. ' And now what of the plan for to-day ? How will you lead the Puma past the keeper at the gate ? I told her, early this morning, that the Python lay dead, the thief, like an old ship's hawser on the road, and she purred with joy, and told me how she herself had once fought with a great snake and killed it, but was so bruised in the battle that she lay a week scarce able to move, and was near death from starvation before she could hunt again. Come, make haste, she is thirsty for her freedom.'

' If freedom, for her, means the danger of being

squeezed to death by a python,' said Dorinda, ' don't you think she might like to stay in her cage?'

' Never!' cried the Falcon. ' Never, never! Freedom is worth all peril in the world, freedom's the noblest thing, we live at ease who freely live. Now what's your plan? What shall I tell her?'

' We shall come to her cage as soon as possible,' said Dinah, ' and the plan is very simple. We shan't be looking like kangaroos, of course. We shall be in our proper shape.'

' Girl children,' said the Falcon. ' Fair-haired or dark?'

' Dorinda is dark, but I'm fair,' said Dinah.

' One of each is fairness itself,' said the Falcon. ' So good-bye, Kangaroos, and hurry, Children, hurry!'

Then he flew swiftly away, and Dinah uncorked the bottle.

' Remember to wish properly,' she said. ' Wish very hard to be Dorinda, or anything may happen.'

' I'll remember,' said Dorinda solemnly, and having drunk exactly half of what was left, gave the bottle to Dinah.

The next thing Dinah remembered was someone saying, ' You've got very dirty feet.'

She looked at Dorinda's feet, and answered indignantly, ' So are yours!'

' Oh, Dinah,' cried Dorinda, ' it's worked!'

' Oh, Dorinda, isn't it lovely to be a girl again!'

' Even with dirty feet,' said Dorinda.

' We'll have a bath to-night.'

' And a proper supper at a proper table.'

' And a proper bed to sleep in.'

' Aren't we lucky to be girls ? '

They began to dance round the nearest willow-tree, but the visitors to the zoo were already arriving, and when they saw some people in the distance

they hurriedly got their clothes and dressed themselves, a little clumsily because they were out of practice, and then stood and looked at each other.

' We're not very smart,' said Dinah. ' Our frocks are terribly crumpled, and mine is rather damp.'

' Your hair needs brushing,' said Dorinda.

' So does yours.'

' Are your shoes uncomfortable ? '

' Horribly uncomfortable.'

' So are mine. Oh, how I hate wearing clothes ! '

' We've got to now,' said Dinah. ' I suppose we'll get used to it in time. But I don't really like clothes. Do you ? '

' I'll *never* get used to them ! ' said Dorinda. ' I wish——'

' No, don't say that ! ' cried Dinah. ' It might happen ! And we've got work to do. Pick up the key — there it is, in the grass — and come and look for Mr. Steeple's motor-car. Then we'll let the Puma out of her cage, and in a very short time we'll be home again.'

Mr. Steeple the Vicar went to the zoo every Sunday afternoon, and having stayed there for exactly an hour, drove away in his motor-car, which was the oldest car in Midmeddlecum, but also the most dignified and the most comfortable. It was so handsome and old-fashioned that it looked more like a carriage that should be drawn by a pair of horses than a motor. Dinah's plan was to put the Puma on the back seat, cover her with a rug, and then tell the Vicar that she and Dorinda were very tired, and would like to be driven home.

' He's so kind,' she said, ' that he's sure to say yes, and he's very fond of company, so it won't be a hardship for him.'

' We'll have to make the Puma promise to keep perfectly still,' said Dorinda.

' I've just thought of something,' said Dinah. ' I

wonder if we can still talk like animals and understand what they say ? '

' Kea yark urbaneesh eeeern gnarrh uh,' said Dorinda.

' How funny that sounds ! '

' But you know what I mean ? '

' Oh, yes. Perfectly.'

' Well, that's all right,' said Dorinda.

They found the Vicar's motor-car, where it stood with a lot of others on a broad part of the road, and for a little while they looked curiously at all the people from Midmeddlecum who had come to spend Sunday afternoon at the zoo and stare at wild animals. Their appearance, thought Dinah, is really far more odd and comical than any of the animals I know, except, perhaps, the old Baboon who isn't allowed out of his cage, and the Dancing Cassowary, and the Wart-hog.

' And Mr. Parker,' added Dorinda, who had guessed her thoughts.

' You could make quite as interesting a zoo by putting people in the cages.'

' But you wouldn't be allowed to,' said Dorinda.

' No,' said Dinah regretfully, ' I suppose you wouldn't. Well, let's go and wait for a good opportunity to open the Puma's cage.'

In the blue lift of the sky, far above the cage, there was a little speck of matter that no one saw. It was the Silver Falcon watching like a sentry from his lonely post, and when he perceived that two small girls had halted by the cage and were pressing their faces between the bars, he turned a somersault for sheer excitement and joy, dived through the sunny air for eight hundred feet and roughly breasted the rising air to stop his swift descent, threw himself on to his back, rolled one way and then the other, and crying hoarsely, ' Freedom's a noble thing ! ' climbed again to the silky fringe of a little cloud.

' Puma, Puma ! ' whispered Dinah. ' Here we are ! We're going to let you out as soon as those people have gone.'

The Golden Puma lay on a rock, motionless and with unblinking eyes, about three yards away. She paid no attention.

' You're talking English,' said Dorinda. ' What's the use of that ? '

' I quite forgot ! ' exclaimed Dinah. ' Puma, Puma — gnirk arkee ur bagrccr zy rook, shim salee, gnaaar pupu, roor myaah nyiih kling. Shrings kraugh ? '

Then the Puma turned her head, and her agate eyes, as if a lamp had been lighted behind them, shone suddenly with a wild joy. Swiftly she rose, and with the same movement leapt to the bars. ' Now ? ' she asked. ' Are you going to let me out now ? '

' Wait till those people are out of sight,' said Dinah. She explained what the Puma had to do, carefully described the Vicar's motor-car, and told her where to find it.

The Puma listened, purring with happiness, her whiskers stiff with excitement, her eyes like lighted lamps, and her restless tail sweeping the ground from side to side.

' Now ! ' said Dorinda. ' There's no one in

sight. Quickly, Dinah!'

Dinah slipped the key into the lock and opened the door. Stretching her golden body in a great leap for freedom, the Puma bounded from the cage and a moment later was out of sight among some bushes on the other side of the road. Dinah locked the door again and she and Dorinda hurried away.

Before going to the Vicar's car they went to see Lady Lil, and found her sitting proudly on her nest with at least twenty people standing round, and Sir Bobadil beside her with a very virtuous look on his face — 'She's forgiven him,' said Dorinda — while Mr. Parker was pacing slowly behind the ring of spectators like a policeman on his beat. He was obviously determined that never again would an egg be stolen so long as he was there.

'We have made Lady Lil happy again,' said Dinah.

'And Mr. Parker looks quite pleased with himself,' said Dorinda. 'I'm sure he thinks it was all due to him.'

'I would like to speak to him,' said Dinah, 'and tell him who we are. But he might make rather a fuss.'

'He might be baffled again,' said Dorinda.

'So we had better go and look for Mr. Steeple.'

They returned to the Vicar's motor-car and were greeted by a low growl from underneath it. Dinah knelt down. 'Did anyone see you?' she asked.

'No one,' said the Puma. 'How long must I stay here? This machine has a most horrible smell.'

Dinah opened the door. 'Get inside,' she said,

and the Puma slid nimbly in. ' But don't scratch the cushions,' she added, and covered the Puma with a dark-blue rug.

They waited for ten minutes and then the Vicar came.

' What a lovely afternoon ! ' he exclaimed. ' But you weren't in church this morning, and you weren't in church last Sunday, or the Sunday before, and I'm not sure of the Sunday before that. Why not ? '

' We've been away from home,' said Dinah.

' Then I hope you have had a happy holiday,' said the Vicar. ' And now, I suppose, you are waiting to see if I shall offer to drive you home ? '

' We're feeling very tired,' said Dorinda.

' Then climb in,' said the Vicar, ' and off we shall go. And as there are three of us we may as well pass the time by singing a round. Let us sing *Hot Spice Gingerbread.*'

So they drove out of the zoo, and the gate-keeper opened the main gate for them, and took off his hat to the Vicar, and Dinah held Dorinda's hand very tightly and both of them thought : ' I wonder what the gate-keeper would say if he knew that he had opened the gate for two Kangaroos and a Puma ? ' But with perfectly innocent faces they looked straight in front of them and loudly sang :

' Hot spice gingerbread,
Ho ! come buy my hot gingerbread smoking hot !
Hot spice gingerbread,
Ho ! come buy my hot gingerbread smoking hot !
Who's for a ha'porth of hot gingerbread, ho !
Smoking, smoking hot ! '

Then, when the round was finished, the Vicar sighed deeply and said, 'These are sad times we live in. My poor wife is still in prison, and so are all the other people, unhappy souls, who could not agree to find Mrs. Taper guilty, and would not consent to find her not guilty. Mr. Justice Rumple keeps them all in prison still.'

Dinah and Dorinda knew nothing about that, because it was on the very morning when they became kangaroos that Mrs. Steeple and all the other Members of the Jury were sent to prison — that was the procession, of prisoners and their friends, which they had so badly frightened — so the Vicar told them the whole story of the trial of Mrs. Taper and its dreadful consequences. And by the time the story was finished, they had reached home.

Dorinda opened the door of the car, and the Puma slipped quietly out. The Vicar did not look round. They thanked him very politely, and as he drove away they could hear him singing *There is a Tavern in the Town*. Then they hurried towards the long garden at the back of the house, the Puma following them in the shadow of the hedge, and when the rhododendron thicket was between them and the house the Silver Falcon, swooping from the sky, came down to meet them.

'But you mustn't stay here,' said Dinah, as the Falcon and the Puma greeted each other. 'It wouldn't be safe. You would be seen, and caught again, and taken back to the zoo.'

'Never!' exclaimed the Puma. 'Never again shall I be taken captive. Rather death than that.'

' But you don't want to die if you can help it,' said Dorinda sensibly.

' Go to the Forest of Weal,' said Dinah. ' The Falcon knows the way. And as soon as we can — we shall have to do lessons every day, you know — we'll come and meet you near the tree where we hid our clothes. The Falcon knows where that is.'

' Then I shall wait till then,' said the Puma, ' to thank you for your most noble gift to me.'

' Come soon ! ' cried the Falcon, leaping high into the air. ' Follow me, Puma. Come and taste your freedom in the Forest. Good-bye, children ! '

' Till to-morrow,' said the Puma. ' Good-bye till then ! ' And with a bouncing joyful movement, like a kitten at play, she crossed the grass and jumped the hedge and was out of sight.

' Yesterday,' said Dorinda jealously, ' we could jump as well as that.'

' And to-day,' said Dinah, ' we can sit in a comfortable chair, and have our tea, and read a lot of books, and go to sleep in our own beds. Come on, Dorinda. We've got to go and see Mother.'

' Are we going to tell her what happened to us ? '

' No ! ' said Dinah. ' Grown-up people would almost certainly say that it's extremely naughty to turn oneself into a kangaroo, and they might think it wrong of us to let the Puma out of the zoo. So we had better say nothing about it.'

' Then it's going to be extremely awkward,' said Dorinda, ' to explain why we've been away for so long.'

But when they went in they found their mother

standing by the fireplace with a letter in her hand and a worried look on her face, and all she said to them was, ' Children, you're late for your tea again ! Now go and wash your hands and brush your hair, and do try to be quick.'

Chapter Nineteen

'Very well,' said Miss Serendip, 'if you won't tell me, freely and willingly, where you have been, then I certainly shan't try to compel you. All I shall say is this : any children with a proper sense of affection for their teacher, and a natural courtesy, would *not* behave as you are doing. Your mother, as you know, has been very seriously worried by certain news from Bombardy, where your father, it appears, is now in circumstances of considerable danger. I do not propose to add to her worry by asking her to find out where you have been and what you have been doing all this time, because I presume, from your reluctance to speak, that you have been *up to no good*. And your mother, if she discovered that, would be very much distressed. But I am made of sterner stuff! I have known you for two years now, and nothing you can tell me would shock or surprise me. So I shall give you one more chance to behave as children should behave to a teacher who has lavished so much care on them. Dinah, will you tell me where you have been ? '

'Please, Miss Serendip, I'd rather not.'

'Dorinda, have you no manners either ? '

'Yes, Miss Serendip.'

'Then will you tell me ? '

'I promised I wouldn't, Miss Serendip.'

That was more than a week after their return. Every day Miss Serendip had done her best to discover where they had been, but neither Dinah nor Dorinda would offer the smallest explanation, and Miss Serendip, because she could not satisfy her curiosity, was in a very ill humour.

'Very well,' she repeated, 'if you won't, you won't. But I shan't think any the better of you for this wanton, wilful, woeful display of hateful, horrible, heinous manners. And now to our lessons. We had begun, I think, the study of Geography.

'Geography is the science that describes the earth. It is a very useful science. It teaches you that Coal comes from South Wales, Tapioca from Brazil, Tigers from Bengal, Nougat from Montélimar, and Sleepy Sickness from Portuguese Angola. When you are a little older you will also learn Philosophy. Philosophy is more difficult than Geography, because it tries to explain why, and for what purpose, there is coal in South Wales, tapioca in Brazil, tigers in Bengal, nougat in Montélimar, and the tsetse-fly which carries sleepy sickness in Angola. But do not think about such difficult questions in the meantime. For the present we shall occupy ourselves with Geography only, which is a good straightforward subject, and would be quite easy if it were not so big. But it happens to be a very big subject indeed, because the diameter of the Earth, measured round the Equator, is 24,901·8 English miles.

'If we found ourselves upon the Equator in the middle of the South Atlantic — which, however, is unlikely to happen — and from there decided to travel westward, we should come in time to the mouth of the River Amazon, which drains four-fifths of South America, and for that, if for no other reason, must always be esteemed. If, however, we travelled eastward along the Equator, we should arrive on the coast of Africa a few miles south of the River Gabun, which is not really a river but an estuary of the sea, and was discovered by Portuguese navigators near the end of the fifteenth century. I

would not, however, advise you to continue your journey any further in that direction, because it would be highly unpleasant and most unhealthy.

' To find a really healthy climate, I should rather suggest your going to Bournemouth, in the county of Hampshire, which has an area of 1623·5 square miles and several streams where there is very good trout-fishing. It was invaded in A.D. 495 by the West Saxons under Cerdic and Cynric. Cerdic later gave the Isle of Wight to a nephew of his called

Stuf. Little did he think that many years later it would be the scene of Queen Victoria's death. Queen Victoria was born in Kensington Palace, but her parents, the Duke and Duchess of Kent, had previously lived in Franconia, which was not without amenities of its own, and much cheaper to live in than Kensington.

' Franconia was one of the principal duchies of mediaeval Germany. It lay along the valley of the River Main, which is 310 miles long, and winding its way among vine-clad hills, washes the walls of the University city of Würzburg.'

' Are they dirty ? ' asked Dorinda.

' Kindly refrain from interruption,' said Miss Serendip. ' Würzburg is an interesting city where they make bricks and vinegar. The art of making bricks dates from very early times. Many are to be found in the ruins of Babylon, and the Great Wall of China, which is 1500 miles long and from twenty to thirty feet high, is partly constructed of brick. . . .'

Miss Serendip went on and on, talking in this manner about all sorts of things, until it seemed that even the Great Wall of China could be no longer than her idea of a geography lesson. And immediately after lunch, Dinah and Dorinda were horrified to hear her say : ' In the ordinary way you would be receiving instruction this afternoon in Music and Dancing. But your teacher in those subjects, Mr. Casimir Corvo, is unhappily still in prison. We shall therefore take a walk in the Forest of Weal and pursue the study of Botany.'

But no sooner had they entered the Forest than Dinah and Dorinda took to their heels, ran down a ride, dodged behind an oak-tree, scampered along a twisting path where undergrowth concealed them, trotted up a soft and leafy slope under the shadow of enormous smooth-sided beeches, hurried over a low crest where holly grew, and in a little while were far away from Miss Serendip, who, having no wish to study botany all by herself, went home again and wrote long letters to most of her sisters.

'And now,' said Dinah, 'we'll go and look for the Golden Puma and the Silver Falcon.'

They found them beside the old and ruined tree in which they had once hidden their clothes. The Falcon, bolt-upright in his snowy plumage, sat on a dead branch, and the Puma in a pool of sunlight lay stretched on the warm turf.

'Greeting!' cried the Falcon, lifting his small and lovely head. 'Greeting, my noble children!'

But the Puma rose and walked towards them, slowly and not speaking. She stopped before Dinah, looked up at her, and then with a light and easy movement laid her fore-paws on Dinah's shoulders. First on the one side, then on the other, she rubbed her head against Dinah's face, purring like a great cat, and Dinah felt on her cheeks the warm harsh fur, the wiry bristles, and the thin dark lips of the Puma. Dinah kissed her between the eyes and laughed aloud. Then the Puma greeted Dorinda in the same way, and Dorinda kissed her, and she too laughed with sheer delight because she had for a friend so beautiful a being as the Golden Puma.

'Children,' said the Puma, 'let me tell you this. You have done me the greatest service in the world. You have given me freedom, and I am grateful.   You have given me life again.

' All last night I walked in the Forest with the smell of the trees and the rich ground in my nostrils, and the darkness was beautiful, the sky with a few stars looked through the branches, and a little while before morning the late moon came out, a small and yellow moon.   Then a little breeze ran through the Forest and I caught another smell.   I had not known there were deer in the wood till I smelt the draught of their movement.   So I turned and followed up the wind, and in the first dawning found a stag going to drink.   But the wind played me false, he scented me, and ran.   So we had a chase, and I was slow and stiff because I had lain so long in a cage. But presently I felt, like a brook running more strongly after rain, the returning tide of strength in my legs.   Faster I went, fast and easy, till the morning air was whistling past my ears and the forest floor slid below my feet like a torrent racing down a mountain, and the labouring haunches of the stag came nearer.   I drew closer to him then — we were now on green turf, and his hooves were cutting the surface, and flinging crumbs of damp soil in my face — I drew near-level with him, he glanced backward, checked a moment, and in that moment I leapt upon his shoulder.   Down he went with a thud and thump on the grass, and as the sun came up I made my kill.

' For that glorious moment and the headlong chase in the morning, thank you.   For the life you have given me, thank you.   For the freedom of to-day and the liberty of to-morrow, thank you.   I shall never cease to be grateful, and if I can ever serve you, in a little thing or a great thing, then tell me and I shall be with you.'

Both Dinah and Dorinda were somewhat horrified to learn that the Puma, so soon after regaining her freedom, had killed a deer. Deer were pretty creatures, and another reason for not killing them was that all those in the Forest of Weal belonged to Mr. Bevidere FitzGarter. The children began to realise that what they had done was rather serious. It seemed that you could not release a Puma, and set her at liberty in an English county, without some awkward consequences. And the longer she remained at liberty, obeying her instincts and satisfying her hunger, the more and more numerous the awkward consequences would be. Not only were there deer in the Forest, but in the neighbouring fields there were cattle and sheep. Dinah and Dorinda, while listening to the Puma's story, felt more than a little anxious about the future.

But then they remembered — both together, for they often had thoughts in common — that the Puma was their friend, and there was no use having a friend if you were going to complain about everything that he or she did. You had to understand her point of view ; or his. Few things were pleasanter than having a great number of friends, but the only way to keep your friends was to make allowance for them. And the Puma, of course, didn't know that all the deer in the Forest belonged to Mr. Bevidere FitzGarter. And as to her killing one now and then — well, was that any worse than buying a leg of lamb which the butcher had killed ?

All these thoughts passed through the children's

heads, and when the Puma had finished her story they said nothing to show they disapproved, but agreed with her that the hunt must have been delightful. They thanked her for the friendship she offered them, and all promised to be good friends together : the Falcon and the Puma and Dinah and Dorinda.

Then the Falcon said that he had news to tell. He had been to the zoo that morning, and talked with several of the birds and animals there. They were all in a state of great excitement.

Sir Lankester and Mr. Plum, it appeared, had been extremely worried and alarmed when they discovered that not only the Puma but the two young Kangaroos had escaped. There had been far too many strange happenings in the zoo, Sir Lankester had said. And Mr. Plum had declared that never in his life had he known anything like it. Then Sir Lankester, in a very bad temper, had shouted at Mr. Plum : ' I have always done my best to make my animals happy, but if they are not grateful to me, I shall try no longer. Go round the cages, open every door, and those who want to escape may do so. I shall keep none here who does not stay of his own free will.'

' And have they all gone ? ' asked Dinah.

' Very, very few,' said the Falcon. ' Very few indeed. Most of them are indignant against Sir Lankester for trying to turn them out. Bendigo, and Mr. Parker, and Marie Louise are especially angry, and say that nothing will ever make them leave.'

' Poor Bendigo,' said Dinah. ' Dorinda and I

are going to send him *The Times* every day so that he won't have to steal it from Sir Lankester, and on Sundays we're going to take him a cigar. Father left quite a lot behind when he went abroad.'

' And we ought to give Mr. Parker a present of some kind,' said Dorinda. ' What do you think he would like ? '

So they talked about the animals in the zoo, and the Falcon described the nest where he had been hatched on a mountainside all white with snow in Greenland, and how frightened he had been when he made his first flight. But the Puma, who was tired after her night's hunting and lazy after the great breakfast she had eaten, fell asleep in the sun and lay dreaming on the turf. And when it was late in the afternoon, Dinah and Dorinda went home.

Every morning they had their weary lesson from Miss Serendip, but later in the day they often escaped from her and went into the Forest to meet the Falcon and the Puma. There they learnt more than Miss Serendip could teach them. They learnt to see things.

They would play hide-and-seek with the Puma, and at first the Puma could lie within three or four yards of them and not be found. She would choose a place where the leafy ground in the sunlight was nearly the same colour as her coat, and there she would lie without a single movement, so still that she might have been the fallen dead branch of a tree all covered with lichen. Dinah and Dorinda, searching in all directions, might pass within three paces of her, and not see her unless she made a movement to attract their attention. But after a good deal of practice they grew more clever, and the Puma had to hide herself with the greatest care if she wanted to avoid discovery.

Then she taught them, when they were hiding, to lie as still as she did, and choose a place to lie in where the frocks they were wearing would match their background of shady bushes, or rocks and grass, or dead leaves. And often, when they lay like that, the birds of the Forest would come within a few feet of them, or a rabbit would sit down beside them, or a weasel with its little darting eyes would walk by no more than a yard away.

Sometimes they would climb to the topmost branches of a tall tree, and the Falcon would sit beside them and point his head towards little movements in the bushes below that otherwise they would never have noticed. Birds were there, and small animals. There was far more life in the Forest than they had ever guessed, and the Falcon taught them to see it. The Falcon saw everything.

They learnt to know, by the smell of the wind and the look of the sky, whether to-morrow was going to be fine or foul. They learnt to remember the look of a certain tree, as if it were a man or a woman whom they knew, and when they had learnt that, they could go anywhere in the Forest without losing their way. They learnt to be interested in everything they saw or heard, and because of that they even learnt something from Miss Serendip's dreary lessons.

But they learnt neither Music nor Dancing, because Mr. Casimir Corvo, who had taught them both these subjects, was still in prison.

Chapter Twenty

Every day Mr. Justice Rumple used to go to Mid-meddlecum Prison to see the twelve Members of the Jury whom he had committed because they would not agree that Mrs. Taper the draper's wife was Guilty of trying to steal some stockings ; nor would not acknowledge that she was Not Guilty.

Every day the twelve Members of the Jury would assemble in the prison yard. Dr. Fosfar, Mr. and Mrs. Leathercow, Mrs. Fullalove and Mr. Fullalove, Mr. Crumb and Mrs. Crumb, Mrs. Wax, Mrs. Horrabin, Mrs. Steeple, Mr. Casimir Corvo and Mr. Whitloe the drayman — they all gathered in the shady rectangle which was enclosed by the prison buildings, on the outer walls of which grew virginia creeper, and on the inner walls rambler roses. And there Mr. Justice Rumple would march up and down, then halt and stare at them most fiercely, and shout in a threatening voice, ' Well, have you made up your minds yet ? '

' Yes ! ' they would answer, shouting twelve times as loudly as he had.

' But have you all made up your minds *in the same way* ? ' he would bellow.

' No ! ' they would bellow in reply, bellowing twelve times as boisterously as he.

' Then when *are* you going to make up your minds all in the same way ? ' he would demand.

' Never ! ' they would answer.

' Then you'll stay in prison for ever,' he would cry.

' Hurrah ! ' they would reply.

' Because you're a stiff-necked, rascally, rebellious, unruly rout of predestined skilly-swillers,' he would yell.

And then they would all sing, at the top of their voices :

' Rule, Britannia ! Britannia, rule the waves !
BRITONS NEVER, NEVER, NEVER SHALL BE SLAVES ! '

After that Mr. Justice Rumple, looking as red and swollen as a turkey-cock, would march out of the prison yard muttering fearful threats, and the twelve Members of the Jury would make speeches.

All the speeches were always on the same subject, and everybody agreed that every British citizen had the right to hold his own opinion on any matter whatsoever, and talk freely about it, whether it was a good opinion or a bad opinion, a silly opinion or a sensible opinion, an opinion he had formed for himself or an opinion he had picked up in a train. Even Mr. Casimir Corvo, who was really a foreigner, had lived so long in Midmeddlecum that he shared this noble faith and made speeches with the best of them.

Then, after everyone had made a speech, they went to dinner with a good appetite. And because Mrs. Jehu the gaoler's wife was an excellent cook, they always had a very good dinner indeed, beginning with soup and finishing with cheese, but not forgetting roast beef and apple tart in the middle. After that they played darts and dominoes, draughts and chess, or read good books and the newspapers. Then it was time for tea. After tea they talked about a hundred and one different things, and then it was time for supper. And after supper they practised *Rule, Britannia,* and then it was time for bed.

The beds in Midmeddlecum Prison were quite comfortable. Mrs. Jehu the gaoler's wife changed the sheets and pillow-slips every week, and anyone who wanted such a thing could have a hot-water bottle when the weather was cold. Eleven Members of the Jury slept soundly every night, and every morning woke in the glad assurance that they were suffering in a good cause and for a noble principle. The principle, that is, that every British subject can make up his mind in his own way, and no one shall dictate to him.

But Mr. Casimir Corvo slept badly, and when he woke he could hardly refrain from tears at the thought of yet another day in prison. Like the others, he firmly believed that a man has the right to his own opinions, and he had no intention of giving in to Mr. Justice Rumple. But he wanted, above all things, to play the piano and teach people to dance ; and so long as he remained in prison he could do neither, because there was no piano there, and the Members of the Jury preferred making speeches to dancing. So Mr. Corvo was desperately unhappy, and every night he prayed for release.

And that was the state of affairs in Midmeddlecum Prison.

Chapter Twenty-one

One afternoon in the Forest of Weal, Dinah and Dorinda were lying on the grass with the Golden Puma between them, and the Silver Falcon stood on the stump of a dead tree a few feet away. Dinah had asked them how they came to be captured and brought to England, and the Puma answered, 'By the treachery of an Indian.'

'To satisfy the greed of a white man,' said the Falcon.

But afterwards they spoke of happier things, telling tales of life in the hot Brazilian forest, and adventure among the cold white cliffs of Greenland, and then they were all silent while they thought about what they had heard. Then Dinah said, 'Whenever I hear stories about other people doing exciting things, I want to do something exciting myself.'

'It's a long time since we did anything interesting,' said Dorinda with a sigh. 'All we do nowadays is to listen to Miss Serendip, and that gets duller and duller.'

'We have lessons from her all day,' said Dinah, 'except, of course, when we run away.'

'Which you do fairly often,' said the Falcon.

'Who wouldn't?' asked Dorinda.

'We used to have music or dancing twice a week,' said Dinah, 'but Mr. Corvo, who taught us, is still in prison, so now we have neither.'

'Why do you not fetch him out of prison?'

asked the Puma. 'You helped us to escape from the zoo, which was a hard thing to do, and if you think well and use all your wits, I daresay you will find some means by which he may escape from prison.'

'I don't think he would come,' said Dinah. 'You see, there are twelve of them in prison, and all because they won't agree whether Mrs. Taper the draper's wife did or did not try to steal some stockings. If they would agree, they could come out to-morrow.'

'And did the woman try to steal the stockings?' asked the Falcon.

'I'm sure she didn't,' said Dinah.

'I think she did,' said Dorinda.

'You see,' said Dinah, 'we don't really know, but we all have our own opinion, and naturally we don't mean to give it up.'

'I am glad that I am not a human being,' said the Puma. 'It must be very difficult to be happy when your minds are so much at the mercy of ideas.'

'They have no wings to fly,' said the Falcon, 'they have no feathers to keep them warm, no beak to cut their food, and their eyes are very dull. But they have ideas, and ideas make them strong. Human beings took us captive, my friend, and human beings set us free.'

'I do not dislike them, nor underrate them,' said the Puma. 'But sometimes I am sorry for them.'

'Sometimes we are sorry for ourselves,' said Dorinda. 'Especially when it's raining, and we can't run away from Miss Serendip.'

'Go and talk to your music teacher,' said the Puma, ' and try to persuade him to change his mind. Tell him you are unhappy because of his imprisonment. Put into his head the idea that his duty is to escape, and perhaps that new idea will drive out the old one that keeps him in gaol.'

' It sounds rather complicated,' said Dinah, ' but I suppose we had better try.'

' It will be something to do,' said Dorinda.

Then for an hour or so they played Touch under rules of their own making, by which the Puma had to walk on her hind legs, Dinah and Dorinda go on all-fours, while the Falcon flapped about using only one wing. After that Dinah and Dorinda, with their frocks torn by brambles and stained by grass, with mud on their elbows and their knees, went home to tea and were soundly scolded by Miss Serendip.

The following day was Thursday, and Tuesdays and Thursdays were Visiting Days at the prison. So in the afternoon they went to see Mr. Casimir Corvo.

About forty people from Midmeddlecum had also gone to visit their friends, taking with them baskets well packed with buns and ham sandwiches and lemon tarts and thermos flasks of tea and bottles of ginger-beer, and they were all sitting on the grass of the prison yard, having a picnic with the Members of the Jury. Mr. Horrabin the ironmonger had brought a gramophone, which was playing *Land of Hope and Glory*, and though they were all enjoying themselves thoroughly, the Members of the Jury managed to look noble and virtuous as well.

Mr. Casimir Corvo, however, was not in the
happy group of picnickers. Dinah and Dorinda
had to search the whole prison before they found
him, at last, on the top floor in a little room that
was used for drying clothes. He was sitting on a
wooden stool under a clothes-line from which hung
a pair of flannel trousers belonging to Mr. Jehu the
gaoler, an apron of Mrs. Jehu's, Dr. Fosfar's best
shirt, three pocket-handkerchiefs, a bath-towel,
and a damp pillow-slip. He rose when Dinah and
Dorinda came in, and greeted them with a mournful
smile.

'My dear friends,' he said. 'My favourite
pupils! You have come to visit your old master?
That is so kind of you.'

He was a small man with a handsome clean-
shaven face as white as a chicken bone. He had
large dark eyes under thick dark eyebrows that
moved up and down whenever he became excited.
Sometimes the left one appeared to rise half-way up
his forehead, and sometimes the right one descended
in a fearful one-sided frown. His hair was thick
and rather curly, and grew to a point in the middle
of his pale brow. He made frequent gestures with
his hands, which were long and delicate, and he
walked with a light and graceful step. People in
Midmeddlecum thought he wore strange clothes,
but in Dinah's opinion his dark-green velvet jacket
and yellow corduroy trousers suited him very well,
and Dinah greatly admired his red waistcoat with
brass buttons and his white silk shirt. He spoke
perfect English, but he filled it with unusual sounds,
with trilling *r*'s, and *t*'s that made you think some-

one had struck a tuning-fork on the table, and long vowels with a song in them.

' You will suppose,' he said, ' that this is a strange place in which to find me, this room in which people hang their clothes to dry. But I had to bring my pillow-slip here, because this morning, when I woke up, I was filled with sadness to think that I must stay in prison. So I began to cry, and it became quite wet. You, because you are English, will think it silly for a grown-up man to cry. But in my country, when people are sad, they all cry, whether they are big or little. And when they are happy, they laugh. The biggest and the littlest together, they all laugh.'

' It was very sensible of you to hang up your pillow-slip before going to bed again,' said Dinah.

' If you had gone to sleep on it while it was wet,' said Dorinda, ' you would have caught a cold, and that would have made you sadder than ever.'

' So I thought,' said Mr. Corvo, ' because I am not altogether silly. Indeed, when I consider many other people whom I know, I often think that I am a very sensible kind of person.'

' Would you like to escape from prison ? ' asked Dinah.

' Alas ! ' said Mr. Corvo, ' I cannot. I must remain here with all the other Members of the Jury. It is my duty. But tell me this : have you forgotten all the music I taught you, and all the dances ? Or are you remembering them, and practising every day ? '

' It's very difficult to remember much without you to help us,' said Dorinda. ' We used to enjoy our music and dancing more than anything else, and we shall continue to be thoroughly unhappy until we resume our lessons with you.'

She spoke very clearly and carefully, as though she were repeating a poem that she had learnt by heart. She and Dinah, indeed, had earnestly considered what they should say to Mr. Corvo, and on the way to the prison had rehearsed their speeches over and over again. Now it was Dinah's turn.

' You have a duty to us, your pupils,' she said, ' as well as to your fellow-prisoners. Perhaps it is your duty to think of that duty first and the other duty second, like remembering to brush your teeth before going to bed, and if so you ought to make up your mind to escape, and we shall do our utmost to help you.'

' We are very good at helping people to escape,' said Dorinda, ' and all the benefit of our long experience is at your service.'

' You can rely on us,' said Dinah.

They stood there, between the clothes-lines, with trousers and towels in front of them, and tea-cloths and pyjamas behind them, and stared at Mr. Corvo with earnest, anxious eyes. Mr. Corvo stared at them. His eyebrows began to move up and down, first one and then the other, and before he spoke he made several beautiful gestures with his long white hands. Then he said ' No ! ' and sat down again.

Dinah whispered, ' It's your turn, Dorinda.'

' I've forgotten what comes next,' murmured Dorinda.

' *In addressing. . .*'

' In addressing a final appeal to you,' said Dorinda firmly, ' we rely on the affection that you have so often shown us . . .'

' No, no ! ' cried Mr. Corvo, jumping from his stool and waving his hands as though he were conducting an orchestra. ' You must not appeal to my affection. That is not fair ! I want so much to escape, more than anything in the world I want to come out of prison and teach you again to dance and play the piano, but it is my duty, my horrible but so necessary duty, to remain here. I have sworn that I shall never give in to Mr. Justice Rumple, and if I were to escape it would be like running away from him. It would be running away from my duty, which is to resist him and resist all tyranny wherever it appears.'

' Then you may have to stay in prison all your life,' said Dinah.

Mr. Corvo struck an attitude. He stood very straight and still, with his head proud and high. He laid the long fingers of his left hand on his heart, and raising the other hand towards a corner of the ceiling he declared, ' If it has to be so, it will be so. I shall never give in ! '

But a moment later he turned and covered his face with the drying bath-towel, wiped away a double stream of tears, and cried, ' But I hope it will not be so ! I want to come out of prison very soon. I shall do my duty, but oh, I do not want my duty to be more difficult than I can bear ! '

' Well,' said Dinah, ' we really did come here to help you, and if there is anything you can suggest . . .'

' You must not ask me to escape.'

' Then what else can we do ? ' asked Dorinda.

'There is only one way out of the difficulty,' said Mr. Corvo. 'Neither I nor any other Member of the Jury will ever give in, and therefore Mr. Justice Rumple must give in. Make him change his mind, persuade him that he is in the wrong, and then we can all go free. That is the only way.'

'Oh dear,' said Dinah, 'that isn't going to be easy.'

'It would be far, far easier to plan your escape,' said Dorinda.

'You do realise, don't you,' said Dinah, 'that what you have asked us to do is very, very difficult indeed ?'

'It is so difficult,' said Mr. Corvo in a melancholy voice, 'that I fully expect you to say it is impossible.'

'No, I wouldn't say that,' said Dinah thoughtfully.

'We have done several things,' said Dorinda, 'that a lot of people would have considered *quite* impossible.'

'It's really surprising,' said Dinah, 'how much you can do if you make up your mind to do it.'

'Sometimes it is *very* surprising,' said Dorinda.

Mr. Corvo shook his head in a mournful fashion, and took his pillow-slip off the line. 'It is dry now,' he said. 'But by to-morrow morning, I daresay, it will again be full of tears. Good-bye, my dear friends, my favourite pupils. Come again to see me.'

'The next time we see you,' said Dinah firmly, 'you will be in your own house in Holly Street.'

Chapter Twenty-Two

On Saturday morning they walked with Miss Serendip into Midmeddlecum to do some shopping, and on the way Dorinda said to Dinah, ' Have you thought of anything yet ? '

' Not yet,' said Dinah.

' It was very nearly a promise that we made him,' said Dorinda. ' I mean, when you said that the next time we saw him he would be in his own house in Holly Street. That was practically a promise.'

' It was a promise,' said Dinah, ' and we shall have to keep it. But I don't know how.'

' Shall we have to keep our promises even when we are grown-up ? ' asked Dorinda.

' Yes, I think so,' said Dinah. ' You just can't get out of them.'

' I thought life would be a lot easier when we grew up,' said Dorinda with a sigh.

' When we are very old and cautious,' said Dinah, ' I daresay we shan't make any promises. And that will save trouble.'

' Look ! ' exclaimed Dorinda. ' Those two men in bowler hats — oh, I've forgotten their names ! '

' Mr. Hobson and Mr. Jobson,' said Dinah.

' They're lawyers, aren't they ? '

' I think they're called barristers.'

' Well, it's the same sort of thing. It was they who had to argue with the Judge and the Jury when Mrs. Taper was tried.'

Mr. Hobson and Mr. Jobson

' They have to be paid, of course,' said Dinah thoughtfully. ' How much money have you got ? '

' Seven shillings in my money-box, and eightpence in my pocket.'

' And I've got nine and threepence altogether. That makes sixteen and elevenpence between us.'

' It's a lot of money,' said Dorinda.

' Do you think we should ask them to help us ? '

' They know how to argue with people,' said Dorinda. ' Especially with Judges.'

' It's a good idea,' said Dorinda. ' But we shall have to lose Miss Serendip first.'

They were walking along Ash Street towards the Square, and Mr. Hobson and Mr. Jobson were a little way ahead of them. The two barristers were knocking at every door in the street, Mr. Hobson on the left of the road, Mr. Jobson on the right, and whenever a door was opened, Mr. Hobson — or Mr. Jobson, as the case might be — would immediately begin to talk, in a very earnest way, to the person who had opened it. But what they were talking about neither Dinah nor Dorinda could guess.

They and Miss Serendip continued to walk along Ash Street, turned the corner into Wallflower Street, and came into the Square.

Then Miss Serendip stopped and said to them in a brisk and businesslike way, ' Now, girls, I have quite a lot of shopping to do, and as you would only hinder me, you had better go and talk to those children beside the statue. But remember this : I don't want you to leave the Square ! '

' No, of course not, Miss Serendip,' said Dinah and Dorinda in their politest voices. But no sooner had she gone into the nearest shop than Dinah exclaimed, in a very scornful way, ' As if we would go and talk to Catherine Crumb ! '

' Or to Robin and Robina Wax ! ' said Dorinda with equal scorn.

' Come and look for Mr. Hobson and Mr. Jobson,' said Dinah, and hurrying down Wallflower Street they turned into Ash Street, and found Mr. Hobson ringing the bell of the corner house.

' Good-morning,' he said to the lady who came to the door. ' Good-morning, Mrs. Wellaby. Have you committed any crime to-day ? Petty Larceny or Grand Larceny, Fraud or Sacrilege or Sorcery, Blackmail or Theft by Forcible Entry, Assault or Battery, or Assault *and* Battery ? '

' No, nothing to-day,' said Mrs. Wellaby.

' Are you sure ? ' asked Mr. Hobson in a very anxious tone of voice. ' *Quite* sure, Mrs. Wellaby ? Remember that the germ of crime is universally present in mankind, ever ready to show itself under conditions favourable to its growth. Are you quite, quite sure, Mrs. Wellaby, that you haven't committed even the least little tiny tort in the last few days ? Because I am ready, now as ever, to defend you against any accusation whatsoever, no matter whether it be barratry or illicit diamond-buying, forgery or coining, breach of promise to marry, or armed resistance to capture. Are you quite sure, Mrs. Wellaby ? What about perjury or fire-raising ? Surely you've done something wrong ? '

Mrs. Wellaby was fifty-two, she had grey hair, a kind round face, and steel-rimmed spectacles. She thought for a few moments, and then said regretfully, 'No, Mr. Hobson, I'm sorry, but there's nothing at all to-day. Nothing at all.'

'Well, well,' said Mr. Hobson cheerfully, 'if that is so, it can't be helped. Better luck next time, Mrs. Wellaby. I'll just leave this small handbill, and you'll remember that any time when you want my assistance, I shall be entirely at your service. Here is the handbill, and now good-morning, Mrs. Wellaby. Good-morning!'

The handbill which Mr. Hobson presented was inscribed in this way:

Does Prison Stare You in the Face?
Don't be Downhearted!

MR. HOBSON, K.C.

Is

At Your Service!
He will blow your crimes away!
No Matter What *Offence* You
Have Committed—
Entrust Your *Defence* To Him!

MR. HOBSON, K.C.

The Best Lawyer In England ! ! !

———

OUR CLIENTS ARE ALWAYS RIGHT

———

P.S. Simply to show Good Faith, and to make his name more widely known, MR. HOBSON, K.C., is prepared to defend any New Customer and First Offender against a Charge of Assault, Theft, or Cruelty to Children, for the Nominal Fee of
Five Shillings Only!
(Win, Lose, or Draw)

N.B. This remarkable offer may never be repeated.
Take advantage of it
NOW

Meanwhile, on the other side of the street, Mr. Jobson was ringing the bell of Mr. Bostockle's house, and when Mr. Bostockle came to the door, Mr. Jobson, having wished him good-morning, immediately enquired, 'Now what about some

quiet, pleasant, profitable litigation to-day, Mr. Bostockle? Has anybody been blackmailing you lately? Has anyone stolen flowers or vegetable marrows out of your garden? Have you been knocked over by a cyclist, run down by a motor-car, injured in train, tram, aeroplane, bus, or other public conveyance ? If so, Mr. Bostockle, don't let the grass grow under your feet, but take the case to court *now* ! '

Mr. Bostockle was an old man with a long white beard who walked with great difficulty and the aid of two sticks. He thought for some time, and then said slowly, ' No, Mr. Jobson, nothing of that sort has happened to me for a long while now.'

' Now don't be in a hurry,' said Mr. Jobson. ' Take time, think carefully, jog your memory. Are you quite sure that you haven't been bitten by a dog, gored by a mad bull, swindled out of your inheritance, trapped in an elevator, or had your pocket picked ? '

' No,' said Mr. Bostockle, ' there's been nothing like that at all. I think maybe I'm getting too old for things to happen to me nowadays.'

' What about your neighbours ? ' asked Mr. Jobson. ' Haven't any of them been slandering you ? '

' Not that I've heard of,' said Mr. Bostockle. ' But I've scarcely been out of the house for the last ten days.'

' Well, if you do hear of anything, you'll let me know, won't you ? ' said Mr. Jobson. ' I shall always be delighted to represent you, Mr. Bostockle, in any court in England, civil or criminal, before a Bench of Local Magistrates or the Judicial Committee of the House of Lords. And remember this, Mr. Bostockle : litigation is not only pleasant, it can be profitable ! Permit me to leave with you this useful handbill. Don't lose it, and don't forget that I am always at your service. Good-morning, Mr.

Bostockle, good-morning ! '

This was the handbill that Mr. Jobson gave to Mr. Bostockle :

The Latin Word for a Lawsuit was
LIS
The Latin Word meaning ' To bring a lawsuit ' was
LITIGARE
Hence That Most Beautiful of All English Words—
LITIGATION !
Do You Do Enough Of It ?
If Not

MR. JOBSON, K.C.
Is Here To Help You.
. . . .
JOBSON IS THE MAN TO GET DAMAGES!
. . . .

Litigate with Jobson, and Earn while you Learn !

If you live in a Bad Locality where your neighbours
are constantly maiming your cattle, setting
fire to your house, kidnapping your
children, blackmailing your
mother, stealing your furniture,
throwing stones at your green-
house, borrowing your lawn-
mower, and maligning
your character
REJOICE
AND SEND FOR JOBSON ! ! !
He Will Make Them Pay.

If you litigate often and take my advice
You will all become healthy, and wealthy, and wice.*

* I mean *Wise*, of course, but that wouldn't rhyme
so well.

Mr. Hobson and Mr. Jobson then met in the middle of the street, and each of them pushed his bowler hat to the back of his head and said, ' Well, that's that ! '

' Done well ? ' asked Mr. Hobson.

' Not bad,' said Mr. Jobson. ' And you ? '

' Fair to middling,' said Mr. Hobson. 'Shall we go and do Oak Street now, or shall we have lunch first?'

' Lunch first,' said Mr. Jobson.

' Could you spare a few minutes, please, to talk to us ? ' asked Dinah.

She and Dorinda had waited patiently until Mr. Hobson and Mr. Jobson completed their business with Mrs. Wellaby and Mr. Bostockle, and now, still in the middle of the street, they confronted the lawyers with such an air of grave importance that Mr. Hobson and Mr. Jobson immediately straightened their bowler hats and assumed an expression as serious as the children's.

' You have committed a crime ? ' demanded Mr. Hobson. ' Tell me all about it.'

' We have committed several, I think,' said Dinah, ' but we're not worrying about them.'

' Not a bit,' said Dorinda.

' Then somebody has injured you, threatened you, maltreated or maligned you ? ' asked Mr. Jobson. ' Confide in me, and all will be well.'

' Thank you very much,' said Dinah, ' but we wouldn't take up your valuable time about anything like that. We want your advice on something really important.'

' Then don't waste another minute,' said Mr. Hobson. ' Open your mouth wide, talk clearly, and tell us the whole story.'

' Have no doubt, have no hesitation,' said Mr.

Jobson. 'Speak fully, and yet be brief. Be natural, but articulate with care. You may rely upon us.'

'We want to know,' said Dinah, 'how to make Mr. Justice Rumple change his mind.'

'Good heavens!' said Mr. Hobson.

'Bless my soul!' said Mr. Jobson.

'A Judge,' said Mr. Hobson, '*never* changes his mind.'

'Never,' said Mr. Jobson. 'It would be unnatural.'

'But Mr. Justice Rumple has *got* to change his,' said Dorinda, 'because we promised he would. Or, at any rate, we promised to do something which we can't do until he has. So you see how important it is that he should.'

'You are setting us an almost impossible task,' said Mr. Hobson.

'And yet,' said Mr. Jobson, 'it would not be like us to shrink from difficulty.'

'No true lawyer,' said Mr. Hobson, 'is ever dismayed by difficulty.'

'Nor even deterred by impossibility,' said Mr. Jobson.

'And yet,' said Mr. Hobson, 'it is not often that a lawyer is asked to undertake such a case as this.'

'But if we succeed,' said Mr. Jobson, 'we shall acquire immortal fame.'

'How right you are!' said Mr. Hobson. 'To make a Judge change his mind would be a truly historic feat.'

'So let us go into the Square,' said Mr. Jobson, 'and sit down comfortably on the bench beside the statue of Queen Victoria, and there we shall discuss the whole matter fully and minutely.'

Chapter Twenty-Three

As a result of the conversation they had, Mr. Hobson and Mr. Jobson might have been seen, about three o'clock that afternoon, walking with firm and decided steps up the drive that led to Mr.

Justice Rumple's house on the north side of the River Brill. The Judge, as it happened, was playing clock-golf with his Cook, and his two maids were watching, so there was some delay before the visitors were admitted. They had, indeed, to wait for about twenty minutes, until the game was finished. But then they were shown into the library.

Mr. Justice Rumple had won his game of clock-golf, and in consequence of that was in a very good temper. He was wearing white flannels, a red belt, and his wig. He gave Mr. Hobson a cigar, and Mr. Jobson — who did not smoke — a piece of nut toffee, and asked what he could do to help them.

' We should like you to answer some questions,' said Mr. Hobson.

' Certainly,' said the Judge. ' What sort of questions are you going to ask me ? '

' Well, to begin with,' said Mr. Jobson, ' how often do you change your shirt ? '

' Every day,' said the Judge. This was not quite true, but the Judge thought it would set other people a good example in cleanliness if they were told that he had such splendid regular habits.

' And your socks ? ' asked Mr. Hobson.

' Every day,' said the Judge, who was still in a happy temper.

' And your vest ? ' asked Mr. Jobson.

' And your pocket-handkerchief? '

' Every day,' answered the Judge, because he felt that now he was creating a great impression. ' Every day, and sometimes *twice* a day.'

' Well, well ! ' said Mr. Hobson, as though he were lost in admiration.

' And your sheets and your pillow-slips ? ' asked Mr. Jobson. ' How often are they changed ? '

' You would have to ask one of the maids about that,' said the Judge a trifle haughtily. ' But you can take it from me that they are changed regularly and often.'

'That's fine,' said Mr. Hobson. 'Isn't that fine, Jobson?'

'It's magnificent,' said Mr. Jobson. 'Now tell us, Judge, did you have a good lunch to-day?'

'Why, of course I had,' said Mr. Justice Rumple. 'I always have a good lunch. To-day I had cream of asparagus soup, two lamb chops with peas and new potatoes, a cherry tart, and a piece of Wensleydale cheese. There's nothing wrong with that, is there?'

'Indeed there isn't,' said Mr. Hobson, 'but did you eat it all off one plate?'

'Of course not!' said the Judge indignantly. 'I had four plates at the very least!'

'So you change your plates even oftener than you change your socks?' asked Mr. Jobson.

'I do indeed,' said the Judge.

'Very interesting,' said Mr. Hobson. 'I find that extremely interesting, don't you, Jobson?'

'Absolutely enthralling,' said Mr. Jobson.

Then Mr. Hobson pointed to a book that lay on a small table by the Judge's chair, and said, still in a tone of fervent admiration, 'I suppose you are a great reader, sir?'

'That is a book,' said the Judge, 'which I have lately been reading with close attention. It is about Ancient Egypt. Or else it is about Ancient Greece, or Ancient Mesopotamia. I haven't got very far in it yet.'

'And do you always read the same book?' asked Mr. Jobson.

'Good gracious, no!' said the Judge. 'As soon as I have finished one, I start another.'

'So you change your books?' said Mr. Hobson. 'You change them quite often, in fact?'

'Naturally,' said the Judge. 'Who doesn't?'

There was a little pause after that, and the Judge was beginning to wonder why Mr. Hobson and Mr. Jobson wanted to know so much about his personal habits, when Mr. Jobson suddenly asked him another question. At this point both Mr. Hobson and Mr. Jobson leant far back in their chairs and gazed upward at the ceiling as though they were profoundly meditating.

'You remember the case of Mrs. Taper?' asked Mr. Jobson.

'I do,' said the Judge, rather stiffly.

'The Jury,' said Mr. Hobson, 'are still in prison.'

'And there they will stay,' said the Judge in a loud fierce voice. 'There they will stay, as I solemnly warned them many weeks ago, until they come to a unanimous decision whether she is Guilty or Not Guilty.'

'You have made up your mind about that?' asked Mr. Jobson.

'I have,' said the Judge.

'Why don't you change your mind?' demanded Mr. Hobson.

'I *never* change my mind!' shouted the Judge.

'What, never?' asked Mr. Jobson.

'Not even once a month?' said Mr. Hobson.

'I said NEVER!' roared the Judge.

'How disgusting!' said Mr. Jobson.

'How insanitary!' said Mr. Hobson.

'You change your shirts and your socks,' said Mr. Jobson.

'Your pillow-slips and your sheets,' said Mr. Hobson.

'Your dinner-plates and your pocket-handkerchiefs.'

'Your books and your vests.'

'And yet you never change your mind!' said Mr. Jobson. 'It's almost unbelievable, isn't it, Hobson?'

'It is undeniably dirty,' said Mr. Hobson.

'Do you notice a curious smell in the room?' asked Mr. Jobson.

'There *isn't* a smell in the room,' bellowed the Judge.

'Oh yes, there is, and a very nasty smell too,' said Mr. Hobson, holding his nose.

'You really ought to change your mind,' said Mr. Jobson, also holding his nose.

'Get out of my house!' shouted the Judge.

'With pleasure,' said Mr. Hobson.

'We shall feel all the better for some fresh air,' said Mr. Jobson.

Then they both stood up, and putting on their bowler hats — which, when they came in, they had laid on the floor beside them — walked out of the library in a dignified manner, and closed the door carefully behind them. The Judge was in such a furious temper that he took off his wig, threw it on the floor, and began to jump on it.

He had jumped on it three times when the door opened a little way and Mr. Jobson again appeared in the narrow entrance. He was still holding his nose.

'By odly reasod for returdig,' he said, 'is to rebide you that cleadlidess is dext to godlidess.'

Chapter Twenty-Four

At about nine o'clock that night Dinah and Dorinda
heard someone whistling in the garden. They had
gone to bed but they were still wide awake, and as
soon as they heard the whistle repeated they got
up, put on slippers and dressing-gowns, and going
quietly downstairs, went into the garden through the
french window in the dining-room. In a corner of

the rhododendron shrubbery they found Mr. Hobson and Mr. Jobson.

They listened with great interest while the two
lawyers described their interview with the Judge,
and were filled with admiration of their cleverness.

' Now we have done all we can,' said Mr. Hobson, ' but whether we shall be successful or not
depends on what you can do.'

' We have cut the bread, but you must toast it,'
said Mr. Jobson.

' I don't quite see what you mean,' said Dinah.

'We have put a certain idea into the Judge's head,' said Mr. Hobson. 'Namely, that a person who doesn't change his mind is no better than a person who doesn't change his shirt or his socks.'

'And you,' said Mr. Jobson, 'must show him the dreadful consequence of *not* changing his mind.'

'Of course !' said Dinah. 'Now I understand.'

'So do I,' said Dorinda, 'and I've thought of something already. Something we can do, I mean.'

'In that case,' said Mr. Hobson, 'Mr. Jobson and I will go home and start work on our next case. We are busy men, we lawyers.'

'We're very, very grateful to you indeed,' said Dinah, 'and now will you please tell us how much we owe you ? '

'How much have you got ? ' asked Mr. Jobson.

'Sixteen and elevenpence,' said Dinah. 'Did you remember to bring it with you, Dorinda ? '

'Here it is,' said Dorinda, taking a knotted handkerchief from the pocket of her dressing-gown.

'Sixteen and elevenpence is what we always charge for a case of this kind,' said Mr. Hobson politely.

Dinah untied the knots and spread the handkerchief out on the grass. 'I'm afraid you'll find it rather difficult to divide it evenly between you,' she said.

Mr. Hobson and Mr. Jobson knelt down, and with their forefingers stirred the coins on the handkerchief.

'Not at all,' said Mr. Jobson. 'I see there are twice as many half-crowns as shillings, and the number of ha'pennies is the same as the number of shillings and half-crowns added together, including that very shiny bob with the head of Queen Victoria on it. Then, if you add to that the number of two-shilling pieces, the total is one and a half times the number of pennies. Now let me see . . .'

' There are two single shillings,' said Mr. Hobson, ' and if you multiply the number of half-crowns by that you will get the exact number of pennies. It's perfectly easy, Jobson. We divide the sixteen shillings and elevenpence into two exactly equal halves by taking eleven coins each. There are no complaints and nothing left over. — Good heavens, what's that ? '

It was growing dark by now in the shadow of the bushes, and from the depths of the shrubbery, facing Mr. Hobson as he knelt on the grass, there had suddenly appeared two small and golden lights, as though a pair of tiny lamps were shining there.

' Don't be alarmed,' said Dorinda kindly. ' It's just a friend of ours.' And softly she called, ' Good-evening, Puma.'

She was answered by a curious sound that was half a cough and half a growl, and at the same moment there was a rushing noise in the twilit air, and something with great wings came swooping down, and abruptly soared again.

' And *that* ? ' asked Mr. Hobson in a trembling voice. ' What was that ? '

' Another of our friends,' said Dinah, and putting her hands to her mouth she cried upwards to the sky : ' Hullo, Falcon ! '

Mr. Hobson and Mr. Jobson rose to their feet.

'I think,' said Mr. Jobson, 'that it's time we were going.'

'It's getting late,' said Mr. Hobson, and looked nervously at the little golden lamps in the shrubbery.

'So good-night,' said Mr. Jobson, 'and good luck.'

'We're terribly grateful,' said Dinah and Dorinda. 'Terribly grateful!' they cried more loudly, for by now the two lawyers were hurrying away as fast as they could.

Then the Falcon, stooping out of the darkening sky, dropped swiftly down and landed, light as a feather, on Dinah's shoulder, while the Puma came noiselessly out of the shrubbery and put her head between Dorinda's hands. They all made themselves comfortable on the grass, and had a long talk.

It was Dinah and Dorinda who talked most, for they were eager to tell of the progress they had made towards getting Mr. Corvo out of prison, and to describe what they meant to do next. They had made all their plans by now, and they wanted the Falcon to help by bringing them half a dozen mice.

'Alive or dead?' asked the Falcon politely.

'Oh, dead!' said Dinah hurriedly. 'Quite dead, please.'

'You are busy creatures, you human beings,' said the Puma with a yawn. 'You are always planning something, making something, or talking about something. It must be very tiring.'

'What have you been doing to-day?' asked Dorinda.

'Nothing,' said the Puma. 'Nothing at all, except living.'

' It was so fine a day,' said the Falcon. ' One of the loveliest days I have ever seen.'

' Was it?' asked Dinah. 'We have had so much to think about that we hardly noticed what it was like.'

' That was foolish,' said the Puma.

' I think it was wicked,' said the Falcon. ' You wouldn't waste food or drink, would you? Then why do you waste fine weather? '

' But we had things to *do*,' said Dinah.

' That's the worst of being human,' said the Puma.

' You know the north end of the Forest? 'asked the Falcon. ' The ground climbs to a hill, and then falls steeply away. Near the highest part of the hill there was a landslide, many hundreds of years ago, and the rock is still naked there, a cliff rises out of the sloping wood. That is where we spent the day. I sat on a ledge of the rock, with fifty miles of landscape below me, and the Puma lay upon the branch of a great tree, with the sun sifting through the leaves upon her.'

' Some time,' said the Puma, ' when you are tired of doing things, you must come and spend a whole day with us. Not doing anything, but simply being. You will feel all the better for it.'

' But didn't you get hungry? ' asked Dorinda.

' I had a good supper last night,' said the Puma. ' I killed a fat lamb.'

' Whose was it? ' asked Dinah.

' How should I know? It was mine when I had killed it.'

They talked for a little while longer, and then the Puma and the Falcon went back to the Forest, Dinah and Dorinda to bed.

But they didn't go to sleep very quickly, because they were rather worried to hear that the Puma had begun to kill sheep.

'And it's no use telling her that it's wrong to kill them because they belong to someone,' said Dinah unhappily. 'She simply wouldn't understand.'

'But you're not sorry that we let her out of the zoo?'

'No, of course not, we couldn't do anything else after we'd made friends with her. But whenever you do anything, something always seems to happen because of it. That's what makes life difficult.'

'Well, she'll be very hard to catch,' said Dorinda comfortingly. 'I shouldn't think a farmer could ever catch her.'

They talked for a little longer, then grew drowsy without noticing it, and when they woke in the morning they found that the Falcon had already been to visit them, and had left six dead field-mice on their window-sill.

'Go and get one of Father's big handkerchiefs, and we'll make a little bag to carry them,' said Dinah.

Dorinda went along the passage to her father's deserted dressing-room, and found a handkerchief. She stood thinking for a moment, and then, with a sudden idea that delighted her, ran back to their own room, and exclaimed as she threw open the door, 'Dinah! I know exactly where we ought to put them.'

'Where?'

'Wait till we get there,' said Dorinda, 'and I'll show you.'

Chapter Twenty-Five

' Do you remember,' said Dorinda after breakfast, ' that quite a long time ago, before Father had gone abroad, we went down to the river, and I happened to have a fork, and we caught two eels ? '

' And put them in a bottle that we found,' said Dinah.

' And then put a cork in the bottle, to prevent them from getting out.'

' And took the bottle home, and left it behind the tool-shed, and then we forgot all about it.'

' The eels must be dead by now,' said Dorinda.

' Horribly dead,' said Dinah thoughtfully. ' It was very naughty of us, but all the same they may be useful.'

' That's just what I was thinking.'

' And the three kippers that we bought yesterday are beginning to smell already.'

' We've got all we need now except the post-cards,' said Dorinda, ' and we can write them while we're doing our lessons.'

In the afternoon they walked over the fields to Mr. Justice Rumple's house on the other side of the river. They avoided Midmeddlecum, because they were carrying several parcels which they did not wish to be seen. They had chosen the proper time to arrive — the time when the Judge, with his Cook and his Tablemaid and his Housemaid, usually went out to have a game of clock-golf — and because the dining-room window was wide open, and the sill no more than two feet from the ground, they got in quite easily, without anyone seeing them, and without having to ring the bell or knock at the door.

Then, quietly and quickly, they went upstairs and found the Judge's bedroom. They knew it was his, because on a table in a corner there were three busts, of Caesar and Shakespeare and the Duke of Wellington, and each of them was wearing one of the Judge's spare wigs.

' And now,' said Dinah, ' what do you want to do with the mice ? '

' Come here,' said Dorinda, who had crawled under the bed, and when Dinah followed her, she pointed to the spiral springs on which the mattress rested.

' They look rather like little cages, don't they ? ' she asked. ' It would be a very appropriate place to put mice, and nobody will ever think of looking for them there.'

Dinah agreed, so they pushed the six dead field-mice into six of the spiral springs that supported the Judge's bed, and crawling from under it, looked through the window at the lawn where the Judge was playing clock-golf with his Cook, his Tablemaid, and his Housemaid. Then they set to work again.

' This must be his dressing-room,' said Dinah, opening another door.

' What a lot of clothes he has ! ' said Dorinda, looking into a wardrobe.

' And dozens and dozens of shirts,' said Dinah, examining a chest of drawers.

Some of the postcards which they had written

were concealed in the neat array of shirts, and others thrust into the pockets of his various suits, and when that was done Dinah said they must look for the library.

That was on the ground floor, and as soon as they went in they saw, on a very ornamental marble

mantelpiece, two tall Greek vases of the sort which Miss Serendip had taught them to call an amphora.

' The very thing ! ' said Dinah, and drawing a chair to the mantelpiece she climbed up, and having pulled the cork from the bottle containing the dead eels, she hid it in the nearer vase.

' Isn't it horrible ! ' cried Dorinda, as she sniffed the dreadful smell that came from the uncorked bottle.

' It's worse than horrible,' said Dinah. ' If that doesn't make him change his mind, nothing will.'

' And we still have the kippers,' said Dorinda.

' I think the dining-room is the proper place for them. You remember those enormous oil-paintings which are probably his father and his mother? And another, of sheep walking over a mountain? We could pin the kippers to the wall behind them with these drawing-pins that I brought.'

Dorinda had no better suggestion to make, so that was quickly done, and they left the house through the open dining-room window, and walked into Midmeddlecum. They wanted to see Catherine Crumb, the baker's daughter.

They both heartily disliked Catherine, with her wicked face and her long thin legs, and they had by no means forgiven her for what she had once done to them when, after eating too much, they had swollen into something very like balloons. But they knew that Catherine was the most useful person in the village for their present purpose, because she had a natural gift for mischief and loved nothing better.

She was very much surprised, and rather frightened, when they arrived at her house and told her they had something very secret to talk about. But no sooner had they explained their plan to her, and described what they had done already, and made clear what they wanted her to do, than her wicked face grew pale with excitement, her dark eyes gleamed with pleasure, and she pulled the joints of her fingers so that each of them made a noise like a stick breaking.

' You can depend on me,' she promised. ' All the children here will do what I tell them, and if the Judge doesn't change his mind within a week, you can stick more pins in me than I ever stuck into you.'

' Thank you,' said Dinah, a trifle haughtily, ' but we never stick pins in people.'

' Don't if you don't want to,' said Catherine. ' It won't make any difference to what I've promised.'

Then for a day or two Dinah and Dorinda waited impatiently to see how their plan was going to work, and before long they had very good news of it. The Judge was beginning to look thoroughly unhappy, and his Cook reported that he had entirely lost his appetite.

After finishing his game of clock-golf, on the afternoon when Dinah and Dorinda left the mice and the eels and the kippers in his house, the Judge had gone into the library to read, and was immediately aware of a strange smell in the room. So he rang the bell and the Tablemaid came in, and when he told her to sniff she sniffed, and looked rather surprised, but answered, ' I smell nothing but your cigar.'

Then he rang for the Housemaid and made her sniff. ' I smell nothing but the nice leather smell of your armchair,' she said.

Then the Judge, growing angry, sent for the Cook, and made her sniff all round the room like a bloodhound. But the Cook, in a very determined voice, said, ' I smell nothing but that bowl of lovely roses, which I cut for you myself, and which I myself put on your desk.'

The truth was that all of them could smell the strange odour in the room, but none would admit it, because they worked very hard to keep the house tidy and clean, and they refused to believe there could be anything dirty or out of place in it.

So the Judge sent them away and tried to persuade himself that the smell was nothing but imagination, and after an hour or two he became used to it and did not notice it. But on the following morning, going to breakfast in the dining-room, he sniffed and sniffed, and summoning again his Cook and his Tablemaid and his Housemaid, declared, ' There is a disgusting smell in this room also. What is it, what causes it, and why do you permit it ? '

But all of them, looking very smart and clean in their print dresses and white aprons, with their faces newly washed, indignantly replied that the room smelt sweet as a garden, and always would while the house was in their charge. So the Judge ate his breakfast unhappily and went out quickly. But on his way through Midmeddlecum he passed several little boys and several little girls who, when they saw him coming, hurriedly avoided him and held their noses in a very ostentatious way.

The smell in the library was much worse that evening, and when he went to bed he lay awake for at least an hour, sniffing from time to time, and saying to himself, ' It is only imagination. It can be nothing but imagination.'

In the morning, however, the smell of mouse was undeniable, and rising early he searched the room for the source of it, but found nothing. He did find, however, in the folds of a clean shirt, a postcard on which was written :

HAVE YOU CHANGED YOUR MIND TO-DAY ?

This made him very angry, but as soon as he went into the dining-room he felt more worried than angry, for by now the room was smelling unmistakably of bad fish. Quickly he felt for his handkerchief — and found in his pocket another postcard with the inscription :

HAVE YOU CHANGED YOUR MIND TO-DAY ?

In Midmeddlecum that morning at least thirty little boys and girls, in the most pointed manner, held their noses while he passed, and twice he heard Catherine Crumb explaining to them in her shrill voice : ' He hasn't changed his mind for weeks and weeks ! '

This state of affairs lasted for several days, and the Judge grew more and more worried, and the several odours of mice and kippers and eels grew worse and worse in his house, for though the Cook and the Tablemaid and the Housemaid dusted and cleaned from morning till night, and searched again and again for the source of the smell, they never thought of looking in the springs under the bed, or in the Greek amphora, or behind the paintings of the Judge's father and mother. So in a few days' time he became thin and haggard, and wherever he went he heard voices saying, ' He hasn't changed his mind for weeks and weeks ! ' He began to wonder whether that indeed was the cause of all the disagreeable odours in his house.

And then one night he could not sleep at all, for the smell of mouse was stronger than ever, and the dining-room had smelt abominably of fish, and the smell of decay in the library had been perfectly disgusting. He sat up in bed and turned on the light, and looked at his watch. It was four o'clock. Quite soon he would have to get up, and walk into Midmeddlecum, where all the little boys and girls would hold their noses when they saw him coming, and ostentatiously avoid him.

'Oh, what shall I do, what shall I do?' he exclaimed, and tore a strip off the top sheet before he realised what he *was* doing.

Then he seemed to hear a mysterious voice say to him: 'Tearing sheets won't help you, what you've got to do is to change your mind. *Change your mind.* CHANGE YOUR MIND!'

A hundred and fifty-seven times the voice repeated its message, and then the Judge lost his temper and shouted, 'All right, all right. I heard you the first time! I'll change it, if that's the only way to get rid of these confounded smells. I'll change it, I tell you, but give me a chance! I've got to get my trousers on first.'

He got up and dressed as quickly as he could, and walked through Midmeddlecum to the prison, which was on the other side of the town. The sun rose as he crossed the Square, and the windows of the houses blinked in the morning light, and the bowl of the sky was like a Chinese tea-cup that you can almost see through, and a flock of little clouds stood perfectly still, like sheep when a strange dog first appears. Mr. Justice Rumple felt happier than he had been for a long time, and hurried to the prison as fast as he could. How delighted the poor Members of the Jury would be, he thought, when they heard that he had decided to release them ! They would probably give him three cheers, he decided.

He pulled the big brass bell at the prison gate, and heard it ring far inside : *Inkle-bangle-bankle-bang. Inkle-bangle-bankle-bang. Inkle-bangle, inkle-bangle, bang.*

No one came to let him in, so he pulled it again and again : *Inkle-bangle, inkle-bangle, inkle-bangle-bankle-bang* . . .

Then a window opened, and another and another and another, and all the prisoners put out their heads and shouted, ' Who's making all that noise ? '

' I am ! ' shouted the Judge. ' I've come to tell you that I've changed my mind, and you can all go home. You can go home at once ! '

' I'm not going home at this time in the morning for you or anyone else ! ' shouted Mr. Whitloe the drayman, and shut his window with a bang.

' Aren't we even allowed to sleep ? ' yelled Mrs. Leathercow, and shut her window with a still louder bang.

' You don't think we're going before we've had breakfast, do you ? ' exclaimed Mr. Fullalove, and shut his window too.

' Go away ! ' shouted all the others. ' Wait till we've had our breakfast ! ' And they all shut their windows very firmly indeed.

An expression of great sadness settled on the Judge's face, but making an effort he decided to be patient, and sitting down on a grassy bank opposite the prison gate he lighted a cigar and prepared to wait until nine o'clock, which was the usual breakfast-time at Midmeddlecum Gaol.

Far above him, while he sat there smoking, a great bird crossed the sky, then turned in a wide sweep, circled above him, and presently flew swiftly to Major Palfrey's house, where he landed on a window-ledge and with his beak tapped loudly on the glass.

Dinah and Dorinda woke immediately and let the Falcon in.

' I think your plan has worked,' he said. ' The Judge is sitting outside the prison, waiting, I suppose, till the slugabeds wake and let him in.'

' He has changed his mind ! ' exclaimed Dinah.

' And Mr. Corvo will be free,' said Dorinda, clapping her hands.

' So it appears,' said the Falcon.

' We must go at once,' said Dinah, ' and take away the kippers and the mice and the eels before the Judge gets back. Hurry up and get dressed, Dorinda. Good-bye, Falcon, and thank you for coming. We'll see you very soon ! '

So the Falcon flew away, and Dinah and Dorinda got dressed in three minutes, and ran all the way across the fields to the Judge's house.

Just before they reached it they saw the Cook and the Tablemaid and the Housemaid hurrying in the direction of Midmeddlecum, for the news had spread rapidly, and everybody by now had heard what was happening, and practically all the inhabitants except very small babies and people who were bedridden were on their way to the prison to see the release of the Members of the Jury.

So Dinah and Dorinda found it quite easy to remove the mice from under the bed, and the kippers from the dining-room wall, and the eels from the Greek vase, and quickly they buried them in one of the Judge's own flower-beds. Then they washed their hands and ran to the prison too.

They were in plenty of time, for the Members of the Jury still refused to leave until they had had their breakfast, and would not even allow Mrs. Jehu to serve it half an hour before the usual time.

But at half-past nine they came out, looking very serious and important, and the Judge stood on a chair and politely announced that he had changed his mind, and so they would be released from prison and could go where they liked and do as they pleased — ' Within reason, of course, always within reason,' he quickly added.

Then the Members of the Jury all wanted to make speeches in praise of Freedom and Justice and the British Constitution, but the Vicar had already formed a choir, and soon everybody was singing *Lilliburlero*. Then they marched into Mid-meddlecum, singing to the tune of *Greensleeves* :

> ' As I went through the North Countrie
> The fashions of the world to see,
> I sought for merry company
> To go to the City of London.'

All the way they sang, with Constable Drum marching beside them and shouting, ' Left, right ; left, right ; left ! Pick up the step, you miserable

He announced that he had changed his mind

sinners, or I'll see that none of you get any dinners. Left, right ; left ! '

And in Midmeddlecum Square they gathered round the statue of Queen Victoria and sang till they were so hoarse they could sing no more.

Chapter Twenty-Six

Only to Mr. Casimir Corvo did Dinah and Dorinda explain the part they had played in securing the release of the Members of the Jury, but he thanked them so handsomely, and appreciated their cleverness in so understanding a way, that they were perfectly repaid for the trouble they had taken, and wanted nobody's gratitude but his. This was just as well, because all the other prisoners thought they had been released because of the firm stand they had taken, and no one of them was prepared to show gratitude to anyone. Catherine Crumb, indeed, spread the tale that she had made thirty children hold their noses whenever they saw Mr. Justice Rumple, and she told everyone that Dinah and Dorinda had filled his house with dead animals; but it was well known that Catherine was a wicked girl who told lies every day of her life, so no one believed a word she said. The result was that in all Midmeddlecum the only grown-up person who ever knew the whole truth of the matter was Mr. Casimir Corvo.

He said to them, a few days after he regained his freedom, when they came for their dancing lesson, ' If I had stayed in that prison for another week, I would have gone mad. If I had gone mad, I would have thrown myself out of a window. If I had thrown myself out of a window, I would have broken my neck. If I had broken my neck, I would have become altogether lifeless. But instead of that,

I am now full of life, I am leaping and singing for joy like a trout in a stream and a cuckoo in the woods, and that is all due to you. My very dear Dinah — my charming Dorinda — I am your servant ! And now let us dance. I shall teach you a magnificent Spanish dance in which you must be swift as a storm, and light as a bubble, and gay as a clown. It is called the Jaleo de Jerez.'

Mr. Corvo never taught his pupils any of those dances in which people do little more than walk about, with now a hop and now a slide in this direction or that ; for in his opinion that was worth nothing at all. He liked the old dances of England and Spain and Scotland, of France and Poland and Russia, that were stately and vigorous, and these he taught with such tremendous enthusiasm that many of his pupils became so exhausted, after two or three lessons, that their parents had to take them away to the seaside for a long rest. But Dinah and Dorinda, having been kangaroos and learnt to jump, were now so strong that they could dance a Fandango and a Foursome Reel, a Schottische, a Mazurka, an Irish Jig, a Sailor's Hornpipe, and Lumps of Pudding, one after the other, without being tired at all.

They enjoyed their lessons with Mr. Corvo, and for two or three weeks lived very happily indeed. Their mother had gone to London, and Miss Serendip had hay-fever, so they were able to spend a lot of time with the Puma and the Falcon, who taught them how to do nothing. This is more difficult than it sounds, and only the animals are really expert at it. But Dinah and Dorinda made good progress in their studies, and soon were able to do *almost* nothing.

But then their mother came home. They went to meet her, and as soon as they saw her they realised that she was very worried. She was leaning out of the window as the train came into the station, and the long string of blue and yellow beads that she was wearing had in some way twisted round the handle of the carriage door. It took them several minutes to disentangle it and let her out, and then they discovered that she had lost all her luggage except a bag of plums that belonged to someone else.

'Poor Mother,' they said. 'Come home and have some tea.'

Then she told them that she was very anxious about their father, because she had not heard from him for several weeks. She had been to London to try and get news of him, but nobody could tell her anything about him. 'And I shall not have a moment's happiness,' she said, ' till I get a letter in his own handwriting assuring me that he is safe and well, and on his way home again.'

Now Dinah and Dorinda, though they often thought of their father, had never really worried about him. He was, they believed, perfectly able to look after himself in any circumstances, however dangerous. But when they saw how anxious their mother was, they could not help feeling anxious too, and like her they began to wait for the postman, and look for his coming, with growing impatience.

One day they saw him walking slowly down the road, and going to meet him they found him standing at the garden gate with a single letter in his hand. He was staring at it in a very curious way, and he gave it to Dinah without a word, though usually he was a friendly and talkative man.

The envelope was rather dirty, and on one corner there was a dark red stain.

' That's blood,' said Dinah.

' That's Father's handwriting,' said Dorinda.

' I know,' said Dinah, and both of them looked at the bloodstain with frightened eyes. Their faces were white, and each could hear her heart beating.

' I'm going to open it,' said Dinah.

' But it's addressed to Mother.'

' Suppose there is bad news in it ? Mother isn't strong, and it might make her ill.'

' But if it's bad news we shall have to tell her about it.'

' We might be able to do something first,' said Dinah, and putting her finger into the flap of the envelope, tore it open.

The letter was quite short. Their father had written : *Though my news is not good news, you must not worry about me. I was arrested three weeks ago, and am now in a dungeon in the Castle of Gliedermannheim. I am quite well and I feel sure that I shall be released before long. The dungeon is not very comfortable, but I am not ill-treated, and my worst hardship is that I am forbidden either to write or receive letters. I send you this note by the hand of a friend who is going to England on business, and has consented to take it, though at great risk to himself. I ask you again to have no fear for me. Be patient, and all will be well. By good fortune I was wearing winter underclothing at the time of my arrest, so I am quite warm, though the dungeon is unheated.*

It was some little time before either Dinah or Dorinda could speak. They were horrified by what they read and by the thought of their father in a dungeon. They could imagine its darkness, the dank smell of a cave, the moisture on the rough stone walls, and the narrow shaft of light steeply descending from a little barred window in an upper corner. Their poor father ! And how bravely he had written, making light of his misfortune and anxious only to comfort their mother, though he himself must be suffering both in mind and body. Perhaps he was chained to a wall !

' We must rescue him,' said Dinah suddenly.

' He's a long way from here,' said Dorinda.

' Gliedermannheim is the capital of Bombardy.'

' Its chief industries are the manufacture of musical instruments, chinaware, casks, and beer, while the surrounding country is rich in beech-woods, cherry-orchards, clay-pits, and ' flocks of geese,' said Dorinda. ' Miss Serendip taught us that.'

' Gliedermannheim is where Mr. Corvo comes from. He'll be able to tell us how to get there.'

' I had forgotten that,' said Dorinda. ' Oh, he's

sure to help us, and I expect we shall need all the help we can get. We've never rescued anyone from a dungeon before.'

' Till a few months ago we had never rescued anyone from anywhere. But we have a lot of experience now.'

' Not with dungeons,' said Dorinda. ' I feel that dungeons are very difficult. I wonder if Mrs. Grimble knows anything about them ? '

' She may,' said Dinah. ' But you know she doesn't really like being asked to help people.'

' Perhaps she would give us another bottle of medicine or a powder that would make us invisible. She knows how to make herself invisible.'

' But if we both became invisible we should probably lose each other,' said Dinah. ' And what about our clothes ? Would they become invisible too, or would we have to take them off and go into a very cold dungeon with nothing on ? And I suppose you want us to take some of the medicine to Father, so that he could become invisible too. But the bottle itself wouldn't be invisible, so the bottle would have to be carried by nothing, or by you or me looking like nothing, and what do you think the soldiers guarding the Castle would do if they saw a bottle swimming through the air towards them ? '

' They might think they were dreaming,' said Dorinda, '' or they might pretend they saw nothing at all, for fear the others would laugh at them if they suddenly said, '' I see a bottle ! '' '

' It's far more likely,' said Dinah, ' that they would guess what had happened. Everybody, at one time or another, must have thought what fun they could have if only they knew how to become invisible, and if a lot of soldiers saw a bottle floating about, they would probably say at once, " There's an invisible man ! " Then they would feel jealous of him, and begin to beat the air with their rifles, like beaters driving pheasants out of a wood.'

' Would you feel a beating if you were invisible ? ' asked Dorinda.

' Perhaps you would and perhaps you wouldn't,' said Dinah. ' If you simply became transparent, like glass, I suppose you would ; but if you changed into something like a cloud, you wouldn't. But I'm sure we'll have to think of something else, a more *ordinary* way of rescuing Father.'

' You say that because you don't want to be invisible,' said Dorinda, who had been rather hurt by Dinah's objections to her idea.

' Let's go and talk to Mr. Corvo,' said Dinah, bringing the argument to an end because she could not properly explain, even to herself, why she disliked the thought of becoming transparent. Dorinda continued to grumble a little, and finding a large round yellow tin on the road, kicked it before her all the way to Mr. Corvo's house.

Just as they arrived the door opened and two of Mr. Corvo's pupils came out. They were a fat little boy and a stout little girl, and both were dripping with perspiration and so tired they could hardly walk. Mr. Corvo had been teaching them a Cossack dance.

They could hear him playing the piano in a bold and brilliant manner and singing a fine cheerful song in some foreign language. But he stopped as soon as they went in, and greeted them warmly, pretending, as he often did, that they were fashionable ladies who had come to call. Then he saw how serious they were, and becoming serious himself, asked what was the matter. Dinah showed him the letter.

Mr. Corvo read it carefully and then said slowly, ' I was born in Gliedermannheim. It is a beautiful town in a beautiful country, but now it is ruled by a cruel man, a tyrant, and all my people are suffering as never before. Your father is in great danger.'

' We are going to rescue him,' said Dorinda.

Mr. Corvo smiled sadly. ' That is not possible. There are many thousands of people in prison, throughout Bombardy, and as many people who dream of rescuing them. But never do their dreams come to life. The prisons of Bombardy are strong, the prison guards are fierce and cruel, and the country is ruled without mercy by the iron hand of its Tyrant, Count Hulagu Bloot. You can do nothing, my poor children. Nothing at all.'

' We got you out of prison,' said Dinah.

' And we got the Golden Puma and the Silver Falcon out of Sir Lankester Lemon's zoo,' said Dorinda.

' You shouldn't talk about that,' said Dinah with a frown.

' Why not ? '

' Because it's a secret.'

' It isn't now,' said Dorinda, and she proceeded to tell Mr. Corvo the story of how they had become kangaroos and lived, for quite a long time, in Sir Lankester's zoo.

Dinah felt very uncomfortable while she listened
to all this, for she felt that the story was really their
own affair — hers and Dorinda's, the Puma's and
the Falcon's — and that in some curious way it
would be spoilt by other people knowing of it. A
secret was such a splendid thing to have, but as
soon as you told the secret, you lost the feeling
entirely. Dorinda, so Dinah thought, was spoiling
everything.

But was she ? For Dinah could not help seeing
that Mr. Corvo was very much impressed by the
story. To begin with, he was astonished. Then he
grew serious, and stared at Dorinda with bright
enquiring eyes and a frown on his forehead. And
when he heard of the Python's death he clapped his
hands and cried ' Hurrah ! ' and did a very difficult
dancing-step called an *entrechat-dix*.

He was certainly impressed, and Dinah realised
that their only chance of persuading him to help
them was to impress him very deeply indeed. So
Dorinda, it now seemed, had done the right thing
in telling him the story of the zoo, and Dinah, admit-
ting to herself that she had been wrong, listened with
growing admiration to her sister.

When the story was finished, Mr. Corvo walked
up and down the room several times without
speaking. Then he stopped and said : ' When I was
a boy, and living in Bombardy, I often used to hear
stories of people who could change themselves into
birds or animals. It was said in the villages that
there were certain very wicked men who, when the
moon was full, became wolves and went hunting in
the forest. We were told about an old woman who

could turn herself into a crow in order to listen to what people were saying in the fields where they were working. And a cousin of mine, who ran away and went to sea, came home and described the great birds that followed his ship when she was far from land, and these birds, he said, were really the souls of dead sailors, and they followed the ship to see if the younger sailors were as good as they had been, and worked as hard, and were as brave when the storm-winds blew.

' These stories,' said Mr. Corvo, ' and others like them, I had quite forgotten. But now, when you tell me that you have lately been kangaroos, I remember many things. I feel humble, as I did when I was a child ; but also I feel glad and strong, because it may be true, as I thought then it was true, that nothing is impossible.'

And Mr. Corvo, very beautifully and neatly, did another *entrechat-dix*.

' Then you will help us,' said Dorinda, ' to go to Bombardy and rescue Father ? '

Mr. Corvo began to walk up and down the room again, with his hands behind his back and a deep frown on his forehead.

' It will be difficult and dangerous,' he said. ' Oh, so difficult, and ah, so dangerous ! '

' After we got you out of prison,' said Dinah, ' you said that you were deeply indebted to us.'

Mr. Corvo stood perfectly still in the middle of the room. Then he placed his left hand on his heart — or rather, on that part of his yellow waistcoat which lay nearest his heart — and raising his right hand towards the ceiling, he said in a high ringing voice, ' Yes, and now I shall discharge my debt ! Listen while I tell you how we shall go to Bombardy, and make our entrance even into the Castle of Gliedermannheim, the Castle of the Tyrant of Bombardy, Count Hulagu Bloot ! '

Chapter Twenty-Seven

Count Hulagu Bloot hated all the countries of the earth except his own, and his own he despised. He despised it for two reasons. When he was young, his fellow-countrymen had never been able to see how clever he was ; and after he became the Tyrant of Bombardy — by various cruel, dastardly, ingenious, and horrible means — they never saw how easy it would be to get rid of him, but allowed him to rule them as he liked. And what he liked more than anything else was to make people suffer.

He hated England and France and Germany and Russia and America and Holland and Turkey and Italy and Spain and Austria and Sweden and Portugal and Switzerland and China ; but that did not prevent him from buying English bulldogs and French wine and German sausages and Russian caviare and American ice-cream and Dutch tulips and Turkish delight and Italian pictures and Spanish onions and Austrian hats and Swedish matches and Portuguese men-o'-war and Swiss milk chocolate and Chinese puzzles, or anything else, no matter where it came from. For he was very rich.

Quite lately, as it happened, he had decided to refurnish his Castle from top to bottom, except the dungeons, and hearing that the Duke of Starveling, who lived near Midmeddlecum and was very poor, had decided to sell all the furniture and pictures and silver plate and carpets and so forth in *his* castle, Count Hulagu had sent him a telegram offering to buy the lot. The Duke of Starveling at once said yes, and a week later an envoy from the court of Bombardy arrived with a cheque for £85,471 : 6 : 9, which was the price of the furniture and pictures and silver plate and carpets and so forth at Starveling Hall, and began to make arrangements to have them packed up and sent to Gliedermannheim.

This man, the envoy, was called Professor Bultek, and when they were both small boys, he and Mr. Corvo had lived next door to each other. He had come to see Mr. Corvo as soon as he arrived in England, to show him the cheque, which was written in gold ink, and to tell him the latest news from Bombardy.

So much Mr. Corvo explained to Dinah and Dorinda. Then he said : ' And when my friend Bultek goes home, he will take the Duke of Starveling's chairs and tables and beds and pictures and tapestry with him in five enormous furniture vans. Huge and tremendous vans, the biggest that can be found. So big there will be room — do you not think so ? — for you and me to hide ourselves among all that furniture, and go to Bombardy with no difficulty, and make our entrance into the Castle of Gliedermannheim. Then, if you are still as clever as you were when you rescued me from prison, and the Golden Puma and the Silver Falcon from the zoo, then you will think of some way to bring your father out of his dungeon. Do not ask me how. That is for you to say. And by and by the furniture vans will be sent back to England with big labels on them saying : EMPTY. RETURN TO OWNER. But they will not all be empty. In one of them, if

we are clever and lucky, there will be you and I,
and your father too.'

'It sounds quite easy,' said Dorinda. 'It sounds
the easiest thing we have ever done.'

'No, no, no!' said Mr. Corvo. 'Do not deceive
yourselves. All I can do to make it easy, I shall
do — if my friend Bultek agrees — but like the stone
in a plum, the middle part will be hard and difficult
and dangerous. We go into Bombardy: good!
We go into the Castle: excellent! But to get your
father out of the dungeon, and ourselves out of
Gliedermannheim, may be as difficult as breaking a
plumstone between your thumb and your little
finger. Do not be light-hearted about that. Think
deeply, make your plans with care.'

'What sort of a professor is Professor Bultek?'
asked Dinah.

'He looks like a frog,' said Mr. Corvo, 'and he is
a Professor of Palmistry.'

'He tells fortunes, you mean?'

'By looking at the lines on your hand,' said Mr.
Corvo. 'It is all great nonsense, I think, but our
Tyrant, Count Hulagu, believes in it, and so Bultek
has become a favourite of his.'

'And does Professor Bultek himself believe in the
fortunes that he tells?'

'It would not be kind to ask him that,' said Mr.
Corvo. 'He cries too easily. Ever since he was a
little boy, and looked in a glass and saw that he
was like a frog, he has cried a great deal. But now
you must go and make your plans and preparations,
and I shall write a letter to Bultek.'

Chapter Twenty-Eight

On the following day Dinah went to see Mrs. Grimble. She went alone. Dorinda had pleaded with her to be allowed to go too, but Dinah, after much thought, had refused to take her. She told Dorinda, as she had told her before, that Mrs. Grimble could be very difficult, and was far more

likely to be difficult with strangers than with people she knew. That was perfectly true, but Dinah had two other reasons, about which she said nothing, because she didn't want to. In the first place, she was frightened that Dorinda might laugh at Mrs. Grimble, who had the habit, when talking, of opening the right side of her mouth and closing her left eye ; and then, sometimes in the middle of a sentence, she would begin to use the other side of her mouth, and open her left eye and close the right. She did this, she said, because her face got easily tired, and by using only half of it at a time, she could rest the other half. But people who were not used to her appearance often found it upset them.

Dinah's second reason was one that she was very properly ashamed of. She was proud of knowing Mrs. Grimble and wanted to keep her all to herself, as if Mrs. Grimble were a secret. She knew how selfish this was, and therefore wrong, but it was a very pleasant form of selfishness and she could not make up her mind to part with it. Not yet. But she gave her word that if they succeeded in rescuing their father she would take Dorinda to see Mrs. Grimble as soon as they returned.

' And that,' she said firmly, ' is a *promise*. And I promise, too, that I shall ask her if she knows about any medicine to make people invisible. But I don't suppose for a moment she does.'

So Dorinda had to find what comfort she could in these two promises, and wait, as patiently as might be, for Dinah's return. She spent most of the time in making a list of the things they would have to take if they went to Gliedermannheim in a furniture van.

Then Dinah came back and her first words were : ' Mrs. Grimble wasn't even a little bit pleased to see me, and when I asked her if there was any way of becoming invisible she said : " There's only one way I know of, unless you were born with the gift of it like I was, and that's to take off all your skin and put it on again inside out, and I'll tell you the name of a tailor who'll do it for you, if you want to know, but the last man who went to him was hurt so bad that he took to his bed afterwards, and that didn't do him any good either, for not a soul could see him by that time, so there he lay and got no attention at all, and my advice is that you should have nothing to do with such a notion, and my second piece of advice is to go home and leave me in peace, for I had a leg of pork for my dinner that the Puma brought me for a birthday present — I'm ninety-eight to-day — and after eating all that meat I'd rather sleep than listen to you and all your nonsense." '

' And did you go away ? ' asked Dorinda.

' No,' said Dinah. ' I let her sleep for an hour, and then I woke her up by tickling my nose with a piece of grass and sneezing three times, very loudly. I told her the whole story of what had happened to Father, and how we meant to go and rescue him, but I don't know whether she was listening or not, she seemed to be half asleep again. Well, after I had finished she didn't say anything for quite a long time, and then she opened one eye and asked, " What do you want me to do ? "

' " I want you to help us," I said. " I want you to suggest some way of getting Father out of the dungeon."

' Then she got quite angry and said, " Learn to help yourselves, that's the best help, instead of coming to worry an old woman who's got plenty to worry her already, with all the things she hears about that are going on in the world."

' She was quite different from the last time I saw her. I suppose she's getting older,' said Dinah.

' And did she give you nothing at all ? ' asked Dorinda.

' Well, at last she seemed to feel sorry for us, or sorry about Father, because presently she got up and said, " I'm going to give you two things, and one of them is a piece of good advice, and the other is a little bag full of something that smells. And here's the advice to begin with :

" Remember that honey
Is better than money,
    And friends are the sweetest of all ;
A star in a stream
Will teach you to dream —
    But always look over the wall !

Plough and sow your own brain,
You'll get plenty of grain
    And reap a fine harvest and tall ;
Then open your eyes
And learn to be wise,
    And always look over the wall.

In your garden you need
To stoop and to weed,
    To kneel and be humble and small ;
Then up tiptoe to see
Great hills and the sea
    That lie over, far over the wall !

Be honest, my sweet,
Be cleanly and neat,
    And pick yourself up when you fall ;
Make the most of your youth,
And then seek for the truth
    That is over, far over,
    And far-away over,
    A hundred miles over the wall ! " '

' Do you know what it means ? ' asked Dorinda.

' I'm not quite sure,' said Dinah. ' Anyway, it seems to me that good advice is never so helpful as the people who give it think it is going to be. It doesn't really tell you what to do, it only makes you stop and think. And that can be very tiresome.'

' I don't like good advice,' said Dorinda. ' Where is the bag she gave you ? And what use will it be ? '

' I left it on the garden seat, because it has rather a strong smell. And I don't really understand how it's going to help us either. But Mrs. Grimble said we must use it to draw a circle round the house after tea this afternoon. It has to be a big circle, at least a hundred yards across, and we must be careful not to leave any gaps in it.'

' But why ? ' asked Dorinda.

' I don't exactly know,' said Dinah. ' You see, after I told Mrs. Grimble that we meant to go to Gliedermannheim whether she helped us or not, she said, " You'll need a friend, a strong friend and a brave friend, and I have something here that will keep your friend safe, and that's all I can do for you, so don't trouble me any more." Then she went to her cupboard, and her magpie was sitting on it, but he'd been eating pork too and was almost as sleepy as she had been. He opened his beak and seemed to yawn. Then she took out the bag with the smell, and gave it to me.'

' And was that all she said ? '

' Just as I was going she called me back and whispered, " The Puma has been on the warpath again. She's killed a pig, and she's killed another lamb, and last night she killed a calf. They'll hunt her with men and they'll hunt her with dogs, and you and your sister are the only friends she has, and she'll be a good friend to you if she gets the chance. Remember that, and now be off home and don't come worrying me again, for I'm an old woman and I like my peace." '

' It's very wrong of the Puma to kill things,' said Dorinda, ' even though she doesn't know the difference between what is hers and what is somebody else's. But they'll never catch her, will they ? '

' I hope not,' said Dinah.

' Nothing can run as fast as she can. Not even a horse.'

' There are two packs of foxhounds not far away,' said Dinah, ' and Captain Bilbo's beagles, and Mr. Haggle's bloodhounds, as well as hundreds of terriers and setters and pointers and bulldogs. If they hunt her with all those, it will be very difficult for her to get away. Oh, poor Puma ! It was very generous of her to give Mrs. Grimble a leg of pork. And it's our fault, in a way, that she's in danger, because it was we who let her out of the zoo. I'm terribly worried about her.'

' The Falcon will give her plenty of warning,' said Dorinda. ' She'll be all right.'

Then they went in and had their tea, and after tea they took the little bag with the smell in it and rubbed it on the ground so as to draw a circle, at least a hundred yards across, all round the house. This took them a long time, and it was later than usual when they went to bed.

They were half asleep when they heard the Falcon's wings at the open window and his voice

248

calling to them. Dorinda rose quickly and pulled up the blind to let him in. A silvery light came with him into the room, making his feathers gleam, for the moon was rising.

' The Golden Puma is in danger,' he said. ' She has been killing too many beasts, though there are so many in the fields that no one could think their owners would miss a lamb or two, or a young pig, or even a calf. Your farmers must be greedy men, as well as good counters, for now they are angry and have made up their minds to hunt and kill the animal that is feeding on their flocks. Yesterday they went to those men who are Masters of Fox-hounds, one pack on this side of the Forest of Weal, and one upon the far side. They went to a man who has a pack of bloodhounds, great ravening beasts, and to another who hunts with a score of those little dogs called beagles. Many others have joined them with lurchers and greyhounds, terriers and retrievers. The men have guns ; some are on horseback, some on foot. This evening they gathered all their strength and surrounded the Forest. We first saw them coming from the east, and were not alarmed, the Puma and I, because we knew that she could out-distance them. But then I flew high, soaring above the Forest, and to the west I saw others, and others to the north and south. They were closing in upon the Forest to make a ring all round it. So I flew down and told her what I had seen, and she bade me come here and ask if she could find harbour with you.'

' Of course she can,' said Dinah and Dorinda, speaking together.

' Listen ! ' said the Falcon. ' You can hear them now.'

Out of the moonlit night, clear enough though still far away, rose the cry of hounds. And in that distant chorus there was a wild and cruel excitement that made Dinah's heart beat faster, and Dorinda felt her skin prickling as though a cold wind blew.

' Quickly ! ' exclaimed the Falcon. ' Go down and open the door, but quietly, so that no one hears.'

They ran downstairs together, turned the key in the front door, and carefully, so that it would not creak, pulled it open. A little nervously, they looked out at the empty garden. Already the cry of hounds was louder. They were coming nearer.

Then swiftly a lithe shape crossed the lawn and the Puma, panting a little, stood in the doorway.

' Will you give me harbour ? ' she asked.

' Yes, yes,' they whispered.

' Where shall I go ? '

' Come to our room,' said Dorinda, and led the way while Dinah, as carefully as she had opened it, closed and locked the door. Then, following Dorinda, she locked their bedroom door and put the key under her pillow.

' Did they nearly catch you ? ' asked Dorinda.

The Puma lay on the hearth-rug, still panting. ' There were too many of them,' she said. ' They were coming from all sides.'

' You're quite safe now,' said Dinah, but even as she said it they heard a new and louder noise, so fierce that they felt as though a hand were tightening round their throats.

This new noise came from the back of the house,

They looked out at the empty garden

where suddenly another pack of hounds gave tongue. Their voices seemed to fill the night. There were high voices and deep voices, hounds that bayed and hounds that babbled, a yelping chorus.

' Forty or fifty yards from your door,' said the Puma, ' there was a scent that rose like a wall before me. It stopped me, I did not know what it was. Then I leapt across it.'

' We made that,' said Dorinda.

' Mrs. Grimble gave us a bag,' Dinah explained, ' and told us to make a circle round the house by rubbing it along the ground. But we didn't know what good it was going to do.'

' You made the circle complete ? ' asked the Puma. ' You missed nowhere ? You left no gaps ? '

' We did it very carefully indeed,' said Dinah.

' Look how we scratched ourselves, getting through the hedges,' said Dorinda.

' It will keep them out,' said the Falcon.

' Let us hope so,' said the Puma, and rising from the hearth-rug paced slowly up and down the room. The fur on her neck was bristling and her eyes were very bright.

Now the hounds, in full cry, encircled the house, and their terrible voices came from all sides. Some were shrill and some were deep, some were as clear as a bell and some nearly as hoarse as a ship's siren. There were those that babbled and those that bayed, and one like a wolf caught in a trap howled most horribly. And that was not unreasonable, for in a way they were all caught in a trap.

As soon as they came to the scent that Dinah and Dorinda had laid, they had to follow it. It was so strong that it held their doggy noses as if they had been chained to it. It filled their simple doggy minds, and led them round and round the house, at full gallop, and round again.

There were two packs of foxhounds, Sir Leopold Livery's hounds from one side of the county and Mr. Vortigern's from the other, and Captain Bilbo's beagles, and about thirty or forty setters and pointers and spaniels and lurchers and terriers of one sort or another, and Mrs. Fumer's pack of otter-hounds from Watercress Court a dozen miles away, who were always bad-tempered, and her two poodles, and a Bedlington terrier that was out on its own and up to no good, and Mrs. Steeple's lion-hearted Pekinese that got in the way of the great hounds, who were continually tripping over it and tumbling and falling.

Round and round they went, barking and baying and yelping in the moonlight, and the men who had brought them — Sir Leopold Livery and Mr. Vortigern and their two huntsmen, and eight or nine farmers, and Captain Bilbo and Mrs. Fumer's husband — some of whom were on horseback and some on foot, went round and round as well, till they saw what was happening, and then they tried to call off their hounds, shouting and bellowing and making almost as much noise as the hounds themselves, but all to no purpose. For the scent was so strong that nothing could persuade even the little dogs to leave it, while the big ones were nearly mad with pleasure and excitement and the ridiculous belief that all the time they were getting nearer and nearer to something they could kill.

About this time Mr. Haggle arrived with his bloodhounds. They were late in coming because they hunted much more slowly and deliberately than the foxhounds ; for a foxhound that has lost the scent will cast forward to look for it, but the sagacious and thoughtful bloodhound will cast back. The other packs, and the setters and terriers and spaniels and so on, had by now galloped round the circle eleven times at full speed, and some of them were a little tired. They were all hunting in the same direction, running round the circle like the hands of a clock, though much faster.

But when the bloodhounds arrived and found the scent, they gave tongue like thunder and with ears flapping and their noses to the ground immediately began to gallop round in the opposite direction; or anti-clockwise. The first thing that happened was that a bloodhound called Hannibal met a foxhound called Ranter, and knocked him over. Then two bloodhounds called Hengist and Horsa, who were brothers, collided with two otter-hounds called Danger and Ranger. The otter-hounds, who were quite unused to running so far and so fast as this, were hot and tired and more bad-tempered than usual. So Danger bit Hengist and Ranger bit Horsa, the first in the ear and the second in the leg, and the Bedlington who was out on its own and up to no good, seeing that a fight had started, thought it would be good fun to join in and bit Ranger the otter-hound in the left cheek. Then Ranger, who as well as being hot and tired was rather confused in his mind, howled like a banshee and bit a very handsome foxhound called Dairymaid who had stopped for a moment to see what was going on.

Now Dairymaid was one of Mr. Vortigern's favourite hounds, and when Mr. Vortigern saw that she had been attacked he became so excited that he fell off his horse. The horse galloped away and knocked Sir Leopold Livery off his horse, which also ran away, with Sir Leopold's huntsman in close pursuit. Mr. Vortigern in the meantime, sprawling on the ground, had been bitten on the nose by the Bedlington ; and a foxhound belonging to Sir Leopold, who had tripped over a fat spaniel and was rather out of humour in consequence, knocked him flat on his back again when he tried to get up. Then eight or nine hounds of one sort or another fell over him, and the Bedlington, who was a quick-witted and happy dog, bit four or five of them so swiftly that none knew who had done it, and they began to fight among themselves.

Where the circle of scent crossed the road to the left of the Palfreys' house, the hounds had made gaps through the hedges, and here there was now a traffic block of a very noisy and serious kind. The bloodhounds were largely to blame for it, because they still insisted on hunting in the opposite direction to all the others, but as the fast-running foxhounds grew tired they more and more often tripped and fell over the smaller and slower beagles, and that added to the confusion. The gaps in the hedges were full of hounds struggling to get through, and thirty or forty of all kinds were fighting on the road while Mr. Vortigern's huntsman and the eight or nine farmers stood and shouted at them. Mrs.

Fumer's husband had been bitten by Mrs. Steeple's lion-hearted Pekinese, and was sitting in a ditch crying.

From the window of their bedroom Dinah and Dorinda had been able, in the bright moonlight, to see the wild running of the hounds as they crossed and recrossed a field. The Falcon stood on the window-sill, and the Puma, on her hind legs, stood between Dinah and Dorinda. For about a quarter of an hour they had watched the extraordinary spectacle, but now there were only a few hounds on the roundabout, some running aimlessly to and fro, for most of them were either fighting on the road or in the other battle which had started over Mr. Vortigern. — Mr. Vortigern himself, pursued by two otter-hounds called Dimple and Daffodil, who wanted to tear off his breeches, was on his way home. — Mrs. Fumer's poodles, who were clever enough to keep away from the fighting but not clever enough to see that they were going round in a circle, still ran wearily one way, and so did three stubborn old hounds called Varlet and Vagabond and Venomous ; while a huge bloodhound, whose name was Horatius and who looked the very picture of sorrow, went shambling and shuffling with equal persistence in the opposite direction. Here and there, their tongues lolling out and their sides heaving, lay dogs in utter exhaustion, and the voices of those who still ran, or still were fighting, were cracked and hoarse.

' What a good thing that Mother went to London again ! ' said Dinah. ' She would have been terribly frightened by all this noise.'

' I wonder if Miss Serendip was frightened ? ' said Dorinda. ' I expect she put her head under the bed-clothes.'

But Miss Serendip, though indeed she had been more frightened than ever before in her life, had not been frightened out of her wits. She had telephoned to Constable Drum and told him that all the dogs in the county had gone mad and were running round the house, while several Masters of Hounds and a lot of other men, who also appeared to be mad, were having a riot. Would Constable Drum please come as quickly as possible and put a stop to it ?

Constable Drum had a keen sense of duty and a good brain. He went to the Fire Station, woke up the Firemaster, and ordered him to bring out his fire-engine.

Dinah and Dorinda heard it coming, with its great bell ringing, but only the Falcon saw what happened then. He flew from the window to the topmost branch of a tree that grew by the roadside and saw Constable Drum take command of the situation.

There was a hydrant not far from the house, and quickly a hose-pipe was coupled to it. Then, with the bright brass nozzle of the pipe in his hands, the Constable bravely approached the forty hounds who were still fighting on the road.

' To avoid further slaughter, please turn on the water ! ' he shouted to the Firemaster.

A great jet of water leapt from the pipe. The brass nozzle shone like pale gold in the moonlight, and the stream of water, as thick as a man's wrist, glittered and hissed and knocked the hounds off their feet. Foxhounds and otter-hounds, terriers and spaniels and the sad-faced flop-eared bloodhounds, staggered and fell and were battered out of the fight. It was all over in half a minute, and half a minute later not a hound was to be seen. They ran for home, with their tails between their legs, and their frightened yelping grew fainter and fainter.

Then Constable Drum aimed the hose at the huntsman and the farmers and knocked them over too, exclaiming in a loud voice : ' What a horrible riot have you been provoking ! You'd better go quiet or I'll give you a soaking ! '

He gave them a soaking indeed, for by now the road was like a beach when the tide is coming in, and some of the farmers were trying to swim, and as soon as they struggled to their feet the jet of water knocked them down again as though it had been a battering-ram.

When the last of them had been driven away, Constable Drum went into the field, with the hose-pipe trailing behind him, and broke up the fight that was going on there, and drove off the straggling dogs and the limping dogs, and woke up the dogs that had gone to sleep, and sent them all home. Then he shouted to the Firemaster : ' The battle is won, you're a very fine chap, and I am another, so turn off the tap ! '

Then they rolled up the hose and drove back to Midmeddlecum in the moonlight, feeling very pleased with themselves indeed, and the great bell on the fire-engine ringing loudly all the way.

Chapter Twenty-Nine

The Golden Puma slept on the hearth-rug, and Dinah woke early to let her out. But she warned her not to go far.

The Puma said gravely, ' Had I not better go away ? So far away that you will never see me again ? I am causing trouble here, and if I stay longer I shall cause more, and that would embarrass you. It might even distress you.'

' It would distress me a great deal if you got into trouble.'

' Then shall we say good-bye ? Shall I go and look for some freer, more generous part of England, where I can eat my fill in peace, without bringing angry hunters on my track every time I kill a sheep ? '

' I don't think you would find such a place very easily,' said Dinah. ' Not in England. And quite apart from that, there's something else we ought to think about. Do you realise that when Mrs. Grimble gave me the bag with the smell in it, she must have known that you were going to be in danger and would need help ? '

' She is far-sighted,' said the Puma.

' But I had gone to Mrs. Grimble to ask her to help us. To help Dorinda and Mr. Corvo and me to rescue Father. He's in a dungeon, you know.'

' You have told me his story,' said the Puma. ' I am not likely to forget it ; for I myself was once in a cage.'

'Then you can sympathise with him,' said Dinah. 'But the point is this : did Mrs. Grimble mean to help us rescue Father by first of all helping us to help you so that you could help us in return, if you see what I mean ? '

'I understand,' said the Puma. 'But what help can I give ? '

'You're very strong, and you can fight. And if we get inside the Castle of Gliedermannheim, we may need somebody who can fight.'

'I shall come with you,' said the Puma.

'I know it's asking a great deal of you,' said Dinah, 'because it may be very dangerous.'

'You gave me freedom,' said the Puma, 'and therefore I am your faithful friend and servant. You saved my life from the hounds, and therefore my life is yours. I am in danger here, and by going with you I shall merely exchange danger of one sort for danger of another. That is no hardship. And now, under the edge of that cloud — no, higher, look higher ! There to your left, where the cloud is lighted by the sun — I see the Falcon. I shall tell him of my decision and suggest that he too comes with us. Then we shall make a good company.'

Dinah knelt and put her arms round the Puma's neck. 'Dear Puma,' she cried, 'how can I say thank-you so that it will sound real and true ? I don't know enough words to say what I feel ! '

'Say nothing,' said the Puma, 'except this : We are friends. That is sufficient.'

Then she ran softly along a hedgerow and into a field where she waited for the Falcon, and Dinah went back to wake Dorinda and tell her the good news that they had gained an ally for their adventure.

Three days later Mr. Corvo sent them a postcard on which he had written : *Come this afternoon. A decision has been reached of which I shall inform you.*

The sternness of the message and the dignity of his language impressed them very much, and when they came to his house and saw how he was behaving, they were at first surprised and then filled with awe.

Mr. Corvo, with a stately stride, was pacing up and down the room where he taught dancing. He wore a green hat with a feather in it, and carried a large walking-stick. ' Sit down and watch me,' he said, and continued to pace the floor with a firm and measured tread. Now and again he pretended to recognise a friend, to whom he lifted his green hat with a flourish, and then suddenly turning he shouted, ' Ha, you villain ! Too late, too late ! Your last hour has come ! ' And twisting the handle of his walking-stick, he pulled from it a thin bright sword and made a terrific lunge in the direction of his imaginary enemy.

There was a picture on the wall of a bowl of goldfish and a cluster of yellow chrysanthemums in a lustre vase. The point of Mr. Corvo's sword pierced the canvas in the very middle of the goldfish-bowl, and for a moment Dinah expected to see water trickling out, and was disappointed when nothing happened. But Dorinda politely asked, ' Who was the villain, Mr. Corvo ? '

' Any one of the numerous enemies whom we

shall encounter in Gliedermannheim,' he answered.
' I am preparing myself not only to meet danger,
but to overcome it. I have bought this swordstick,

and every day I practise myself at fencing. Watch
me ! '

Mr. Corvo assumed the attitude of a fencer. He
raised his left arm in an upward curve with his

fingers hanging gracefully down. His feet were planted firmly apart, his knees were slightly bent, his sword arm pointed at the throat of an invisible enemy, and his expression was extremely fierce. He lunged and returned on guard, and lunged again. Then, it seemed, his enemy began to retreat, and Mr. Corvo with swiftly sliding steps pursued him, presently killed him, and immediately wheeled about to engage another. Having killed half a dozen opponents, he threw his sword away and said, ' Now I am disarmed — or so they will think. But I have made my preparations. Look ! '

From his waistcoat pocket he took a fountain-pen.

' Is that to write your last message with ? ' asked Dinah.

Mr. Corvo smiled in a superior way and un-screwed the top of the pen to show them, instead of a nib, a sharp steel point. ' It is not a pen,' he said, ' but a dagger ! No, no, be careful, you must not touch it. For as a fountain-pen is full of ink, this is full of poison ! '

' What a good idea ! ' said Dorinda.

' Do you think we shall have to do a lot of fighting ? ' asked Dinah.

' It is a good thing to be prepared for the worst,' said Mr. Corvo gravely.

' Then I think you will be glad to hear that the Puma is coming too. The Golden Puma, you know, that we helped to escape from Sir Lankester's zoo.'

' I have never travelled with a Puma before,' said Mr. Corvo. ' It will be an interesting ex-perience.'

' When are we going to start ? ' asked Dorinda.

' Very soon,' said Mr. Corvo.

' Have you persuaded Professor Bultek to let us go in a furniture van ? ' asked Dinah.

' Bultek is my very good friend,' said Mr. Corvo. ' I felt sure that I could persuade him to accommodate us among the furniture. But, as it turned out, very little persuasion was required. I told him who you were, I told him your father's name, and he at once exclaimed, " I shall do anything I can to help the brave and magnanimous Major Palfrey ! I brought with me, when I came to England, a letter to his wife. He is my dear friend." Then he told me a story.

' He was reading the lines on a gentleman's hand one day, in Gliedermannhcim, and telling his fortune. " Next week," he said, " you will be going on a long sea voyage." Then the gentleman gave a shout of anger and began to beat Professor Bultek with a stick. Poor Bultek ran from his house and the gentleman pursued him. He always became deadly sick when he went to sea, and he was so angry with Bultek for giving him such a bad fortune that he would probably have killed my unhappy friend if he had been able to catch him. But your father happened to be walking along the pavement, and Bultek called to him for help. So your father struck the angry gentleman a tremendous punch on the jaw and broke several of his teeth. Then the gentleman said to Bultek with a smile, " You are a liar, you see ! I cannot go on a voyage next week, for I shall be going to the dentist." So Bultek says that your father saved his life, and he will be very pleased to do all he can for you. He will arrange to have the furniture in one of the vans stowed in such a way as to leave plenty of room for us to live there. And the day when we shall start is next Wednesday.'

Chapter Thirty

Dinah and Dorinda, sitting side by side at the nursery table, were making a list of the stores they would require for their journey to Gliedermann-heim. Dinah had already written :

1 primus stove	3 small plates
1 frying-pan	3 big plates
1 saucepan	3 cups
1 kettle	1 meat dish for the Puma
1 teapot	

' How are we going to wash the plates ? ' asked Dorinda. ' We can't take very much water with us in a furniture van.'

' You don't need a lot of water if you have plenty of dish-cloths to wipe them with,' said Dinah. And she wrote :

1 sheet from the spare bedroom for dish-cloths
All the hot-water bottles, lemonade bottles, and
    other bottles that we can find, full of water
Some salt and pepper
12 eggs

' Do we need as many as that ? ' asked Dorinda.

' Mr. Corvo said the journey would take about three days, so that means three breakfasts. One each for us and two for Mr. Corvo, multiplied by three, makes twelve. What do you think we ought to take for the Puma ? '

' A leg of mutton for the first day, a leg of pork for the second, and a sirloin of beef for the third,' Dorinda suggested.

'It's going to be very expensive.'

'Then ask her to kill another sheep and bring that.'

'It wouldn't be quite honest,' said Dinah, 'and I don't think we should like travelling with a dead sheep either. It would get in the way, and it might smell. I think we had better be honest and tidy, even though it is extravagant. How much bread shall we need?'

'I like biscuits,' said Dorinda.

'We must have some bread,' said Dinah, and wrote:

> 1 loaf of bread
> 2 large tins of mixed biscuits
> 1 pound of butter
> 3 pounds of sausages

'Cocoa and jam and condensed milk,' said Dorinda.

'Tooth-paste, soap, a pork pie, and some apples,' said Dinah.

'Chocolate,' said Dorinda.

'Books and a pack of cards and a tin-opener,' said Dinah.

'What's the tin-opener for?'

'To open tins, of course.'

'But we haven't got any tins.'

'I was just going to write them down,' said Dinah, and wrote:

> 3 tins of pineapple chunks
> 3 tins of tinned pears
> 3 tins of peaches

'And sardines,' said Dorinda, 'and I'm going to wear my corduroy trousers, and we ought to take our winter overcoats because it may be cold in the dungeon.'

' We don't mean to stay in the dungeon,' said Dinah.

' No, but we may have to,' said Dorinda.

' Then we ought to take some more books,' said Dinah, ' and some cushions to sit on.'

' I hope Professor Bultek leaves plenty of room for us in the furniture van.'

' We do seem to be taking rather a lot, but even so we've probably forgotten some of the most important things of all. Let's go over the list and see.'

' Sugar,' said Dorinda, ' and spoons.'

' Towels,' said Dinah.

' Won't the sheet do for towels ? '

' It might. But we ought to have a map.'

' And a file,' said Dorinda.

' What do you want a file for ? '

' There may be a window in the dungeon with bars over it.'

' That's a *very* good idea,' said Dinah. ' And we must take an electric torch, and some matches in case it doesn't work.'

' And some cheese.'

' I'm not very fond of cheese.'

' Neither am I, but there are sure to be mice in the dungeon, and we can use the cheese to tame them and make pets of them, in case we get in and can't get out again.'

' We shan't be making pets in the dungeon,' said Dinah. ' We'll be making plans. Plans to get out of it.'

'We can't spend all our time making plans, or we'd have so many we wouldn't know which one to choose.'

'Oh, well,' said Dinah, 'if you want to tame mice, I suppose you must. But when we're going to Gliedermannheim simply to rescue Father from a dungeon, I don't feel it's the proper thing to be making preparations to enjoy ourselves.'

'Then why are you taking so many books?'

'You can learn about all sorts of things from books.'

'And you can learn a lot from animals too, and mice are animals, aren't they?'

'Very little ones.'

'The biggest animal in the zoo,' said Dorinda, 'was Mr. Parker. And he was really the stupidest. So it's silly to despise things for being small.'

'You're quite right,' said Dinah.

'Well,' said Dorinda, 'I shall tame some mice if I want to.' And she took the pencil from Dinah and wrote:

A quarter of a pound of cheese

Then both were silent for several minutes, for neither could think of anything else, and at last Dinah said, 'That's enough for the present. Let's take the list and show it to Mr. Corvo.'

Mr. Corvo was looking worried. He also had been trying to make a list of necessary stores, but all he had written was:

My swordstick and fountain-pen dagger
A pair of slippers
Olive oil

' What is the olive oil for ? ' asked Dinah.

' It is very good for cooking things in,' said Mr. Corvo.

' But what are you going to cook in it ? ' asked Dorinda.

' I do not know,' said Mr. Corvo. ' I am not a good housekeeper, and I cannot imagine what I shall want to eat in a furniture van.'

' We have a list of things here,' said Dinah, and showed him what she had written.

' But this is magnificent ! ' said Mr. Corvo. ' You have thought of everything. How clever you both are ! I have been thinking all day, but to no more purpose than you see — slippers and olive oil are very useful, but we shall need something more on a journey of three days — and now you come with the complete and perfect catalogue of all we can possibly require. Brilliant and charming Dinah ! Exquisite and accomplished Dorinda ! I admire you, I am devoted to you, I salute you ! '

And raising first Dinah's hand, then Dorinda's, to his lips, Mr. Corvo kissed them in turn with the utmost courtesy.

' It's going to be rather difficult,' said Dinah, ' to collect all our stores and pack them properly. A lot of them, of course, we can get at home, but others we shall have to buy. And how shall we take them to the furniture van ? We don't even know where it is.'

' The furniture vans,' said Mr. Corvo, ' will be at Starveling Hall, the Duke's house, where some are already being loaded under the supervision of my friend Bultek. Do not worry about the packing and transport of our stores. I shall provide everything and have them sent in good time to Starveling Hall. Then, if you will come here on Wednesday afternoon, there will be a motor-car waiting, and we shall follow them to Starveling and embark upon our journey. Ah, Gliedermannheim, my poor city, I shall see you again ! It is so beautiful a city, it will break my heart — and Count Hulagu Bloot is so villainous a tyrant, he may break my neck ! Courage, my children, we must be brave and cunning and very resolute ! Go now, and I shall practise fencing with my swordstick for an hour.'

'What sort of clothes should we wear ? ' asked Dinah.

' Clothes that have not many buttons,' said Mr. Corvo. ' It is a great nuisance when buttons come off.'

Mr. Corvo, who had already begun to fence, was clearly not interested in the subject of their travelling clothes, so they said good-bye and went home.

The Falcon came to their window at bedtime and asked what their news was. They told him of the arrangements they had made, and then he said, ' I too shall come to Bombardy. I had intended, very soon, to return to Greenland, but I do not like to let you and the Puma go on such an adventure without me. No, do not thank me. I owe you my liberty, and that is a boon I can never repay. Nor is it difficult for me to travel wherever I wish, and it will be good to see yet another country. I shall have many tales to tell my own people, who are not numerous, when at last I go home.'

A little while later he asked, ' What shall I tell the Puma ? '

' Tell her,' said Dinah, ' to be at the cross-roads on the other side of Midmeddlecum, where the long row of beeches begins, at six o'clock on Wednesday. Mr. Corvo is taking us to Starveling Hall in a motor-car. We'll stop at the cross-roads and pick her up.'

' You will not see her till then,' said the Falcon. ' She is leaving the Forest, and for the next few days will be hunting far to the west. I found some wilder country where there are sheep in plenty, and I think she can eat her fill there without being harried by the farmers. But truly this country of yours is too small both for her and me. It is a pleasant land, but there are too many people for hunters such as we are, and too little room. And now good-night. Sleep well, and dream of your father's freedom.'

But neither Dinah nor Dorinda found it easy to sleep, that night or the following nights, till Wednesday came ; and every day Miss Serendip's ill-temper grew worse, for they paid no attention to any lesson except geography, and all the geography they wanted to learn was that of Bombardy.

Their mother, by good fortune, remained in London, so they had less need to worry about going away without saying good-bye. On Wednesday afternoon they wrote her a letter and left it on the dressing-table in her bedroom. It said : *Dear Mother, we are going to Bombardy to rescue Father. We thought you would like us to, because he is now in prison. You need not worry about us, we are very good at rescuing people. With love from Dinah and Dorinda.*

Then they went to Mr. Corvo's house and found

a motor-car waiting, but Mr. Corvo was still packing. He had a very small suitcase into which he was trying to squeeze four loaves of bread, three shirts, three pairs of socks, an alarm-clock, a canvas bucket, a jar of raspberry jam, a yellow waistcoat, a large railway time-table, and an omelette-pan.

' All these things are things we may need,' he said. ' Now if you will sit upon the lid, perhaps I can close it. Sit tight ! Good. There it is ! And now — off we go ! '

They stopped at the cross - roads, and while Dorinda occupied the attention of the driver by offering him a piece of toffee, Dinah opened a door and let in the Puma. She had been hiding in a ditch, and looked very well-fed after her hunting in the west country. Mr. Corvo, though a little nervous when introduced to her, quickly became friendly, and they had a pleasant journey to Starveling Hall.

There they met Professor Bultek. He was a fat little man with broad shoulders, a short face, a flat nose, and no neck. He had little eyes, an enormous mouth, a greenish complexion, and as Mr. Corvo had said, he looked uncommonly like a frog, though he wore a purple suit. He spoke English fairly well but seldom more than two or three words at a time, and these he usually repeated.

When Dinah and Dorinda were introduced to him, he bowed and said, ' Honoured, honoured. Your father's children, father's children. Father my friend. Glad to help, glad to help.'

Then he looked at his watch and exclaimed, ' Late, late. Come quick. Van there, van there.'

Five enormous furniture vans stood in a row
before the front door of Starveling Hall. The

drivers and the men who had loaded them were
having their tea, and there was no one about but
the prospective travellers. Professor Bultek gave a
little scream when he saw the Puma and began to

run away, but Mr. Corvo called him back and told him that the Puma was a friend of the family. The Professor was only partly reassured, and walked on tiptoe so as not to attract the Puma's attention. He was frightened again, and gave another little scream when the Falcon came suddenly falling from the sky and settled on the roof of the van that Dinah and Dorinda were to travel in.

'He also is a friend of the family,' said Mr. Corvo.

Professor Bultek said something in his own language that Dinah and Dorinda could not understand, but it sounded as though he were angry. He opened the door of the van, however, and pointed to a little tunnel through the mass of furniture that filled it from floor to roof.

'Go in, go in,' he said. 'Hands and knees, hands and knees. Straight through.'

Mr. Corvo led the way, Dorinda followed him, then came the Puma, and then Dinah. And no sooner was Dinah in the tunnel, which was no broader nor higher than the inside of a barrel, than Professor Bultek closed the door behind her, and swung a long iron bar into position to hold it more firmly, and locked a great padlock on the bar.

Now, thought Dinah, listening to the banging of the door and the clattering of the iron bar, now we must go to Bombardy whether we like it or not, for there's no escape. There's no escape!

Oh dear, she said to herself, why ever did we think of doing something so horribly dangerous, and fearfully difficult, and dreadfully uncomfortable as this?

' It all comes,' she muttered, ' of the wind on the moon that made us naughty for a year. Because there's no denying that it's very naughty indeed to leave home without Mother's permission, or any-one's permission, and the police, I suppose, would consider it really wicked to smuggle yourself into a foreign country in a furniture van. And yet if we do rescue Father and bring him home again, that will be a good thing. But where naughtiness ends and goodness begins, I don't know. I wonder if anyone knows ? '

Then she heard Dorinda calling, ' Dinah, Dinah ! Where are you ? '

' I'm coming,' she answered, and crawling a little farther found herself in a very small room whose walls were made of chairs and tables and packing-cases and a wardrobe and an empty bookcase. It was just long enough to hold a sofa, and it was lighted by an oil lamp that hung from a hook in the roof of the van.

' This is Mr. Corvo's room,' said Dorinda. ' Ours is farther on. Do come and see it.'

Crawling through another narrow tunnel she led the way to a room not unlike Mr. Corvo's, but slightly bigger. One of its walls was the forward end of the furniture van. The left-hand wall was an enormous oil-painting, in a heavy gold frame, of the third Duke of Starveling in the handsome robes of a Knight of the Garter ; and the right-hand wall consisted of a gigantic mahogany wardrobe. The rear wall, through which they had entered the room, was made of two high chests of drawers, or tallboys. There was a carpet on the floor, there were some cushions, a small table, and two sofas.

' And we've got a real window,' said Dorinda. She pulled out the drawers of one of the tallboys so as to make a flight of steps, and, climbing up, opened a small trap-door in the roof of the van. ' We can get in and out if we want to, and if the nights are fine we can sit on the roof and talk to the Falcon.'

' Where is the Puma going to sleep ? '

' In the wardrobe,' said Dorinda. ' There are two rugs in it, so she'll be quite all right, and you and I will have the sofas. Professor Bultek has unpacked all the food and things and put them in that other chest of drawers. Wasn't it tidy of him ? And isn't it a perfectly adorable room, Dinah ? '

' I think we're going to be far more comfortable than I expected.'

' Our journey has begun ! ' exclaimed Mr. Corvo. ' Listen ! '

They heard the slight noise of a motor throbbing, and the walls trembled.

' Come down, Dorinda ! '

' We're off ! ' said Mr. Corvo. ' Three cheers ! Hurrah ! '

The van started abruptly and he fell against the portrait of the third Duke of Starveling. ' He would be very angry if he were still alive,' said Mr. Corvo. ' I beg Your Grace's pardon, Your Grace.'

' I'm hungry,' said Dorinda. ' Let's have supper.'

They set out the primus stove and lighted it, and made cocoa, and put plates on the table, and opened a tin of fruit, and cut bread and butter, and ate a lot of chocolate biscuits, and then opened another tin of fruit, and had some slices of a seven-pound plum cake that Mr. Corvo had brought in case there wasn't enough for them on the original store-list.

' I also brought some tins of salmon and some lemonade,' he said, ' and because this is our first meal together, and therefore a kind of birthday feast, I propose that we shall now have some salmon and lemonade.'

So they all made a very good supper except the Puma, who had eaten so much the day before that she was already asleep in the wardrobe. Then they washed the plates, using a piece of the sheet that Dinah had taken from the spare bedroom, and water from a hot-water bottle. In the bottom drawers of the left-hand tallboy there were twenty-four bottles of various kinds — stone hot-water bottles and rubber hot-water bottles and wine bottles and ginger-beer bottles — all full of water ; and in Mr. Corvo's room, as part of one of the walls, there was a washstand with a jug and two basins, one of which they used for washing the dishes.

Then they sat and talked, and presently Mr. Corvo went to his own room, and they all lay down and slept.

Some time during the night the van stopped, and Dinah, half waking, heard a voice from the tunnel : ' Can I come in, please ? '

' I think,' said Mr. Corvo, who had an electric torch and was wearing a crimson silk dressing-gown, ' that we are now in the railway station at Dover. Now they must unfasten the body of the van, and lift it on to a railway truck. Then we shall make a little journey, a very short one, on the train ferry. We shall be crossing the Channel ! '

They heard voices outside, and men working, and someone climbing to the roof of the van. Then they heard the noise of a crane, and something heavy fell with a crash on the roof. That was the great steel hook by which the van was to be lifted.

The ropes were made fast, there was some more shouting, and jerkily the room began to move. It rose a little with one side higher than the other so that the floor was sloping, then rose with another jerk, swung sideways, travelled forward, and then, jerkily again, began to descend. It met the floor of the railway truck on to which it was being lowered with a bump and a second bump, bang came the hook on the roof, another man climbed up and walked noisily to and fro, on both sides of them people were loudly talking, and someone was whistling *Daisy, Daisy, give me your answer do.*

At last the noises died away, for which they were very glad, and Mr. Corvo cautiously opened the trap-door and looked out. The night was not uncomfortably dark.

'There is no one in sight,' he said. 'If you would like to go out for a little walk, it will be quite safe. But do not go far.'

So Dinah and Dorinda, hurriedly dressing, climbed out on to the roof, and down the side of the van by an iron ladder, and jumped off the truck. The train, of which their truck formed a part, was in a goods yard outside the station. In the darkness

They climbed down the side of the van

the great furniture vans seemed larger than ever, and the deserted yard was cold and cheerless. A wind blew strongly from the sea, and suddenly they both felt very unhappy.

' I wish we weren't going to Bombardy,' said Dorinda.

' So do I,' said Dinah.

' We needn't,' said Dorinda. ' It isn't too late to change our minds and go home.'

' I'm afraid it is,' said Dinah. ' Think how disappointed Mr. Corvo would be. Think of all the trouble that Professor Bultek has taken to make us comfortable. Think of having to explain to the Puma and the Falcon that we're frightened. And think of Father.'

' Oh dear,' said Dorinda, ' there are always so many things to think about, and I hate thinking.'

' Come on,' said Dinah, and taking Dorinda by the hand led her back to the truck. They climbed up and went through the trap-door into their room again. They found Mr. Corvo cutting a hole in the floor with a hammer and a chisel.

' I have found a tool-chest,' he said. ' It is a most useful thing to find. I also discovered that between the bottom of the van and the floor of the truck there is a space of several inches. So when I have cut this hole we shall be able to pour away the dirty water in which knives and plates and forks are being washed from day to day. That will be a convenient arrangement.'

Having cut a hole in the floor, six inches square, Mr. Corvo took the lid of a biscuit-tin, beat the edges flat, laid it over the hole, spread the carpet on top, and proudly declared, ' Now there is no draught and everything is perfect ! Let us all go to bed again, and do not wake until we are at sea.'

They heard in their dreams the noise of shunting, of engines whistling, of trucks clashing their iron buffers together, of men calling, and a ship's siren, but they were tired with the excitement of beginning their journey, and neither Dinah nor Dorinda woke until the table slid down the floor and fell noisily against a tallboy. Then Dinah opened her eyes and saw the walls leaning this way, then leaning the other, and the drawers sliding out of the tallboy, then sliding in again. She heard a hundred noises, of wood creaking, and ropes straining, and the furniture grumbling as it moved to and fro, and the wind howling, and waves thumping and slapping the sides of the ship. She had a curious feeling as though her stomach were swimming like a celluloid duck when you sweep a sponge up and down the bath ; and when she sat up she felt so dizzy that she had to lie down again.

' Oh, Dorinda ! ' she cried.

' Oh, Dinah ! ' cried Dorinda. ' I'm going to be sick ! '

Then softly from the wardrobe the Puma began to howl in a minor key. ' Oh, oh ! ' she cried. ' Why ever did I come to sea ? Oh, misery ! Sorrow is me. Woe, woe, woe ! '

' Poor Puma,' said Dinah.

' Poor us,' said Dorinda.

' You mustn't be sick,' said Dinah.

' I must,' said Dorinda.

THE WIND ON THE MOON

The waves slapped the sides of the ship, the walls leaned this way and that, the furniture creaked and grumbled, the ship strained, and the wind shouted like an angry giant chasing a little giant who had been throwing stones at him. For nearly an hour Dinah and Dorinda were desperately unhappy, and then the sea grew calmer, and Dinah said faintly, ' It was very thoughtful of Mr. Corvo to cut a hole in the floor.'

' It was very useful,' said Dorinda.

A tired voice came from the tunnel : ' May I come in, please ? '

Mr. Corvo crawled in and lay on the floor. ' I do not want to get up,' he said. ' It is more comfortable like this.'

' We're beginning to feel better,' said Dinah.

' I came to see if you want some breakfast,' said Mr. Corvo.

' No ! ' cried Dorinda. ' No, no, no ! '

' Then I shall go back to my own room,' said Mr. Corvo, ' for I do not want any either. How is the Puma ? '

' Would that I had stayed in the Forest of Weal,' moaned the Puma. ' It would have been less pain to be torn to pieces by the angry hounds than to suffer like this ! '

They fell into a half-sleep again and paid no attention to the bustle and busyness and the voices outside, that now spoke French, when the ship docked and the trucks were run ashore and shunted into a siding. In the early afternoon there was more shunting, they became part of a train, and the train set off on its journey. Then, when the train was running smoothly, with a pleasant rhythmical noise, Dinah sat and exclaimed, ' Dorinda ! We're abroad ! Do you realise that ? We're in a foreign country.'

' I'm hungry,' said Dorinda.

' What is there to eat ? ' asked the Puma.

' Can I come in, please ? ' said Mr. Corvo.

' I'm going to look at the view,' said Dinah, and climbed up to open the trap-door in the roof.

Quite suddenly they were all happy again, and everyone felt hungry and excited. They ate an enormous meal, and took turns in climbing up the chest of drawers to look at the flat well-tilled fields of France that went rolling past.

The rest of the day passed quickly, and when night came the train stopped in a little town where it was divided into two, and the furniture van trucks were shunted on to a siding outside the town. There they remained for two or three hours, and Dinah and Dorinda, Mr. Corvo and the Puma, got out and had a walk, and met the Falcon who, high in the sky, had followed the train without difficulty. Then they went back and slept soundly.

The following day seemed very long. The train was running through wooded country, between hills and beside rivers, with here a turreted castle among the trees and there a town at the end of a bridge, and if they had all been sitting comfortably beside a broad window, looking at the ever-changing view, the hours would have gone by pleasantly enough. But they could look through the trap-door only one at a time, and always when they stood with head through the roof they had to come down in a few minutes to take cinders out of their eyes. The day was hot and the room grew stuffy, and the creaking of the closely packed furniture seemed to be getting louder and louder.

Dinah yawned and Dorinda grumbled and they became more and more impatient. They wanted to reach Gliedermannheim as quickly as thought could take them, they wanted to arrive within five minutes, or ten minutes at the most, and see their father. But also, as they came nearer and nearer to Bombardy, they could not help feeling a little frightened of what might happen when they got there. They tried to imagine what the Castle was like, and what the people were like. They looked at Mr. Corvo and wondered if many of the Bombards were like him, or if more resembled Professor Bultek.

' What do people talk about in Bombardy ? ' asked Dorinda.

' When I was a small boy,' said Mr. Corvo, ' everybody talked about buried treasure. There was an old man who lived on the side of a mountain, and one day when he was digging a grave to bury his old sheep-dog, which had died, he found a box with six hundred gold coins in it, many of them very large and heavy. After that nearly everybody began to dig, in their spare time, hoping to find treasure, and wherever you went you met people who would tell you about the holes they had made, and what were the best places in which to look for gold.'

' Did they find a lot ? ' asked Dinah.

' They found none at all,' said Mr. Corvo. ' Nobody, that is, except the old man on the mountain. But nevertheless, for a long time, their conversation was all about buried treasure.'

' And what did they talk about next ? ' asked Dorinda.

' About the holes they had made,' said Mr. Corvo. ' Some were no bigger than a bucket, and some were as big as a barrel. Some were as little as teacups, and some were as deep as a well. But wherever you went, all over Bombardy, there were holes of one sort or another, and a lot of people thought they should be filled up again, and a lot more people said that trees should be planted in them, and a few people were still of the opinion that the earth was full of gold, and all the holes should be dug deeper and deeper till it was discovered. So there was a lot of talk about that.'

' And what did they do with the holes ? ' asked Dinah.

' Nothing,' said Mr. Corvo. ' Nothing at all. They left them alone.'

' What do people talk about now ? ' asked Dorinda.

' Very little,' said Mr. Corvo. ' They have become a silent people, because our infamous Tyrant, Count Hulagu Bloot, has a thousand spies who go everywhere and listen to all that is said, by men and women, throughout the country. And if anyone speaks against Count Hulagu, he is arrested and put in prison. And as there is a great temptation to speak against him, because he is always doing some vile, iniquitous, and cruel thing, the people, to guard their safety, have almost stopped talking. They go about almost in silence now.'

Slowly the day passed. Mr. Corvo told them about Bombardy and its people, and every now and then they would climb on to the roof of the van and look at the view, and then come down again to wipe the cinders from their eyes.

Evening came, and when it was dark the train once more stopped in a siding to let faster trains go by, and they all got out and walked in a field beside the railway, and had some conversation with the Falcon. Then they returned to the stuffy furniture van and slept for a little while, but were wakened when the train started again.

' We must be getting very near Bombardy now,' said Dinah.

' Are you frightened ? '

' Not exactly. I'm not feeling perfectly happy, but I don't think I'm frightened.'

' Nor am I,' said Dorinda, ' but I've got the sort of pain in my stomach that I get when I am, and I thought that if we put the sofas side by side we could sleep together, and that would be more comfortable, don't you think ? '

Hearing the furniture being shifted, the Puma woke in the wardrobe and asked what was the matter.

' We're going to sleep together,' said Dinah.

A moment later they saw beside them the yellow gleam of two bright eyes, and lightly, nimbly, the Puma leapt into the double bed which the pair of sofas made, and lay down between them.

' Feel the muscle of my shoulders and my legs,' she said. ' Put your hands upon my neck, and now upon my jaw. Can you see, in this darkness, how thick and sharp and strong are my claws when I bare them ? Often in my native forest I had to fight, and fight fiercely, and I was never defeated except once by trickery. And now all my strength is here for your protection. Do not be afraid, for I shall look after you.'

The Puma's presence was so comforting, and her words so reassuring, and her silky hide so soft to lean against, that Dinah and Dorinda quickly fell asleep, and though the bed grew rather hot, with all three lying side by side, they slept till late in the morning and had to be wakened by Mr. Corvo. He came in and shook them gently, and when they opened their eyes they found breakfast ready. There was tinned fruit and condensed milk and boiled eggs and bread and butter and buns and jam for Dinah and Dorinda, and the remains of the leg of pork for the Puma.

Mr. Corvo waited till they had finished eating, and then he said, ' We are now in Bombardy. In about four hours' time we shall be in Gliedermann-heim. When we get to the station they will have to take the furniture vans off the railway trucks and put them on to lorries. Then they will drive us to the Castle, which is seven miles from the station. It is unlikely, I think, that we shall reach the Castle before six or seven o'clock, and then it will be too late to start unpacking the vans. — That is my opinion, and Bultek, when we were planning the journey, agreed with me. — So they will leave the furniture vans in the courtyard of the Castle till morning before they open them. But when it becomes quite dark we shall climb out and find our way into the Castle, and begin to look for your father.

' In the courtyard, which is surrounded by high walls, it will be as dark as the bottom of a well, and no one will see us. And there is sure to be some door left open, for all we Bombards are careless about such matters, and wherever we go we lose our keys.'

To begin with, everything happened as Mr. Corvo said it would. The train reached Gliedermannheim, there was more jolting and swaying and swinging and bumping as the vans were lifted off the railway trucks, and then, after a long delay, they began the last stage of their journey, from the station to the Castle. They travelled slowly now, for the road ran steeply uphill, and there were many sharp corners to be turned. As they approached the Castle the noise of the motor echoed from stone walls, and they drove under a great archway and into the courtyard beyond.

When the motor was switched off they could hear soldiers marching, their boots ringing on the pavement, and an officer shouting orders in a strange language. The soldiers came to a halt, all their boots striking the pavement together, and twenty-four trumpets sounded. Then a military band began to play, marching with drums and fifes, and after that there was another fanfare of trumpets. More orders were shouted, there was the noise of marching again, and then silence. All the music and all the marching called a hundred echoes from the great walls of the courtyard, and in the furniture van the noise seemed deafening.

' They were playing the Evening Salute,' whispered Mr. Corvo. ' They play it every evening, an hour after sunset, when they haul down the ensign that flies from the flagstaff on the highest tower. Soon it will be dark.'

Within the van it was already dark, and now with a feverish impatience they waited for night.

Mr. Corvo sat with his watch in his hand — it had a luminous dial — and at last he rose and very carefully, so as to make no noise, pulled out the drawers of the tallboy that made a ladder to the roof, and, climbing up, opened the trap-door. The sky was dark, and through the opening a single star shone brightly. Mr. Corvo cautiously descended.

' I shall go first,' he whispered, ' and look for an open door. You will stay inside until you hear me knock three times on the side of the van. Then climb out as quickly as you can, but quietly. We must be very quiet, remember.'

' Come back quickly,' said Dorinda.

' As quickly as I can,' said Mr. Corvo, and climbing again to the roof, he disappeared.

Dinah and Dorinda, with the Puma between them and their hands on her silky back, waited in painful excitement.

' How long has he been away ? ' whispered Dorinda.

' About five minutes.'

' Perhaps he can't find an open door. What shall we do then ? '

Before Dinah could reply, there was a sudden clamour, of men shouting and iron gates flung open, and the sky above the trap-door quivered and grew bright in the sudden glare of searchlights.

Their powdery radiance poured into the van, and among the startling shadows Dinah stared at Dorinda, Dorinda at her, and their faces were white as paper.

Chapter Thirty-One

The Castle of Gliedermannheim was built on top of a rocky hill. It looked something like a crown on a king's head : a little crown perched on the summit of a huge, knobbly, sallow-coloured, bald head. The city lay on the plain below, a mass of red and yellow roofs with church towers and greenish domes rising among them, and the tops of the trees that grew in the principal streets looking from a distance like hedgerows. The steep winding road that led to the Castle was also lined with trees, and branching from it across the hill, like the veins of a leaf, were lesser roads with villas and rich merchants' houses built beside them.

The Castle was enormously strong and rather ugly. Two square towers, with pointed turrets, guarded the entrance, and above the archway that connected them and led to the outer courtyard were several rooms where the Officers of the Guard lived. The outer courtyard was nearly as big as a football field, and paved with flagstones. To right and left of it were the barracks that housed the soldiers of the Guard, and opposite the archway was the enormous front door of the Castle itself. This was a square building enclosing an inner courtyard, with a square tower at each corner twice as high as the towers that guarded the entrance, and the one at the north-eastern corner highest of all. From the base of its northern and eastern walls the hill fell away as steeply as a precipice, and below these walls were the dungeons. They were lighted only by narrow shafts cut through the rock.

Above the front door was the banqueting hall, and on the same floor in the tower to the right of it was Count Hulagu Bloot's private suite. The banqueting hall was decorated with glittering suits of armour and gigantic oil paintings of the Rulers of Bombardy through the ages, and of scenes of battle ; while the walls of Count Hulagu's private sitting-room were hung with disgusting pictures of people being tortured, and the skins of tigers, lions, bears, and leopards, the heads of which rested on little shelves and glared into the room through great glass eyes, and snarled with bared and yellow teeth. In one corner were some dumb-bells, a skipping-rope, and a Sandow developer for the muscles ; and in another corner a bookcase with a book in it called *How to Make Friends and Influence People.*

Count Hulagu was a middle-aged man with a long yellow face and thick lips the colour of mulberries. His hair grew like stubble in a barley field, he had little greenish glittering eyes, a long nose with a wart on it, and whiskers grew out of his ears. He generally wore a white uniform with gold epaulettes, a purple sash, and a good many medals ; but he never looked really handsome because one of his arms was longer than the other, and his feet were enormous.

On the evening when Dinah and Dorinda arrived in the furniture van, he was walking up and down his sitting-room with a frown on his face. He was feeling bored and also a little sick, because he had eaten too many chocolate éclairs and cream buns at tea-time. He had tried to read, but the book in his bookcase no longer interested him. He thought of sending out for some people to torture, but as well as feeling sick he had a slight headache,

and their screams, he decided, would make it worse. So he walked up and down and looked at the pictures on the walls and the skins of the lions and the tigers, the leopards and the bears; and the pictures, he now perceived, were badly painted, and the skins were dusty and some were moth-eaten. He decided to have them all removed and replaced by new ones. And then, quite suddenly, he remembered that a few weeks ago he had sent Professor Bultek to England to buy the Duke of Starveling's furniture.

Drawing his revolver, he fired six shots at the ceiling. This was to summon the Lord Chamberlain. He used to fire one shot for a page-boy, two for a parlourmaid, three for his valet, four for the butler, five for the Officer Commanding the Guard, and six for the Lord Chamberlain. And as the ceiling was covered with half-inch armour-plate, no harm was done.

The Lord Chamberlain was a tall man with a handsome face, but his mouth had a nervous twitch, and during the three months that he had held office he had developed a stutter.

He opened the door, bowed, and said, ' What does Your Ek-ek-excellency want, Your Ek-ek-excellency ? '

' New pictures and new furniture ! ' shouted Count Hulagu. ' The Duke of Starveling's furniture from England. Where is Bultek ? Why hasn't it arrived ? '

' It c-c-came this evening, Your Ek-ek-excellency. The v-v-vans are in the c-c-courtyard now.'

' Why wasn't I told at once ? Have them unpacked now, immediately ! I want my room refurnished. Unpack, unpack ! '

' But it's d-d-dark, Your Ek-ek-excellency.'

' There are searchlights on the Castle towers. Turn them on ! Let the courtyard be made as bright as day, and then unpack, unpack ! '

While the Lord Chamberlain hurried away as hard as he could, to do what he had been told, Count Hulagu fired three shots at the ceiling to bring his valet, to fetch him an overcoat ; and five shots to summon the Officer Commanding the Guard, to turn out the Guard to help with the unpacking.

Then he went down into the courtyard, the searchlights were turned on, doors were flung open, soldiers and servants appeared from all directions — and in the little room in their furniture van Dinah and Dorinda and the Puma waited with dread and dismay in their hearts.

Fearful thoughts perplexed them. What had happened, and what was going to happen ? What had become of Mr. Corvo ?

Then they heard the door of their van being unlocked and pulled open, they heard rough voices speaking an unknown language, and the scraping, groaning noise of furniture being pulled out.

' They're beginning to unpack ! ' whispered Dinah.

' They'll find us ! ' murmured Dorinda. ' What can we do ? '

' Hide ! ' growled the Puma.

' But where ? ' asked Dinah. ' In the wardrobe ? '

' There's room for us all,' said the Puma.

' But they'll see what's left of the food and the other things we brought,' said Dorinda.

Dinah whispered fiercely, ' Put them away ! Put them into drawers, get them out of sight. But quickly, Dorinda, quickly ! '

' Open the bottom drawer of the wardrobe,' said the Puma. ' There's room for me there. Then lock it and take the key. You can stand, one on either side, in the upper part of it, and keep the doors closed as well as you can.'

The upper part, which had two doors, was divided by a partition, and along the inner side of the left-hand door ran a strong brass rail.

' I'll lock Dorinda in the right-hand side,' whispered Dinah, ' and I can hold the brass rail to keep the other door shut. Listen ! They're much nearer now. Oh, do hurry, Dorinda ! '

' Why don't you come and help me ? ' said Dorinda. She put a jar of raspberry jam and the remains of the Puma's sirloin of beef into a drawer in the tallboy, looked round to see that everything had been cleared away, and climbed into the wardrobe.

The men who were unpacking were working swiftly, and already they had taken out half the furniture. Now their voices came from close at hand, and their boots on the floor of the van sounded loud and threatening. The back wall of the little room was already trembling as Dinah locked the Puma into the bottom drawer of the wardrobe, locked Dorinda into the right-hand side, and climbing into the other, closed the door and held it firmly shut.

Presently, after a lot more noise, the wardrobe was seized, pulled forward, tilted on to its side, and dragged out of the van. The men who were handling it grumbled loudly, and though Dinah and Dorinda could not understand what they were saying, it was easy to guess that they were complaining about the weight of it. But Dinah and Dorinda had no time to sympathise with the men, for they had worries of their own. Now they lay on one side, now they were tumbled roughly to the other, and all the time Dinah had to keep firm hold of the brass rail to prevent the door from flying open.

The wardrobe was lowered to the courtyard with a bump that jarred their backbones, and it stood there for several minutes till the Lord Chamberlain had asked Count Hulagu where it should be taken. Then it was lifted again, lifted high on the shoulders of six men, and now Dinah and Dorinda found themselves lying on their backs. The six men carried the wardrobe through the front door of the Castle, up a flight of stone steps, round a corner, and up more steps ; and while they were going upstairs Dinah and Dorinda lay uncomfortably with their heels higher than their heads.

They were carried along a corridor, and the wardrobe was set down in a room of some sort, more gently this time. They waited in silence, not daring to speak, and for half an hour or more they listened to the noise of men bringing more and more pieces of furniture into the room, and loud voices talking. Then there was silence, and Dinah, tapping gently on the partition between her and Dorinda, whispered, ' Are you all right ? '

' I think so,' Dorinda answered. ' Do you know where we are ? '

' I haven't any idea,' said Dinah. ' I'm going to count a thousand, very slowly, and then, if it's still quiet, I'll look out and see. And if it's safe I'll let you out then.'

She counted a thousand, and gently opening the door, not more than an inch or so, looked out. She could see, on the opposite side of the room, some part of a huge oil-painting of a man in a plumed hat and a scarlet cloak on a dapple-grey charger. The man looked fierce and masterful, but the horse had a kindly eye and an expression of great good-will. A little to one side of the picture there was a handsome suit of armour. The room, which appeared to be large, was dimly lit.

She opened the door a little wider, and saw more pictures on the wall, more suits of armour, and a great many pieces of furniture, in no sort of order, all over the floor. So far as she could discover, there was nobody in the room except themselves.

Cautiously she got out of the wardrobe, and tip-toeing here and there made certain that they were alone. A single electric light shone high on the gilded ceiling. ' I suppose,' she murmured, ' that the men who brought up the furniture forgot to turn it out. That was very careless indeed, but lucky for us, so perhaps I shouldn't blame them.'

Then she unlocked Dorinda's door, and Dorinda, she perceived, was looking pale.

' You haven't been sick again, have you ? ' she asked.

' Very nearly,' said Dorinda, ' but not quite. — Oh, look, Dinah ! Look ! '

From behind a suit of armour on the other side of the room appeared the figure of a man. ' So we are reunited ! ' he said. ' How very fortunate we are ! '

Chapter Thirty-Two

'You gave us rather a fright,' said Dinah severely. 'Why is your face all black?'

'Is it?' asked Mr. Corvo. 'I didn't know. It must be dirt and grease from the under part of the furniture van. I had to conceal myself beneath it when the searchlights went on. I was on my way back to tell you that I had found an open door when suddenly, as though the moon had come down too close upon the courtyard, like a shining lid, everything was staring-white in that fearful brilliance! So I ran, I ducked, I dived, and took cover under the van. And there I lay while they unloaded it, wondering all the time, with agony in my heart, what would become of you when they found you. But they did not find you, and I guessed what had happened. I said to myself, " They have hidden themselves in the great wardrobe! Ah, clever girls! " Then I spoke to myself the second time and said, " I, Casimir Corvo, shall not fail them! " So I watched carefully for a chance to escape, and presently I saw two men carrying a huge and heavy carpet. It had been rolled up like a sausage, but it was beginning to unroll, and the man at the back end was not only staggering under the weight of it, but half hidden by the folds of it. So I crept out and gave him a little prick with my sword. He screamed, dropped his end of the carpet, looked round to see who had pricked him, and ran in the wrong direction. Immediately I gathered up the carpet, which fell all round me, hiding me almost completely, and shouted to the man at the front end, " Ruhry, mai, reeth tse chum a refai ! "   That, is Bombast, which is our language here, and means " Hurry, friend, there is much to do."   So on we went, following the great wardrobe, and came into this room, which is the banqueting hall, and I took a favourable opportunity to hide myself in that suit of armour.'

' It's very comforting to see you again,' said Dorinda.

' And it was very clever of you to hide under the carpet,' said Dinah.

Mr. Corvo bowed his thanks and asked where the Puma was.

' Oh dear ! ' exclaimed Dinah, ' I hope she isn't suffocated ! '

Hurriedly she unlocked the wardrobe drawer and the Puma, yawning widely, lifted a drowsy head.

' There was very little air in that drawer,' she said.   ' To be shut inside it was not a pleasant experience.'

Slowly she got out, and stretching her limbs, yawned again and again.   Then she lay down and went to sleep.

' And what are we going to do now? ' asked Dinah.

' You and Dorinda will sleep in Count Hulagu's bed to-night,' said Mr. Corvo.

' Oh, *no !* '

' Where will he be ? ' asked Dorinda.

' Far away,' said Mr. Corvo.   ' Listen carefully to what I am going to tell you.   While I was hiding in the suit of armour Count Hulagu and the Lord

Chamberlain came and stood in front of me, no more than two feet away. They were planning where all the furniture should go. Then an Officer of the Guard arrived and told Count Hulagu that seven men, who for a long time had been plotting against him, had been captured at a place called Lodoban, which is nearly two hundred miles away. " They will be shot at dawn to-morrow," said Count Hulagu, " and I shall be there to see their execution." — He is very cruel, he likes to see people being shot. — Then he told the Lord Chamberlain to get his motor-car at once, and said that no more furniture need be unpacked to-night. So he has gone to Lodoban. It will take him at least five hours to get there. Then there will be the execution. Then he will have breakfast. Let us suppose that he begins to return at nine o'clock to-morrow morning : he will not be here before two in the afternoon. So it will be quite safe for you to sleep in his bed, and you will not even have to get up early.'

' But what will happen if somebody comes in ? ' asked Dorinda.

' Nobody ever enters the Tyrant's private rooms unless he has commanded the presence of somebody by firing his revolver at the ceiling.'

' Do you know where his rooms are ? ' asked Dinah.

' My friend Bultek gave me a plan of the Castle,' said Mr. Corvo, and taking a rather crumpled piece of paper from an inner pocket he pointed to a room marked *Banqueting Hall.*

' That is where we are now,' he said, ' and this

corridor, you see, goes straight to the Tyrant's suite. It is only a few yards away.'

' But won't the doors be locked ? ' asked Dinah.

With a smile of magnificent triumph Mr. Corvo pulled from another pocket a large bunch of keys. ' These are, or used to be, the property of the Lord Chamberlain,' he said proudly.

' However did you get them ? ' asked Dorinda.

' I told you,' said Mr. Corvo, ' that when I was hiding in that suit of armour Count Hulagu and the Lord Chamberlain stood in front of me. Some soldiers were carrying in a grand piano. It was very heavy, and they were moving slowly. Count Hulagu shouted to them to make haste, and the Lord Chamberlain, to show how eager he was to help, took off his coat and went to assist them. But he made the mistake of hanging his coat on the helmet of my suit of armour, and so it was very easy for me to feel in his pockets to find out if there was anything interesting in them.'

' How lucky ! ' said Dinah.

' When I was a little boy,' said Mr. Corvo, ' I used to be told that heaven helps those who help themselves. And now, if you will wake the Puma, we shall go to our rooms. That is to say, Count Hulagu's rooms ! And then, if you are not too sleepy, we shall think of plans for to-morrow. We have made a good beginning : do you not think so ? And to-morrow, perhaps, we may decide to lie in wait for the Tyrant, till he returns from Lodoban, and take him prisoner. That would be a good thing to do, but not very easy. Come along. We shall think of something else.'

Chapter Thirty-Three

Count Hulagu's bedroom was very large and magnificently furnished. The bed, which was big enough for four people, was made of solid silver, the peach-coloured sheets and pillow-slips were the finest silk, and on it lay a plum-red satin eiderdown embroidered in gold with the Tyrant's arms. The other furniture was equally handsome, and there were two mirrors each six feet high and four feet broad. There were three doors in the room : one opened into the private sitting-room, one into a marble bathroom with a silver bath, and one into a dressing-room which was as big as the bedroom and the walls of which were lined with wardrobes full of the Tyrant's gorgeous uniforms. From large windows in each of these rooms there was a magnificent view over miles and scores of miles of rolling, well-wooded, and watered country.

Dinah and Dorinda were lost in admiration for the marvellous bed, and showed very clearly that what they wanted to do was not to discuss plans, but to get between its soft sheets, and stretch their legs in the huge space of it, and lay their heads on the peach-coloured pillows.

'But first,' said Dinah, 'we must have a bath in the silver bath.'

'Very well,' said Mr. Corvo, shrugging his shoulders. 'Go to sleep now and we shall talk in the morning. I am sorry that you will have so unpleasant a picture to greet you when you wake.'

And he pointed to an enlarged photograph, framed in gold, that hung on the wall opposite the bed.

' What an ugly little boy ! ' said Dinah. ' Who is it ? '

' Count Hulagu, when he was seven,' said Mr. Corvo.

' Let's turn his face to the wall,' said Dinah.

' Look what I've found,' said Dorinda, opening a large paper bag that lay on a bedside table.

' Peppermint creams ! There must be about four pounds of them.'

' The Tyrant is very fond of sweets,' said Mr. Corvo. ' He likes to see people being killed, and he likes peppermint creams. He is a strange man. And now, if you will permit me first of all to wash my face and hands — which I now see are as black as a negro — I shall say good-night. The Puma and I will sleep in the sitting-room, so you will be quite safe. There is a very comfortable sofa for me, and a Persian rug for her. I hope you will have pleasant dreams.'

'Fancy sleeping in Count Hulagu's own bed,' said Dorinda half an hour later.

'Fancy sleeping under the same roof as Father,' said Dinah. 'Isn't it exciting to think we're quite near to him again? Oh, I wish we could let him know that we are here!'

'So do I,' said Dorinda.

'Poor Father, he's probably cold and miserable, while we're enjoying every luxury.'

'I don't suppose we'll enjoy luxury for long,' said Dorinda. 'Not after Count Hulagu comes back.'

'I wish I could think of some way to get him out of his dungeon. Father, I mean. Have you thought of anything yet?'

'No,' said Dorinda, 'but I expect Mr. Corvo has. Or if he hasn't, he will. He's very clever, isn't he? Dinah, I think I'll have just one more peppermint cream before I go to sleep.'

'Don't make yourself sick again.'

'Of course not. You talk as though I were always being sick.'

'You nearly were, in the wardrobe.'

'Well, it's very different being in a wardrobe and being in bed.'

'Don't make a mess of the pillow,' said Dinah sleepily.

'They're not our pillows,' Dorinda answered with her mouth full. And then, almost before she knew what was happening, she too was asleep.

They hardly stirred till eight o'clock, when Mr. Corvo came in to wake them. Drowsy as they were, they could see at once that he was very pleased about something, and almost his first words were, 'I have found some information of the greatest importance ! But I shall not tell you now. Not till we have had breakfast. And do not be alarmed when, in order to get breakfast, I make a great noise.'

Mr. Corvo explained the Tyrant's system of calling his servants by firing a revolver at the ceiling, which Professor Bultek had told him about, and added, ' Count Hulagu went away so hurriedly last night that very few people know he is not here. It will be quite safe, or almost quite safe, to order breakfast. I have found two loaded revolvers in the sitting-room, and three more in the billiard-room which is beyond it.'

' There are some here too,' said Dinah, ' and one in the bathroom.'

' The Tyrant is very fond of revolvers,' said Mr. Corvo. ' When he was a little boy, like you see him in that photograph, he shot his school teacher with one. Now I have written this message, order-ing breakfast, which I will place upon the table. Then I will fire a revolver four times at the ceiling, go quickly into the bathroom, and turn on both the taps, so the butler when he comes will think Count Hulagu is having a bath. This is the message.'

Printed in capital letters on a sheet of notepaper were the following words : *Gribn unjerdee tevi. Chi issu resh grunhy. Gribn chess fosue, telpyn skepc, chum feekfa, satto, titsanpipse, lamrameda dun rubeer, dun eni fabseeket.*

' It is written, of course, in our language, in Bombast,' said Mr. Corvo. ' In English it means :

Bring breakfast quickly. I am very hungry. Bring six eggs, plenty bacon, much coffee, toast, rolls, marmalade and butter, and one beefsteak.'

' That should be plenty,' said Dorinda, ' and we can finish up with some peppermint creams. The beefsteak is for the Puma, I suppose ? '

' Of course,' said Mr. Corvo. ' It is too early for us to eat beefsteaks.'

Picking up a revolver he fired four shots at the sitting-room ceiling, and hurrying into the bathroom, turned on the taps. Dinah and Dorinda, kneeling at the bedroom door, took it in turns to look through the keyhole, and saw the Count's butler come in and read the message. In a surprisingly short time he and a parlourmaid brought in an enormous breakfast on an enormous tray, and as soon as they had gone again, Mr. Corvo locked the door, and they all sat down and ate a hearty meal.

' And now,' said Mr. Corvo, when they had eaten everything there was to eat, ' look what I found last night in Count Hulagu's private desk ! It was in that drawer there. The drawer was locked, but what of that ? I took a poker and broke it open. And this is the result ! A list of all the prisoners in the dungeons, nine hundred and forty-two men and women, and your father, alone by himself, in Dungeon Number 200 ! '

' How do we get there ? ' asked Dinah.

' It is not quite easy,' said Mr. Corvo. ' In the plan of the Castle that Bultek drew for me — here it is — there is shown a secret passage from the Tyrant's suite, but it does not make it clear where

He fired four shots at the ceiling

the passage begins. We shall have to look for it.'

' I know where it is,' said Dorinda. ' It's behind the big silver towel-rail in the bathroom. The towel-rail is fastened to the wall, and if you pull it in a certain way the wall opens like a door, and there are stone steps behind it.'

' But how did you find it ? ' cried Mr. Corvo.

' I was doing exercises on it after my bath last night. You know : leaning on it and pressing up and down to strengthen your arms. And while I was pressing, the door in the wall slowly opened. So I closed it again, and went to bed.'

Hurrying into the bathroom, Mr. Corvo gripped the silver towel-rail and pressed as hard as he could. But nothing happened.

' How did you push it ? ' he asked.

' Like this,' said Dorinda, and showed him. And still nothing happened.

' You are sure that a door opened ? '

' Of course I am ! ' said Dorinda indignantly.

' Then why won't it open now ? ' asked Dinah.

' How should I know ? Unless — well, I don't suppose it makes any difference, but I'd unscrewed that knob first. I wanted to see if it was solid silver or just hollow. It's just hollow. And then I couldn't put the knob back the first time I tried, and it was just after that I did my exercises.'

Mr. Corvo was already unscrewing an acorn-shaped knob at the end of the rail, and as soon as it was off, he pushed again. And now, like a door, the marble wall opened, and steeply descending they could see a flight of dark stone steps.

' The secret passage to the dungeons ! ' cried Mr.

Corvo. 'Are we all ready ? Shall we go now ? '

'We ought to make the bed first,' said Dinah. 'Even if it is a tyrant's bed, we ought to be tidy.'

'Then quickly,' said Mr. Corvo, 'make it quickly, and I shall get an electric torch. There was a big one in the drawer that I broke open.'

When they had made the bed, Dinah and Dorinda found the Puma in the bathroom. She was looking at the narrow steps with sad and disconsolate eyes.

'I do not like these dark passages,' she said. 'We go from one prison to another. I do not like these walls that enclose us. To you, who live in houses, they may not be oppressive, but to me they are misery. I dreamt last night of my native forest, and the sunlight hot upon open plains, and the brown river swirling in its flow. And I woke this morning with the knowledge that I shall never see that land again.'

'Oh, you will, you will ! ' said Dinah. 'When we have rescued Father, he will arrange it. He can arrange anything. You'll go in a ship to any port you like, and then you'll have freedom again. Real freedom in your own country.'

'No,' said the Puma sadly. 'I shall never see the forest again.'

'When Father hears how much you have helped us,' said Dorinda, 'he'll do anything for you. Oh, don't look so sad ! '

'It makes any creature sad to know a thing for certain,' said the Puma. 'But pay no heed to me. Think of your father, who is waiting for you.'

'You didn't eat your breakfast,' said Dinah. 'I knew there was something wrong with you.'

Mr. Corvo reappeared with an electric torch in one hand and his swordstick in the other. ' Forward,' he cried. ' En avant ! '

' Wait a minute,' said Dorinda. ' I want to get something first.'

She returned in a moment carrying the Puma's beefsteak wrapped in a napkin, which she gave to Dinah to carry, and the large paper bag of peppermint creams.

' It would be silly to leave these,' she said. ' There must be nearly three pounds here still.'

Mr. Corvo, having closed behind them the door in the wall, took the lead. The stone steps, narrow and difficult, were worn hollow in the middle. Dinah counted them : there were thirty-six. Then they came to a narrow passage between stone walls. It was unlighted, and the air smelt cold and sour. It led to a spiral staircase, stone steps descending like a corkscrew, seventy-two of them. A rope, fastened to iron rings in the wall, made the descent a little easier, and here and there a narrow slit in the masonry let in some light. There was a door at the bottom with a great iron key in the lock. The lock had been oiled, and turned easily enough.

They found themselves in a broader passage, sloping steeply downhill, and this was fairly well lighted by loopholes in the wall. The stone floor was damp and slippery. A few yards from the door there was a notice that read :

XUA TOCCASH

' That means " To the dungeons," ' said Mr. Corvo. ' We are getting near.'

Fifty yards farther on they came to a corner where two more notices read like this :

XUA TOCCASH   XUA TOCCASH
1–100   101–200

They went straight on, and now they trod softly and went warily. The passage was hewn through the rock and the walls were rough and damp to the touch. There was no light here, but the torch showed little iron-bolted doors on the outer side, each with a number. At the very end of the passage was Number 200.

Dinah and Dorinda were by now trembling with excitement, and Mr. Corvo was so agitated that it took him a long time to find the proper key on the Lord Chamberlain's bunch. Dinah had to hold the torch, and Dorinda his swordstick, while he looked for it. At last he found it — there was a master-key for the odd-numbered dungeons and another for the even numbers — and with trembling fingers opened the door.

A figure, sitting on a heap of sacking in a corner of the dungeon, said wearily, ' What do you want now ? '

' Father ! ' cried Dinah and Dorinda in one voice. ' Father ! '

Before he could rise they were kneeling beside him with their arms round his neck and trying to tell him, all at the same time, how glad they were to see him, and how sorry they were for all he had suffered, and how they had managed to find him, and who Mr. Corvo was, and who the Puma was, and what adventures they had had, and how they would now rescue him almost immediately, though they hadn't quite decided the method, of course, and a dozen other things as well.

After a long time and many questions, Major Palfrey managed to disentangle their story, but still he could not get over his amazement at seeing them. He was deeply moved by their devotion to him, which had prompted them to undertake so dangerous a journey, and full of admiration for their courage and resource ; but when he heard that they had left Midmeddlecum without their mother's permission, and without even saying good-bye to her, he spoke sadly and sternly, and said, ' That was very wrong of you. Very wrong indeed. I am very much displeased to hear that.'

' It will be all right, and beautifully all right, when we have rescued you,' said Dorinda.

' Your poor mother,' said Major Palfrey. ' To deceive her, and to give her this new worry when she was already so gravely worried — I do not know how you could do it.'

' This is just like being at home again,' said Dinah gloomily. ' Whenever we did anything that we thought was particularly good, it nearly always turned out to be particularly bad.'

' Yes,' said Dorinda, ' our lives have been full of disappointment, haven't they ? — Why have you grown a beard, Father ? It doesn't suit you.'

' After my razor was taken from me,' said Major Palfrey, ' I had no choice in the matter.' And then, very politely, he began to talk to Mr. Corvo, and though he still felt ill at ease with the Puma, he thought it would be good manners to stroke her head. But neither he nor the Puma really enjoyed this.

Dinah and Dorinda examined the dungeon, and were horrified to think that their father had been living in so dreadful a place. It measured about twelve feet long by ten feet broad by eight feet high, and the walls and the roof were the natural rock on which the Castle was built. There was no furniture except a low wooden bed with a pair of old blankets, a couple of tin plates and a chipped enamel jug, and the heap of sacking on which Major Palfrey was sitting. The outer wall was at least three feet thick, but a shaft about a foot square had been driven through it to give light, and light also came from a gaping hole in the floor.

The floor was roughly paved. At one time there had been a lower dungeon which could be entered only by lifting a ringed piece of the pavement, but the outer wall of this other cell had fallen away, rotted by frost and rain that found their way into cracks in the rock, and now it stood open like a cave. The paving-stone which had been the entrance to it had disappeared, and through the hole in the floor the wind blew fitfully.

A simple ladder — a stout pole with pieces of wood nailed across it — led to the lower cell, and Dinah and Dorinda, climbing down to see what it was like, looked cautiously out from the open side. Sheer rock stretched above and below them, smooth and precipitous. The view was magnificent, but quite clearly there was no way of escape. They felt slightly dizzy as they looked down at the valley far beneath.

They returned to the upper dungeon and found their father intently studying Mr. Corvo's plan of the Castle.

' I agree with you,' he said to Mr. Corvo, ' that our best course will be to return to Count Hulagu's rooms, and then try to make our way, unobserved, to the banqueting hall, and conceal ourselves among the furniture there till nightfall. Then, if we are lucky, we may find some means of getting out under cover of darkness.'

' We should start immediately,' said Mr. Corvo. ' We have no time to lose.'

' Then come,' said Major Palfrey. ' Are you ready, children ? '

' The peppermint creams,' said Dorinda. ' Where are they ? '

' There,' said Dinah.

' Who's been eating them ? They're nearly all gone.'

' Not I,' said Mr. Corvo.

' Nor I,' said Major Palfrey.

' Oh ! ' cried Dorinda. ' There's a hole in the bag ! I must have been spilling them all the way ! '

' That can't be helped now,' said Major Palfrey. ' We have things more important than peppermint creams to think about. Mr. Corvo, as you know the route, will you be so kind as to lead us ? '

' We must go swiftly and quietly,' said Mr. Corvo. ' Keep close together, make no noise, and be ready for anything ! '

He moved towards the door, but before he could reach it, it was thrown violently open and two soldiers came in with rifles pointed.   Other soldiers could be seen behind them.

And then a more menacing and fearful figure entered.   With a sneer of triumph on his face, Count Hulagu Bloot appeared.

Chapter Thirty-Four

His gorgeous white uniform was rather crumpled, and he had not shaved. After watching the execution at Lodoban he had driven straight back to Gliedermannheim without waiting to have breakfast — he had taken a few sandwiches with him — and so had returned a good deal sooner than Mr. Corvo had thought possible.

Going straight to his bedroom to have a bath and some peppermint creams, he found the bag had disappeared, but on the floor of the bathroom lay a single sweet. Opening the door in the wall he saw another on the third step down, and calling for some soldiers to accompany him, he followed the trail. It led straight to Dungeon Number 200.

Now, with a smile of hideous triumph on his yellow face, he snatched the bag from Dorinda and ate seven or eight sweets, one after another, as quickly as he could. No one dared to say a word.

Then he made a speech.

' Uqi esi stee chi refai ont assi,' he said, ' dun chi refai ont reac. Amsi vendelity esi stee rusovel dun masi nov el Nagsali Palfrey. Laprouce chi sifa esi nemi sornireps. Chi beeli sornireps. Chi beah hundossat nov sornireps. Setse eni nov nemi boshbie a renti meth. El remo el rerimer ! Ehri esi stee, dun ehri esi nezratted dun tro nulit esi stee troms ! Ha-ha-ha ! '

He ordered the soldiers to search his new prisoners, and from Mr. Corvo they took his sword-

stick, his fountain-pen dagger, the Lord Chamberlain's keys, and all the money he had. But neither
Dinah nor Dorinda had anything which they considered worth removing.

Then Count Hulagu felt them all, to see how fat
they were, and laughed again, and said, ' Esi zeers
chum chum rithenn tavan glon, nemi sornireps ! '

Putting the last of the peppermint creams into
his mouth he left them abruptly, the soldiers followed him, and the door was locked:

' Now,' said Mr. Corvo, ' we are prisoners indeed,
and I have lost my swordstick and my fountain-pen
dagger. I never had a chance to use them.'

' Father,' said Dorinda, ' are there any mice in
your dungeon ? '

' None,' he answered sadly.

' That's a pity, because I brought a piece of
cheese to tame them, and I've still got it.'

' Where is the Puma ? ' asked Dinah.

The Puma, with eyes quicker than theirs, had
seen the door beginning to open before they were
aware of movement, and with a swift and silent leap
had dropped through the hole in the floor into the
lower dungeon.

Dinah found her lying on the outermost edge,
where the wall had broken and the rock fell sheer.
She was staring into the distant sky.

' Are we prisoners again ? ' she asked without
turning her head.

' I'm afraid so.'

' Have you a handkerchief? If so, come here
and wave it.'

' Why ? ' asked Dinah.

' Do you see that mote in the sky ? I think it is the Falcon. He cannot see me here, because we are in shadow, but he would see something white and moving.'

Dinah leaned out as far as she dared and waved her handkerchief. ' I'm afraid it isn't very clean,' she said.

A few minutes later the Falcon, on his strong and easy wings, flew past the opening, then circled and came in. He listened gravely to their news, and asked, ' What can I do to help ? '

Dinah thought for a minute or two and said, ' We haven't any money. Father has none, and they've taken away Mr. Corvo's pocket-book. So our only way of getting back to England, if we do escape, will be to go in one of the empty furniture vans. Mr. Corvo said they would be sent back to the firm that owns them.'

' They are still in the outer courtyard,' said the Falcon. ' Not all of them have been unloaded yet.'

' They'll be taken back to the station and perhaps put on a siding somewhere,' said Dinah. ' Could you keep watch on them, and let us know where they are ? '

' Very easily,' said the Falcon. ' What else can I do ? '

' Come and share our company from time to time,' said the Puma. ' It is a dull life to live in prison.'

' I am sorry indeed for you,' said the Falcon, ' but keep a good heart. To-morrow will bring new counsel and new hope.'

' I wonder ! ' said Dinah, and suddenly she felt

more wretched and despondent than ever before. How dismally all their scheming had failed ! Their excitement, their confident expectation of rescuing their father, had been pricked like a balloon and now lay shapeless about them. Now they were all prisoners together, and what hope had they of escaping from this monstrous Castle, from the Tyrant Count Hulagu, and all his well-armed obedient soldiers ? She felt her eyes grow hot and moist, her lips quiver, and total unhappiness possessed her. ' But no ! ' she murmured. ' No, I won't cry ! I may be a prisoner for the rest of my life, but I WON'T CRY ! Because if Count Hulagu heard that I had been crying he would be very pleased, and I'm certainly not going to do anything to give him pleasure ! '

She went back to the upper dungeon and sat down beside her father on the pile of sacking. Nobody spoke very much, and when darkness came they made themselves as comfortable as they could and tried to sleep. With only a blanket between them and the stone floor, Dinah and Dorinda spent a poor night, though the Puma made a good pillow for them. Fortunately the weather was still fairly warm, but from time to time the wind blew through the hole in the floor and made a noise like a banshee howling in the distance.

In the morning a soldier brought them a jug of pea-soup, a loaf of black bread, and a bucket of water.

' What a horrible breakfast ! ' said Dinah.

' It isn't breakfast only,' said Major Palfrey. ' These are our rations for the whole day.'

' Do you mean to say that we shan't get any-thing else till to-morrow ? ' asked Dorinda.

' Nothing else.'

' But I want a lot more, I'm hungry ! ' And suddenly running towards the soldier, Dorinda kicked him hard on the shin.

He was a big man with a fat red face, and being kicked on the shin did not anger him because he had a wooden leg. He spoke to Mr. Corvo in a thick country accent, explaining that he himself had a daughter very like Dorinda to look at. He had, indeed, seven daughters altogether, and five sons.

' And would they,' asked Mr. Corvo, speaking in Bombast, ' be satisfied with a little pea-soup for their breakfast, dinner, tea, and supper ? '

' No, of course not,' said the soldier, ' they have enormous appetites.'

' So have these,' said Mr. Corvo. ' What else can you bring ? '

The soldier went away, and presently returned with two currant buns.

' Thank you very much,' said Mr. Corvo. ' And now will you bring us some more blankets ? We were cold last night.'

The soldier took off his helmet to scratch his head, and after a moment or two said, ' Well, I'll see what I can do.'

' We Bombards,' said Mr. Corvo when he had gone, ' are not a cruel people. It is only that infamous Count Hulagu who makes my people behave so badly.'

Later in the day the soldier brought them three

Dorinda kicked him hard on the shin

old horse-rugs. They were very dirty, but warm and thick.

' Do you think,' asked Dinah, ' that he would bring us some soap ? '

But the soldier laughed at that. Soap, he said, was only for rich people, not for prisoners.

Two days later Count Hulagu came to see them again. He stayed for half an hour, eating peppermint creams all the time out of a bag that his aide-de-camp carried — his aide-de-camp was a tall young man with red hair and a squint — and felt them all to see if they had got any thinner. He made the same speech as he had made before, and then went away laughing loudly.

' What did he say ? ' asked Dinah.

' Just the same things,' said Mr. Corvo. ' That he doesn't know who we are, and doesn't care. We are his prisoners, and that is enough for him. He likes to have prisoners, he collects prisoners, and the more he has the better he is pleased. That is all. He is a strange man, Count Hulagu.'

Day followed day, and every day was dull and miserable, every night cold and uncomfortable. They tormented themselves by trying to think of plans for escape, but nobody could invent any likely way of getting out of the dungeon, to say nothing of getting out of the Castle. Major Palfrey, though he enjoyed having company after living all alone, was more worried about his daughters' welfare than he had ever been about his own, and Dinah and Dorinda thought with bitter longing of home. Even Miss Serendip's dullest lessons now seemed, in comparison with the dungeon, to have given them hours of pure happiness. Mr. Corvo had lost all his high spirits when his swordstick was taken from him, and sat for most of the time with his head in his hands.

Every third day the red-faced soldier was on duty, and brought them a few currant buns, but on other days they had nothing but cold pea-soup and black bread and water. They were always hungry, and from day to day they grew visibly dirtier.

The Puma, for most of the time, lay on the outer edge of the lower cell looking at the great distances beyond and the deep view beneath. The Falcon came regularly to see her, and they sat and talked together in the way to which they had grown accustomed when both were captives in Sir Lankester Lemon's zoo. The Falcon, though he had the whole freedom of the sky, considered himself, because he was bound to them by friendship, almost as much a prisoner as the others, and grew sadder every day. He brought the news that the furniture vans, now unloaded, had been taken to the railway station and then to a lonely siding about five miles from Gliedermannheim, where they waited to be attached to a train that would take them back to England. But still nobody could think of any means to cross the long distance between their dungeon and the railway, so they listened to the Falcon's news without much interest.

Mr. Corvo tried to make friends with the soldiers who brought their rations, but none of the soldiers dared to help them.

Every second day or so Count Hulagu came to look at them, to feel their arms and their ribs to see how thin they were, and to laugh at them. Once he brought a photographer to take their photographs. He spent a lot of time arranging in big albums the photographs of all his prisoners and of the various people whom he ordered to be shot.

The nights began to grow colder, and rain fell nearly every day.

Chapter Thirty-Five

One day, when the Puma as usual was lying on the outermost edge of the lower dungeon, Dinah was about to go down the ladder to sit beside her when she saw her rise slightly and turn her head inwards. The hair on her neck rose bristling, and her lips parted to show her teeth in a half-snarl.

Dinah, from the upper dungeon, looked towards the corner at which the Puma was staring, and saw to her amazement a flagstone moving slightly in the lower floor. One side of it rose, perhaps, half an inch, and fell again. At the same moment she heard what might be — though she could not be sure — the faint and muffled sound of strange voices. Then, while she was wondering what to do, the flagstone rose again, and now its movement was easily visible. It rose on one side an inch or more, and fell back with a little thud. Now the Puma was on her feet and softly snarling.

' Puma, Puma ! ' called Dinah in a fierce whisper. ' Come here, come quickly ! '

The Puma, with a backward glance, came swiftly up the ladder and lay flat beside Dinah, peering into the lower dungeon.

' Father ! Mr. Corvo ! Dorinda ! ' whispered Dinah. ' Be quiet and come here. Don't make a sound ! '

They lay on the pavement, every one of them feeling their heart beating against the stone in wild excitement, and looked down through the hole in the floor. The flagstone rose again, six inches this time, and they heard a voice saying, 'There she goes! Way-hay, and up she rises!'

'He's speaking English!' muttered Major Palfrey. 'Who can it be?'

Then the flagstone in the lower floor rose clear, and they could see two pairs of arms — lean, ancient, skinny arms — pushing it up. It balanced for a

moment on one edge, and then fell backwards with a crash.

They heard a voice from the depths below — an aged, shrill, and crackly voice — say cheerfully, 'And that's another obstacle overcome, Mr. Stevens! Another sap driven, another way made clear. God save the Queen, Mr. Stevens!'

'God save the Queen, Notchy,' said another voice that was equally old, but deep and gruff. '*Ubique* is truly our motto, Notchy. We go everywhere!'

Then they heard the two aged voices laughing,

and one of them began to sing a song in which the other joined. These were the words of it :

> ' Sap, sap, sap, sap, sap a little more,
> Sap and sap till your bones are sore !
> We sap all night and we sap all day,
> And that's how we go *ubique.*
> Oh, there's nothing can stop us when we start to dig,
> For we dig as fast as an Irish Jig !
> Pick, pick, pick, pick, pick with all your might,
> Shovel up the spoil, then strike a light
> And apply it to a charge of dynamite—
> Bang, bang, bang ! Then give three cheers
> For Queen Victoria's Royal Engineers ! '

' Good heavens ! ' said Major Palfrey. ' It can't be true ! '

' Hush ! ' whispered Dinah. ' Here they come ! '

Out of the hole appeared two little old men. Both were perfectly bald except for a fringe of white hair above their ears, and both had long, white, rather dirty moustaches. Their faces were shrivelled and deeply wrinkled, but their eyes, blue as a summer sea, shone brightly still. They wore patched and faded blue trousers, grey shirts, and broad red braces.

Heaving themselves on to the floor of the lower dungeon, they walked to the open side of it and looked at the view.

' What a magnificent panorama, Mr. Stevens ! ' said one of them.

' Remarkably fine,' said the other. ' There is nothing like sapping, Notchy, for teaching you to appreciate the manifold beauties of the world. After several weeks in the bowels of the earth, you emerge with new eyes, refreshed and eager to enjoy the great works of Mother Nature.'

' Perfectly true, Mr. Stevens, and very well expressed, if I may say so.'

Leaning down from the dungeon above, Major Palfrey suddenly addressed them : ' Gentlemen ! Who are you ? '

The little old men were badly startled, and Mr. Stevens might have fallen over the edge and down the precipice if his friend had not caught and steadied him.

Major Palfrey continued : ' We, like you, are English. We are prisoners, and I have been here for a long time. I am Major Palfrey, of the King's Own Brackenshire Light Infantry, and these ' — he pointed to the others, of whom the little old men could see nothing but their heads — ' these are my daughters ; a friend of theirs, Mr. Corvo ; and another friend, who happens to be a Puma.'

' A Major ? ' asked one of the old men. ' Do I understand you to have said that you are a Major ? '

' That is correct.'

' And we in our braces ! ' said the other old man. ' Oh, dear, dear ! '

' Pardon us while we retire for a minute or two,' said the first one, and before anyone could reply they had disappeared through the hole in the floor.

' Who can they be ? ' asked Dorinda.

' Do you think they will come back ? ' said Dinah.

' Let us go down to the lower dungeon,' said Major Palfrey.

They climbed down the ladder, and almost immediately the two old men reappeared. They were now wearing blue tunics, as old and patched and faded as their trousers, and low shakos of a sort that used to be worn very many years ago. As they came up out of the hole they stood side by side, very stiffly at attention, and saluted Major Palfrey with great dignity.

' Very happy to see you here, sir,' they said. ' Would you care to inspect our work ? '

' Thank you,' said Major Palfrey, ' I shall be very interested indeed to see it. But will you not introduce yourselves ? And shall we sit down, though there is nothing, I fear, but the floor to sit on ? '

' I am Mr. Stevens,' said one of the old men, ' and this is my friend and faithful comrade, Notchy Knight. We are Sappers, humble but loyal members of Her Majesty's Corps of Royal Engineers.'

' *His* Majesty's, you mean,' said Major Palfrey.

' *Her* Majesty's,' said Mr. Stevens, rather angrily. ' Her Glorious Majesty, Queen Victoria.'

' But she is dead, you know. She died many years ago.'

' Dead ! ' exclaimed Mr. Stevens.

' Dead ! ' said Notchy. ' The Queen *dead* ! '

' Oh ! ' they cried. ' Oh, oh ! ' And burst into tears.

' Come, come,' said Major Palfrey. ' It happened quite a long time ago, and you owe your allegiance now to her successor, His Majesty King George the Sixth.'

' George ? ' said Mr. Stevens, wiping his wet eyes with the back of his hand. ' What a good name ! My name is George.'

' And he has two daughters,' said Dorinda.

' Daughters ! ' exclaimed Notchy, drying his tears. ' How delightful ! I do like people to have daughters. And how pleased the dear Queen would have been ! Mr. Stevens, I think this calls for an impromptu but none the less loyal and heartfelt demonstration.'

' It does indeed,' said Mr. Stevens.

Again they stood stiffly at attention, and began to sing. The others joined in, and the dungeon echoed and re-echoed the anthem :

> ' God save our Gracious King,
> Long live our Noble King,
> God save the King !
> Send him victorious,
> Happy and glorious,
> Long to reign over us,
> God save the King ! '

' I doubt if it is wise to make so much noise,' said Major Palfrey, just as they were about to begin the second verse.

' Noise ? ' said Mr. Stevens. ' Do you call the National Anthem a Noise ? '

' It certainly isn't silence.'

' It would be a very poor and ineffectual anthem if it were,' said Notchy stiffly.

' Well, don't let us argue about that,' said Major Palfrey. ' I want very much to know where you have come from, and how you happen to be here.'

' It is a long story,' said Mr. Stevens.

' Very long indeed,' said Notchy.

' It began with our cutting a sap.' Turning

politely to Dinah and Dorinda, Mr. Stevens explained : ' A sap is, or may be, a sort or species of tunnel. It is frequently used in military operations, and we who, by cutting, digging, and blasting, make these tunnels or saps, are called Sappers. Is that perfectly clear? Good. Well, my friend Notchy and I were cutting a sap which was one of the longest and most beautiful saps we had then made ; though since then, of course, we have made some which were very much longer indeed. But unhappily the sap of which I am now talking went in the wrong direction : not towards the enemy, but away from him. And so, when at last we emerged from the other end, we discovered to our great surprise and bewilderment that the war was over, the siege had been concluded, and all our troops had gone home.'

' What siege was that ? ' asked Major Palfrey.

' Sebastopol, of course.'

' Sebastopol ! ' exclaimed Dinah. ' But that was in the Crimean War, and the Crimean War was fought in — what was the date, Dorinda ? '

' It was a very long time ago,' said Dorinda.

' Very, very long ago.'

' And what of that ? ' asked Mr. Stevens angrily. ' Many things happened long ago, didn't they ? In fact, most things happened long ago. And how does that discredit them ? '

' I don't suppose it does,' said Dinah, ' but you must be very old.'

' We are,' said Notchy. ' Very old indeed.'

' But none the worse for that,' said Mr. Stevens.

' All the better, in my opinion,' said Notchy.

' And we're good for a few years yet, aren't we ? '
' I should think we are ! '
The two of them, with great enjoyment, stood up once more, bowed to the others, and briskly sang :

> ' Old soldiers never die,
> Never die, never die.
> Old soldiers never die,
> They only fa-ade awa-ay ! '

After that Mr. Stevens went on with his story.

' Imagine us,' he said, ' alone in the Crimea. Abandoned in a foreign country, far from England, Home, and Beauty ! But did we despair ? Not for a moment. We saw in front of us an impassable mountain. Did that create in us even a minute of doubt or perturbation ? Of course it didn't. We sapped ! We sapped and sapped until we had sapped right through it and come out on the other side. When we saw level country before us, we marched. We often marched, but I must confess that we preferred to find ourselves confronted by an insurmountable barrier, for then we could prove the great merit and virtue of our profession by going underneath it.'

' But how did you live ? ' asked Dinah. ' Had you a lot of money ? '

' To begin with,' said Notchy, ' Mr. Stevens had four shillings, and I had two and ninepence. But that didn't last very long.'

' And what did you do then ? ' asked Dorinda.

' We put our heads together,' said Mr. Stevens, ' and asked ourselves : How shall we make some more money ? That led to another question : How

can a great number of people most easily be persuaded to give us money? And that suggested a
third question: What do most people mostly suffer
from? The answer to that was easy. The answer
was: Toothache and Anxiety. So my friend and
comrade Notchy Knight set up as a Dentist, and I
became a Fortune Teller.'

'Like Professor Bultek,' said Dinah.

'Who is he?'

'A friend of Mr. Corvo's.'

'I have not the pleasure of his acquaintance,'
said Mr. Stevens.

'Will you tell my fortune?' asked Dorinda. 'I
want to know when we are going to escape.'

'Have you got any money?' asked Mr. Stevens.

'None,' said Dorinda.

'Then I cannot tell your fortune. If you have
no money, you have no fortune. That's obvious,
isn't it? I wish you wouldn't waste my time in
this way. As I was saying, before you interrupted
me, we became Dentist and Fortune Teller, and
our livelihood was made secure. Set free from
carking care and amply provided for, we were able
to give most of our time and energy to our real
profession — which, of course, is Sapping — and so
moving northward and then westward we presently
arrived, after a leisurely but eventful journey, much
of it very comfortably underground, at the eastern
border of Bombardy. That was quite recently:
eight or nine years ago, I think. We have had an
instructive and agreeable sojourn in this country,
not the least pleasant of our exploits being the
driving of a sap into this beautiful Castle.'

' A labour which has been further rewarded,' said Notchy Knight, bowing in turn to Major Palfrey, Dinah, Dorinda, and Mr. Corvo, ' by making *your* acquaintance.'

' But how extraordinary,' said Dinah, ' that you should find your way here. To this very dungeon, I mean.'

'I see nothing extraordinary about it,' said Notchy.

' Neither do I,' said Mr. Stevens.

' You know what our motto is, don't you ? It's *ubique*. There are several ways of pronouncing it, but I think my way is the right way : Yoo-be-kway.'

' That's my way too,' said Mr. Stevens.

' Now *ubique* means Everywhere. And if our habit and custom is to go everywhere, why shouldn't we come here ? '

' It would be very extraordinary if we didn't,' said Mr. Stevens.

' You ought to think more carefully and try not to make rash observations,' said Notchy.

' I'm sorry,' said Dinah. ' I hadn't thought of it that way.'

' If you were a Sapper,' said Mr. Stevens, ' you would learn to think of everything every way.'

' What I am thinking of,' said Major Palfrey, ' is whether we can use your sap to get out of the Castle.'

' Of course you can, if you want to get out.'

' We do indeed.'

'Then why didn't you say so before? Come along!'

Before anyone could say a word Mr. Stevens had jumped down the hole, and was quickly followed by Notchy Knight, who, just as he was disappearing, shouted, ' Last man replace the stone ! '

Chapter Thirty-Six

'They are certainly eccentric,' said Major Palfrey, 'but we shall have to trust them, I think.'

'We have nothing to lose by it,' said Mr. Corvo.

'Then you will lead the way, and I shall replace the flagstone. That is an obvious precaution to take against pursuit.'

The passage was quite dark and in some places so low that none of them, except the Puma, could walk upright. It twisted and turned, and here it was narrow, there surprisingly broad. On their right-hand side they felt a surface of jagged stone, on their left some patches of cold clay. The old men, it was evident, had found and followed a long continuous fault in the Castle rock.

Though Mr. Corvo had been the first to enter the passage, it was the Puma who led the way after they had gone a few yards. She alone could see in the dark. Dinah followed, holding her tail. Behind Dinah came Mr. Corvo, then Dorinda, and last of all Major Palfrey. The darkness was complete, unrelieved by any glimmer of light, and very soon they began to wonder if the old men had deserted them and left them to wander unguided, perhaps to get hopelessly lost, in the bowels of the rock. Nobody spoke of this dreadful fear, but they all felt it. They lost all sense of direction, and only knew that they were going downhill.

Then round a corner they saw light, and found the two old men sitting with a lantern between them.

There they found the two old men

' Come along,' said Mr. Stevens. ' Where have you been all this time ? '

' We thought you were in a hurry to get away,' said Notchy. ' But instead of hurrying, you've been dawdling.'

' Even with a lantern this would not be an easy route,' said Major Palfrey, rather breathlessly, ' and in total darkness we found it very difficult to move at all.'

' Difficult ? ' said Mr. Stevens with a cackle of laughter. ' You ought to see some of the places that Notchy and I have come through. This is as easy as Constitution Hill compared with a lot of saps that we've used.'

' That may be so,' said Major Palfrey, ' but we haven't the benefit of your unique experience. Perhaps you would tell us where this passage ends ? '

' At the foot of the hill on the far side from the town,' said Mr. Stevens.

' You come out into a cave,' said Notchy. ' It was the cave that attracted our attention and gave us the idea of sapping into the Castle. We're always attracted by holes in the ground.'

' What are we wasting time for ? ' asked Mr. Stevens. ' I hate sitting still and doing nothing. Come along, everybody ! '

In addition to his lantern he carried a pick with a spare helve and a heavy sack, while Notchy had a spade, a crowbar, and a coil of rope. But in spite of their burdens they moved with great speed, and although they now had a light to guide them, the others found it difficult to keep up with the old men, and soon they were all hot and breathless.

They walked for a long time, bumping their shoulders and elbows against the rock, and Dorinda was feeling that she must, within the next minute, ask them to stop for a rest, when Mr. Stevens suddenly halted and held his lantern to the wall.

' Look at that, Notchy,' he said.

There was a deep diagonal crack in the rock, and when Notchy laid his cheek to it, he felt a little draught of air.

' There's something on the other side,' he said. ' A passage, a chamber, a fault in the rock, or another sap. Interesting, isn't it ? '

' Very interesting,' said Mr. Stevens. ' How strange that we didn't observe it when we were working our way upwards. But we must examine this more closely.'

He opened the sack he was carrying, which contained a few personal belongings, some slabs of guncotton, fuse and detonators, and the head of a sledge-hammer. Quickly fitting this on to the spare helve, he began to hammer at the rock as though in a perfect fury.

Shouting through the din that he made, Major Palfrey demanded, ' Is it absolutely necessary that you should do this now ? Can't we go on and get out of this dreadful tomb ? I want fresh air ! '

Mr. Stevens stopped hammering and said in a tone of great severity, ' This promises to be *most* interesting. To pass on without investigating all the possibilities of driving a lateral sap from this most hopeful beginning, into the very heart of the hill, would be a piece of criminal neglect. Please do not interrupt us in our work.'

It soon became obvious that the rock at this point was very thin, little more than a partition, and after half an hour's vigorous work with sledgehammer and crow-bar, Mr. Stevens and Notchy Knight had made a hole in it big enough to crawl through. Mr. Stevens was the first to go.

The others followed, and found him holding up his lantern to admire the arched roof of a narrow but well-constructed corridor.

' Beautiful ! ' he exclaimed. ' Isn't it beautiful ? '

' As noble a work of man as I have ever seen,' said Notchy reverently.

' What is the explanation of this ? ' asked Major Palfrey.

Mr. Corvo yawned. 'It is another secret passage,' he said. ' All the old castles in Bombardy have secret passages. But I am tired of travelling underground. I am weary of tunnels and saps and rock and clay. I want to get out ! '

' So do I,' said Dinah.

' I don't like the smell,' said Dorinda.

' But we must certainly see where this goes,' said Mr. Stevens.

' Of course we must,' said Notchy. ' I should never forgive myself for omitting to explore every yard of so perfect a piece of engineering.'

' Shouldn't we take the nearest way out ? ' asked Major Palfrey.

But already the old men, after a rapid debate as to whether they should go left or right, were hurrying along the corridor, and the others had to use all speed to keep them and their lantern in sight.

The way seemed endless, and though they should

have been elated by the thought of escape, they were oppressed by the gloom of the narrow walls and the stale damp smell of the air.

At last, however, the two old men, now fifty yards ahead of them, came to a halt. They had no choice in the matter, for they could go no farther. The corridor had come to an end. In front of them was a little door, stoutly built and barred with iron.

Chapter Thirty-Seven

'Notchy,' said Mr. Stevens, ' the sledge-hammer, if you please.'

'Do you mean to break it open?' asked Major Palfrey.

'I see no other means of getting to the other side of it,' said Mr. Stevens.

'But you may be forcing your way into private property.'

'Until we break through we cannot tell whether it is private property or public property,' said Mr. Stevens, and, swinging the heavy hammer, struck the door a tremendous blow. It opened immediately.

'It wasn't locked!' he exclaimed. 'How careless people are!'

They now found themselves in what was evidently the cellar of a house. It contained two stone bins full of bottles of wine, three beer barrels, and an old bicycle.

'And now,' said Major Palfrey nervously, ' we must use the very greatest caution. I insist on caution, and I shall take the lead. Follow me and make no noise whatever.'

Stone steps led upward from the cellar to a door that opened easily, Major Palfrey having first made certain, by looking through the keyhole, that the room beyond it was empty. It was difficult to say what sort of a room it was. There were so many books in it that it might have been a small library, but there was also a narrow bed with a mattress but no blankets or pillow, so equally it might have been a spare bedroom. There were also various articles such as a sewing-machine without a handle, a pair of skates, a very old gramophone with a broken horn, some tall china vases all cracked, and a pair of antlers mounted on a wooden shield, which made it look like a lumber-room. But though Dinah and Dorinda were deeply interested in all these things, Major Palfrey paid no attention to them. With one hand held up for silence, he was listening intently at a door on the far side of the room. Listening too, the others could hear a faint murmur of voices.

The Puma, as though to guard Major Palfrey against sudden attack, stood with head alert close behind him. Mr. Corvo, Mr. Stevens, and Notchy Knight shuffled a little nearer. Mr. Stevens still carried his lighted lantern.

For nearly a minute they all stood quite motionless like a group at Madame Tussaud's. But then there was a most unfortunate accident.

The top of the lantern was by this time almost red-hot, and Mr. Stevens, leaning forward very eagerly and paying no attention to it, let it touch the root of the Puma's tail.

With a howl of fear and pain the Puma leapt forward. Head down and shoulders bunched, she leapt against the door, burst it open, and tumbled into the room beyond. Major Palfrey, trying to catch and hold her, followed her and fell as the rug he trod on slid on a polished floor. Mr. Corvo, Mr. Stevens, and Notchy Knight, unwilling to desert him, followed too, and Dinah and Dorinda rushed after them, eager to see what had happened.

What they did see was so unexpected, and so frightening, that it took their breath away. Sitting opposite each other at a small table were Professor Bultek and Count Hulagu Bloot.

Count Hulagu had come, by the secret passage which led from his suite in the Castle, to Professor Bultek's house to have his fortune told. At the moment when the Puma burst open the door his hands had been lying palms upward on the table, and Professor Bultek was telling him that he would soon be going on a long journey.

But Count Hulagu's adventurous life had taught him how to move quickly, and in a moment he was on his feet, and the hands that Professor Bultek had been reading each held a revolver.

' Heneg onti hath oinc ! ' he whispered fiercely.

' Into that corner,' muttered Mr. Corvo in a low frightened voice.

Slowly and reluctantly they huddled together. Professor Bultek, with all his fingers in his mouth, gazed at them in utter consternation, but Count Hulagu, taking a slow pace towards them, looked from one to another with a grim and gloating smile. He began to speak slowly in Bombast, licking his mulberry-coloured lips, and Mr. Corvo, still in a frightened whisper, translated what he said.

' First there was one ' — he pointed a revolver at Major Palfrey — ' and then came three others, a man and the two girls. You are much thinner than when I first saw you. I like to see my prisoners grow thin and suffer, but I do not like my prisoners to escape. No, no ! I am too fond of them to let them escape. But how did you find you way here? Was it these little ancient men, like dwarfs, who came to your rescue? Who are they? Where did they come from? And where did you find that animal?'

The Puma lay in front of the others. Her great eyes were shining with a fierce and steady light, her hair bristled stiffly on her neck, and her teeth were bared. She was softly snarling. Suddenly, as the revolver came down and seemed to threaten her, she leapt, with a savage grinding roar, straight at Count Hulagu's throat.

Two shots rang out, immensely loud in that small room, and then Count Hulagu, stumbling backwards, fell to the floor with the Puma on top of him. For a few seconds they seemed to be wrestling together, and then Count Hulagu lay still and the Puma, with a tired and awkward movement, crawled a little way from him and fell upon her side.

Pulling the table-cloth from the table where Count Hulagu had sat to have his fortune told, Major Palfrey hurriedly covered the dead Tyrant, and Dinah, on her knees beside the dying Puma, took its head on her lap, while Dorinda, crying bitterly, hid her face on its neck.

'And that is all,' said the Puma softly. 'Now I know why Mrs. Grimble let you rescue me from the hounds. I think I have known in my heart, ever since we came here, that something like this would happen, and that, I suppose, is why for a little time past I have been sadder than I used to be. But do not cry! The people of my breed nearly always die in fight, and what does it matter whether the fight be here or in my own country?'

Dinah and Dorinda were both crying so bitterly that neither could properly answer. But the one sobbed, ' I love you so much ! ' and the other, ' I love you more than anyone in the world, except Dorinda.'

' You gave me what I love above all things,' said the Puma. ' You gave me a little while of freedom. Have I repaid you ? '

Dinah felt the noble head grow heavy on her knees, and the bright eyes went dim. With a little trembling of her golden skin, the Puma died.

' Come,' said their father gently. ' Come, my dears, you must leave her. We are not yet out of danger. There is more trouble in the house, and we must compose ourselves. Say good-bye to her, poor creature, and come quickly.'

The other door in Professor Bultek's room opened into a little hall, and on the other side of that was the drawing-room. The hall was now full of excited people, most of them women, and Mr. Corvo was trying to pacify them. Mr. Corvo had completely recovered his nerve, and was talking in a very loud and confident voice, which, however, could scarcely be heard because nine or ten of the women were screaming far more loudly than he. They had been frightened at first by the sound of the shots, then frightened by the discovery that strangers were in the house, and frightened for the third time by the appearance of Mr. Stevens and Notchy Knight.

Mrs. Bultek was screaming louder than anyone because she thought, for some reason, that Professor Bultek had been shot. Then she saw him in the doorway, and, throwing her arms round his neck, immediately fainted. She was much bigger than her husband, and her weight was more than he could bear. They fell heavily to the floor with Professor Bultek underneath.

Seeing this, her friends stopped screaming and hurried to help her. Then, from the deserted drawing-room, came the sound of another voice. A voice that was high-pitched and thin and very piercing. It was a baby's voice, and as soon as they heard it all the women in the party forgot about Mrs. Bultek, and pushed each other out of the way to get back to the drawing-room.

It so happened that Mrs. Bultek had been having a christening-party for her first grandchild, and the baby, very naturally, did not want to be left alone on so important an occasion. So she began to scream. She was only six weeks old, but her voice was so remarkably strong that no one could doubt that when she grew up she would be able to scream louder than any other woman in Bombardy. In three seconds the hall was empty except for the prostrate figures of Professor and Mrs. Bultek.

Major Palfrey at once took advantage of this to go to the front door and open it. There, before the house, he saw a large motor-car decorated with rosettes and white ribbons, which had been hired for the christening-party.

' Dinah and Dorinda ! ' he called. ' Corvo, Stevens, Knight ! Quickly, here's our chance. Into the car with you ! '

Mr. Stevens and Notchy Knight, who had never before ridden in a motor-car, were more inclined to open the bonnet and look at the engine than to get inside, but Mr. Corvo, now full of nervous energy, pushed them into the back with Dinah and Dorinda, shut the door with a bang, and got into the front seat beside Major Palfrey.

' I think I know the way,' said Major Palfrey.

' Right here,' said Mr. Corvo, and they turned a corner at full speed. ' Now you are on the main road to Gliedermannheim.'

Professor Bultek's house was one of those built on the side of the hill below the Castle, and Major Palfrey drove down the steep and winding road at such a pace that everyone they passed stood and stared in astonishment, and all the white ribbons strained in the breeze like the ropes of a racing yacht.

' There is no need to go through the town,' said Mr. Corvo presently. ' Turn right here, then left by those trees. We shall come to a small road that goes very near the siding where the furniture vans are. If they have not already been taken away, that is.'

Twenty minutes later they left the car in a lane, and walked over a field to a little wood. Beyond it, on a siding, there was a short goods train with the five furniture vans together at one end. There was a signal-box not far away, and a man leaning from a window was shouting something to another man on the other side of the line.

' We must hide in the wood till darkness comes,' said Mr. Corvo.

' How do we get into the van ? ' asked Major Palfrey. ' They will certainly all be locked.'

' There is a trap-door in the roof.'

' You realise, of course, that we have no rations for the journey ? '

' Perhaps you would like a piece of cake ? ' said Mr. Stevens, and opening his sack — he and Notchy still carried all their tools — he took out an enormous iced cake which weighed at least ten pounds.

' The christening cake ! ' said Mr. Corvo. ' How did you obtain it ? '

' It was on a table just inside the room where the baby was screaming,' said Mr. Stevens. ' I chanced to look in, and seeing it there I thought it might come in useful.'

'We're very good at foraging,' said Notchy complacently.

At that moment, with his usual rushing noise and swift descent, the Falcon appeared. 'I am very glad you have arrived,' he said. 'I think the train will be leaving to-night. There is an engine coming now, on this line, from Gliedermannheim station. Where is the Puma?'

Dinah and Dorinda, their eyes still red with weeping, told him the story. He listened gravely, and then said, 'She was a good friend, she had a great heart. It brings more sorrow than I had thought possible to hear of her death, and I shall miss her sadly. But it is better, for us who are the great birds and beasts of the world, to die in fight than to grow weary of life and feel strength wasting in a slow disease.'

Notchy Knight, who had been walking in the wood, now came hurrying back and exclaimed, 'Mr. Stevens, Mr. Stevens! Come and see what I have found!'

'What is it, Notchy?'

'A hole! A beautiful deep hole! Do come and see it.'

The hole, no more than thirty yards away, was like a boring for a well. 'It is one of those that I told you about,' said Mr. Corvo to Dinah and Dorinda. 'It must have been dug when people all over Bombardy were digging for treasure.'

Mr. Stevens lay on his stomach and peered down. 'It seems to be *very* deep,' he said. 'This is indeed a welcome find. Make the rope fast to that tree, Notchy. I'm going down.'

' You've no time for that sort of thing now,' said Major Palfrey. ' It will be dark in a few minutes — dark enough to get into the van — and the train may leave at any moment. If you want to come back to England with us, you can't go down that hole.'

' England ! ' said Mr. Stevens. ' It would be very pleasant to see England again. I dare say there have been many changes there since we left for the Crimea.'

' I never cared very much for the climate,' said Notchy thoughtfully, ' and I don't suppose that has changed.'

' I still owe my tailor a bill,' said Mr. Stevens. ' That might give rise to some unpleasantness.'

' This hole,' said Notchy, ' is one of the most promising holes I have seen for a long time. It would be a most interesting experiment to drive a sap from the bottom of it.'

' I don't suppose we should know many people in England now,' said Mr. Stevens.

' Very few indeed,' said Notchy.

' And it's quite improbable that we should find a better hole than this.'

' Most unlikely,' said Notchy.

' I think we shall stay here,' said Mr. Stevens, ' and just go on sapping, which is the profession we have been practising for so long and to which we have now grown thoroughly accustomed. But if you should happen to meet His Majesty King George the Sixth, I hope you will assure him that we are now as loyal to him as we have been, for so many years, to her late Glorious Majesty Queen Victoria.'

'And do not forget to offer our respectful devotion to the two Princesses,' said Notchy.

Then, taking hold of the rope which Notchy had made fast to a near-by tree, Mr. Stevens swung his legs into the hole and began to go down hand over hand. 'Good-bye!' he said, just as his head was disappearing.

Notchy followed him. 'Good-bye!' he exclaimed, and vanished from sight.

Dorinda leaned over the edge and shouted, 'You've left the christening cake. What shall we do with it?'

'Take it with you,' said a voice from far down the hole. 'We can look after ourselves. We're *very* good at foraging.'

A moment later they heard the thud and clink of spade and pick. The old men were already at work. And then their voices rose, small and muffled. They were singing :

'Sap, sap, sap, sap, sap a little more,
Sap and sap till your bones are sore !
We sap all night and we sap all day,
And that's how we go *ubique*.
Oh, there's nothing can stop us when we start to dig,
For we dig as fast as an Irish Jig !
Pick, pick, pick, pick, pick with all your might,
Shovel up the spoil, then strike a light
And apply it to a charge of dynamite—
Bang, bang, bang ! Then give three cheers
For Good King George's Royal Engineers !'

A long shrill whistle followed the song. It came from some distance away.

'The engine!' Major Palfrey rose quickly, the

others following, and returned to the edge of the wood. In the gathering darkness they saw an engine backing down the line towards the stationary train.

' It's scarcely dark enough yet to get in without being seen. Which is the van that we must travel in ? '

Dinah spoke to the Falcon, and answered, ' The one with the trap-door in the roof is the farthest from the engine.'

The engine was coupled to the train.

' No, it isn't dark enough yet,' said Mr. Corvo anxiously, ' but we shall have to risk it.'

' I have an idea,' said Dinah, and spoke again to the Falcon.

' Keea, keea ! ' he said laughing. ' Yes, I can do that.'

He rose swiftly and flew towards the front of the train. Then from a height of three hundred feet, with a rushing noise of his wings, he swooped down upon the engine, screaming harshly.

The engine-driver and the fireman and the man from the signal-box, who had come to couple the train, looked up in great surprise.

' Now,' said Dinah. ' Now is our chance. They won't look at anything else.'

They hurried down to the line, Dorinda carrying the christening cake, and came to the van. The Falcon, rising and stooping again and again, held all the attention of the engine-driver, the fireman, and the man from the signal-box. They grew angry and began to throw pieces of coal at him, but the Falcon easily avoided them.

Major Palfrey, Dinah and Dorinda, and Mr.

Corvo climbed to the roof of the van, opened the trap-door, and got inside. Nobody saw them. The Falcon made a last screaming attack, and then flew high into the gathering darkness of the night.

Five minutes later the train started.

Chapter Thirty-Eight

' It's not as comfortable as it was before,' said Dorinda.

' No,' said Mr. Corvo. ' They were good rooms that Bultek made for us among the furniture. This time we shall not travel in luxury.'

' You do want to come back with us, don't you ? ' said Dinah to Mr. Corvo. ' I mean, Bombardy is your own country, and you haven't seen very much of it, and if you have any relations——'

' All my relations went abroad when Count Hulagu became the Tyrant,' said Mr. Corvo. ' Some went to South America, some to South Africa, and some to Southend. I went to Mid-meddlecum, and there I have my many pupils, whom I wish to instruct. Bombardy is beautiful, but England is more convenient, and I am very glad to be returning. But I wish they had left some sofas and chairs in the van.'

' It might be worse,' said Major Palfrey.

' It might be much worse,' said Dinah. ' We might still be in the dungeon. If the Puma hadn't saved us, we should have had to go back to it.'

' Come,' said Major Palfrey, ' and help me to make the beds.'

There was a good deal of sacking in the van, that the furniture had been wrapped in, and some loose straw. They gathered everything together and made couches on the floor. They were not very soft but nobody complained, and after the long excitement of the day they were soon asleep.

The train ran slowly, often stopping, and they had a long journey back. They finished the christening cake before they got into France, but that night Mr. Corvo found, in the cart-shed of a little farm near the railway, a hen sitting on eleven eggs, and carried them off in his hat. Three of them were bad, but they ate the others raw. They had two each and felt a lot better.

It was on the following night that they went aboard the train-ferry, and then at last they felt perfectly safe. Then they knew for certain that they had really and finally escaped, and would soon be home again. As the ship put out they suddenly became wildly happy. They were hungry and dirty and tired, but that no longer seemed to matter. They were free, they were going home, and nothing else counted.

The Channel was calm as an inland lake, and when Mr. Corvo climbed on to Major Palfrey's back to open the trap-door — that was how they had to get out now, Dinah and Dorinda going next, and then Mr. Corvo would lean down and catch Major Palfrey's outstretched hands and pull him up — when they were all outside and sitting in the shadow of the van where no one could see them, the moon rose over a cloud and shone with a clear silver light. The clouds fell lower, and soon the whole sky was empty but for the radiant circle of the moon. It was very pale, and perfectly calm, and beautiful.

'Do you remember,' said Major Palfrey, 'the night in Midmeddlecum when I was packing and you climbed the apple-tree and tied bells on the branches ? It was just twelve months ago, and the moon — do you remember ? — had a stormy ring round it, and I told you that when there was an ill wind blowing on the moon it might blow into your hearts, if you were naughty, and keep you naughty for a year.'

' I suppose we haven't always behaved really well,' said Dinah, ' but we have learnt a lot of things that we wouldn't have learnt if we had behaved in a perfectly ordinary way.'

' And we have had a lot of fun,' said Dorinda.

' And we have rescued you,' said Dinah.

' Yes, yes,' said Major Palfrey. ' Except for the worry you have caused your poor mother, and the waste of so much time that you might have spent with Miss Serendip, I find it difficult to blame you.'

' It would be very foolish indeed to blame them for coming to save you from Count Hulagu's dungeon,' said Mr. Corvo.

' When I was a boy,' said Major Palfrey, ' I had to obey my parents in everything.'

' I like to think for myself,' said Dinah.

' So do I,' said Dorinda. ' Well, sometimes it's a nuisance, of course, but when it isn't a nuisance I do.'

' The moon is quite calm now,' said Major Palfrey doubtfully. ' Thinking for yourselves, per- haps, won't always have such unusual results as it has had in the past year.'

Presently they went back into the van and tried to sleep. But now they were too excited for that, so Mr. Corvo gave them a dancing lesson. He made them dance a Foursome Reel till they were quite exhausted, and then, when they lay down, they fell asleep immediately. And when they woke up they were in the railway yard at Dover.

' And now,' said Major Palfrey in a very brisk and businesslike way, ' we shall go to a hotel, and have a bath and get some breakfast. I shall telephone to the War Office to report my arrival, and telephone to your mother to let her know that we are safe and shall be home this evening.'

So they climbed out of the van and then, when they looked at each other in the morning sunlight, they began to laugh. For they were all as dirty and shabby and wildly untidy as scarecrows. Major Palfrey had a fully grown beard, and Mr. Corvo a half-grown beard, and both had straw in their beards, and Dinah and Dorinda had straw in their tangled hair. Their faces were filthy, their clothes were dusty and torn, and the longer they looked at each other, the louder they laughed. And while they were laughing they heard a stern voice saying, ' Now, what's the meaning of all this ? Who are you, and where do you come from ? '

They looked round and saw a tall policeman frowning at them. Major Palfrey began to explain, but the policeman interrupted him and said, ' You come along with me and tell that story to the Inspector. Now don't start any trouble, because I don't like trouble, and I'm horrified by people who make trouble, and consequently I become irate and spiteful. So you'll come quietly, won't you ? '

They said they would, and were marched off to a police station not far away. But after Major

Palfrey had spoken for a few minutes to the Inspector they were treated very kindly, and while Major Palfrey was telephoning, a policeman gave Dinah and Dorinda and Mr. Corvo enormous cups of cocoa and bread and jam.

Then Major Palfrey called the Inspector to the telephone, and the Inspector spoke for several minutes, very respectfully because he was talking to

someone at the War Office, and after that he rang up another number, and in twenty minutes' time a smartly dressed man in a bowler hat, a black jacket, and striped trousers appeared at the police station. This was the cashier of a bank in Dover, and though he was very surprised at Major Palfrey's appearance he gave him £50, and Major Palfrey gave him a receipt for it.

By this time they had all had a good wash and looked a little more respectable, though not much. So they said good-bye to the policemen and went out to buy new clothes. Major Palfrey and Mr. Corvo went to a barber's and got shaved and had their hair cut, while Dinah and Dorinda in another part of the shop had their hair cut and washed. By one o'clock they were all as smart as if they were going to a party, and then they went to a hotel and had an enormous meal, and presently caught a train to Midmeddlecum.

Every single person in Midmeddlecum was at the station to meet them, and as the train drew in the Vicar got on to a porter's barrow and conducted his great choir while they sang *See the Conquering Heroes Come.*

Mrs. Palfrey and Miss Serendip were the first to greet them, and Mrs. Palfrey said to Major Palfrey, ' Darling, how tired you look ! I really think you will have to have your breakfast in bed to-morrow.' And to Dinah and Dorinda she said, ' Isn't it nice to have Father at home again ! Thank you so much for rescuing him. I've quite forgiven you for worrying me so dreadfully.'

But Miss Serendip said, ' You have a great deal of lost time to make up, and I hope that you are now prepared to work very hard at your lessons, because I am prepared to work very hard at teaching you.'

Then everybody came and shook hands with them, and presently they formed a great procession and marched home singing *Begone Dull Care,* *Stormalong,* and *Bannocks o' Bere-meal.* Outside their house the people of Midmeddlecum gave them three cheers and another for luck, and then Constable Drum sent them all home. But everybody had so much to talk about that neither the Palfreys nor anyone else in Midmeddlecum went to bed before midnight.

The Falcon was sitting on their window-sill when at last Dinah and Dorinda went upstairs, and because he had been thinking of the Puma's death, and felt sad and lonely in consequence, he came inside and spent the night on the mantelpiece.

He had gone when they woke, however, and they did not see him again for some time.

Chapter Thirty-Nine

They found it very difficult to settle down after their adventurous weeks in Bombardy, but Miss Serendip did everything she could to help them by giving them lessons from morning till night, every day except Sunday. On Sundays they went to the zoo and had long talks with their old friends there. They took presents to several of them, including a whole year's subscription to *The Times* for Bendigo the Bear, a pair of handcuffs for Mr. Parker the Giraffe, which made him feel very important, and some blue ribbon for Lady Lil the Ostrich's daughter, who was running about and being a great nuisance to Sir Bobadil.

By trying extremely hard they behaved, for two or three weeks, so well that their mother was delighted with them, and even Miss Serendip became kindly and gracious. But one day Dorinda said, ' I can't stand this any longer ! ' And Dinah said, ' Neither can I.' So they escaped from Miss Serendip and went into the Forest of Weal.

It was a cold day and by now the trees had lost all their leaves, and their thin tall branches were bare against a cloudy sky. Though it was only a few weeks since they had longed so ardently to be at home again, and thought that nothing else was needed to make them perfectly happy, both Dinah and Dorinda now felt rather depressed, and life seemed painfully dull. They missed the Puma and the Falcon, and they felt hurt because the Falcon, as it seemed, had gone back to Greenland without even saying good-bye.

They walked along, saying nothing because they could think of nothing they wanted to say, and both were bored and rather cross. Then, far above the trees, they heard a familiar rushing sound, and looking up they saw the Falcon stooping. Down through the cold air he came, faster than a falling stone, his wings a little way open, down to the height of their heads, and then he soared again, but only to the height of the trees, and presently settled, balancing with wings half-open that brushed her cheek, on Dinah's shoulder.

They were delighted to see him and asked him a score of questions without giving him time to answer one of them. 'We thought you had gone back to Greenland,' said Dorinda.

'I am going,' said the Falcon. 'As your desire was to come home, so is mine to go home. I have been dreaming of the great cliffs of ice and snow, the frozen sea, and hunting in that crystal air for lemmings and hares and ptarmigan among the rocks. I cannot rest my mind until I see Greenland again. But I have other news for you, greater news than that. I flew back to Bombardy to see what happened after we left. There has been a revolution there. All the many prisoners whom that man kept in his dungeons have been set free, and every night the people are dancing and singing in the streets. They have buried the Puma in the garden of the house where she was killed, and set up a great monument to her with these words upon it :

IN EVER GRATEFUL MEMORY
OF
THE GOLDEN PUMA
WHO SLEW COUNT HULAGU BLOOT
AND FREED US
FROM HIS TYRANNY '

' Well, I'm glad they've done that,' said Dinah.
' It is comforting to know that they realise what she
did for them.'

' Poor Puma,' said Dorinda. ' A monument
doesn't really do much good, does it ? '

' She could not have lived here,' said the Falcon.
' She would have made too many enemies. I too
am making enemies, for a man tried to shoot me
this morning for taking a cock pheasant. It is better
for me to go back to Greenland while my wings are
still whole. I shall go the old road, the Viking road,
by the islands of Orkney to the Faeroes, and so to
Iceland, and thence to the mountains above Godt-
haab where I used to live. Good-bye, Dinah.
Good-bye, Dorinda. And good fortune to you
both ! '

' Shall we never see you again ? '

' Who knows ? ' cried the Silver Falcon. ' I may
be tempted to wander again. I may come back.
But first I must look at the great fields of ice and
snow. Good-bye, good-bye ! '

He rose on his broad wings, snow-white in the
winter sky, circled above them, and then, climbing
still, flew swiftly to the north. They watched him
till he became small as a pin's head, bright against
a cloud, and disappeared.

' And now,' said Dorinda, ' we're lonelier than

ever. We're losing all our friends.'

' There's still Mr. Corvo.'

' Oh yes, but he's an ordinary human being, like us.'

' He looks very handsome in his new suit with a tartan waistcoat.'

' And he's very kind, but still——'

' Dorinda ! I've got an idea ! '

' What is it ? '

' Let's go and see Mrs. Grimble. We won't exactly ask for anything, because she doesn't like being asked for things now, but we'll tell her what a dull time we're having, and perhaps make her feel a little sorry for us, and just see if she offers to help in any way. She might suggest how to make things more interesting.'

' Can I come too ? '

' Yes, I promised to take you the next time.'

' Oh, Dinah, what a good idea, and how very exciting ! Let's hurry. I'm feeling better already! '

They went faster, running parts of the way where the path was firm, and at last through the naked trees they saw the little green house with yellow curtains and a red door where Mrs. Grimble lived. But as they drew nearer they saw something else. There was a notice-board in front of the house, and from twenty yards away they could read the large letters :

TO LET

' She's gone ! ' said Dinah.

' And I never saw her ! ' cried Dorinda. ' Oh, everybody's deserting us ! Isn't it sickening ? '

' It is,' said Dinah. ' I never expected this.'

Now they felt more depressed than ever, and stood there for several minutes, not knowing what

to do. Then Dinah went to the red door and tried the handle. It turned easily, and the door opened.

' Do you think we ought to go in ? ' asked Dorinda.

' Come on,' said Dinah.

The house was spotlessly clean and at first sight

was completely empty. Every piece of furniture had been removed and it seemed as though no one had ever lived there till, on the kitchen mantelpiece, they saw Mrs. Grimble's cuckoo-clock, and under it a sheet of notepaper. Dinah lifted the clock and read what was written : *To Dinah and Dorinda with Mrs. Grimble's compliments. P.S. I got rheumatism very badly and the Doctor says I must go to the Sahara Desert where the climate is nice and dry so I can't help you any more but the Cuckoo will tell you what to do.*

'It's a present. A farewell present. Well, that *is* kind of her ! '

'It's stopped,' said Dorinda.

'Here's the key. Wind it up.'

Dorinda wound the clock, which began to tick with a loud metallic sound, and put it back on the mantelpiece. Then the cuckoo-hatch opened, and the Cuckoo leapt out. He was a disreputable bird with a broken beak and only one eye and a dragging wing, but what was truly surprising was his language. He was more talkative than a parrot.

To begin with, he coughed two or three times to clear his voice, and then he recited a poem :

'Take off your stockings and look at your legs,
  (The world goes spinning round the sun,)
You can walk all the way from Paris to Cathay,
  And when you tire of walking you can run.

With two good eyeballs and wide-open ears
  (The Amazon's a river in Brazil,)

You can learn all the birds, and the difficult words
    Of the great wild poets to repeat 'em when you will.

Higher than your jawbone but under your hair
    (Madrid is the capital of Spain,)
Like a sack of silver pence is your Intelligence,
    Your face don't hide a turnip but a brain !

And all the world over are houses and hills,
    (The Atlas is on the bottom shelf,)
You can knock at any door, you can climb and explore,
    With your wit for a knuckle and some faith in your-
       self. . . .'

Then the Cuckoo began to shake his head so wildly that he nearly fell out of the hatch. ' Oh dear, oh dear ! ' he cried, ' I can't remember any more. Oh, what would Mrs. Grimble say ! There are ten more verses, all of them *most* important and *very* beautiful, and I can't remember another line. Oh, I *am* a silly bird ! Cuckoo, cuckoo, cuckoo ! '

Faster and faster he cried ' Cuckoo ! ' till at last, with a whirr and a clatter and a bang, the main-spring broke and there was dead silence.

Dinah and Dorinda immediately carried the clock to Mr. Sprocket the watchmaker in Mid-meddlecum, who took three weeks to mend it and charged them seven-and-sixpence. For several years it kept the time as well as Big Ben, but the Cuckoo never spoke again except on Tuesdays and Thursdays, about tea-time, when he used to appear and exclaim, in a grave and angry voice, ' Quack, quack ! Quack, quack ! '

Everybody who heard him always used to say,

What an extraordinary bird ! I never heard a Cuckoo say *Quack* before ! '

Then Dinah and Dorinda would say, proudly but a little sadly, ' This Cuckoo used to belong to Mrs. Grimble, you see.'

THE END

ERIC LINKLATER (1899-1974) was born in Wales but grew up on the Orkney Islands. He served as a sniper in the First World War, from which he returned to study English at the University of Aberdeen. In the course of a busy life, he worked as a journalist for *The Times of India*, stood as a candidate for the National Party of Scotland, commanded a wartime fortress in his native Orkneys, searched out lost Italian art after the Second World War, and served as rector of his alma mater. He was also celebrated as a writer. Among his books are *Juan in America*, a comic picture of Prohibition-era America, *Private Angelo*, the story of an Italian peasant in the Second World War, several satires, a history of Scotland, a study of the Icelandic Sagas, and, along with *The Wind on the Moon*, another acclaimed book for children, *The Pirates in the Deep Green Sea*.

The Wind on the Moon began as a story Linklater told his two daughters when they were caught in the rain on a walk. As his son describes it, "It was so good, such a wonderful and entrancing tale, that they begged him to write it down, and so he did." The book later won the Carnegie Medal and was nominated for best book of 1944. "Those dear children, bellowing their anger," wrote Linklater about his daughters' role in inspiring the story. "How grateful I was!"

NICOLAS BENTLEY (1907–1978) was an artist and author, and the art director for the publishing house André Deutsch, Ltd. He drew many pictures for magazines and books, including an early edition of T. S. Eliot's *Old Possum's Book of Practical Cats*, and was a well-known wit. Humor ran in his family: his father, Edmund Clerihew Bentley, invented the comic verse form known as a "clerihew":

George the Third
Ought never to have occurred.
One can only wonder
At so grotesque a blunder.